TACHYON TUNNEL

G Squared Publishing

****

Science Fiction
by
MICHAEL GORTON

Earth is the Cradle of mankind,
But one cannot remain in the cradle forever.
K. Tsiolkovsky

Tachyon Tunnel

Cover Graphic Design: Aiden Lee
Cover Layout: Sara Fluegel
Text and Flow Edits: Shelley Laine
Grammar & Content Edits: Makenzie Ozycz, MA, MFA
+DW

Michael Gorton

G Squared Publishing
www.G2-Pub.com
Author contact: mg@mgalcor.com

Tachyons are theoretical particles that travel faster than light. They have unique properties, such as imaginary mass and the ability to travel backwards in time. In our three-dimensional world, we would perceive them to co-exist before they are created, but tachyons are not subject to the laws of physics as we see them in our limited 3D world. For this reason, understanding tachyons will be critical to our ability to travel in interstellar space. This author predicts the first true interstellar travel will be done in Tachyon Tunnels...

<u>Read this first</u>

About Tachyon Tunnel

During my youth, like most tech nerds, when I wasn't experimenting with rocket fuels, or taking apart cars, and appliances, I could be found reading science fiction novels. I will admit that I wasn't like many of my friends who stayed holed up in their safe places reading and *living* in their fantasy worlds. Instead, I was inspired by the creative thinking of Isaac Asimov and Robert Heinlein. That inspiration led to engineering school followed by a graduate degree in physics.

The bottom line is that, with science fiction, we can paint a picture of the impossible, and pave the pathway to making it possible. It is in fact a tool that will inspire the next generation to accomplish that to which we could only dream.

So, writing this book was a bit of inspiration, mixed with perspiration, and a lot of fun. I wrote Tachyon Tunnel while decompressing after passing the CEO baton in a "change-the-world" company called Recuro, which I had started. It is filled with science, some adult content, twists, adventure, and a nonstop story that will hopefully keep the reader engaged and inspired.

Special thanks to Shelley Laine, Makenzie Ozycz, Tom Loney, Sara Fluegel, and Aiden Lee for putting the polish on the pages and cover. Special thanks to Mr. Hall, a high school teacher who inspired generations and whose impact will never be fully calculated or appreciated.

Enjoy. I know I did!
Michael Gorton

1

UNFORTUNATE BIRTHDAY

*If time flies, then let's study the aerodynamics,
and build the wings to soar on it.*
- Michael Gorton

Alex Durant stared at the monitors and listened to the hum, which he had come to recognize as a unique part of traveling in tachyon space. He tried to remember what day it was, but lack of sleep was having a bigger impact than he had thought.

"Emily, what day is it?" Alex posed to his onboard AI computer system, to which he had given the name Emily.

"Alex, that is not a logical question," Emily answered. "We are in a tachyon tunnel. Your understanding of linear time does not work here."

Alex pondered her response and became lost in thought. He had named the AI interface to his entire computer network Emily after a GPS he had used with that name over twenty years earlier. This version seemed like she was improving her understanding and communication abilities. Though a little perplexed at how she answered the question, it certainly seemed appropriate, albeit unusual. "Okay, Emily, let me rephrase the question: How many hours have passed since we began this trip?"

"Seventy-four hours, thirteen minutes, and eleven seconds," she answered.

"Okay, thanks," Alex answered. "As a rule, providing the number of seconds is unnecessary. When I ask the time, I am only interested in a response or level of precision in hours and minutes."

"Alex, as calculated with a biological clock, we have been traveling for just over three days. In the current programming, we will return home three days later, but that could be modified to return on any day you choose."

Alex had long since considered the repercussions of time travel from the standpoint of age. It was entirely possible for him to travel somewhere, stay for ten years, and then return home within minutes of his original departure. That, of course, would have a paradoxical impact on his age.

"Alex, we are emerging from the tunnel at your calculated coordinates now," Emily broke his thoughts. "The current date is March 2, in the year 2025."

Alex turned to focus on his display panel which suddenly scabbled in nonsensical characters. Simultaneously, he could feel the temperature in his craft dramatically and unexpectedly rising.

"Cabin temperature one hundred degrees Fahrenheit," Emily reported.

"Cabin temperature two hundred-fifty degrees Fahrenheit," Emily reported a second later.

Alex tried to ascertain what was happening.

"Cabin temperature is now three hundred twenty-five degrees Fahrenheit," Emily added.

Within fractions of a second, the accelerated increase in heat stifled him, taking his breath away and knocking him to the floor. His reaction was to gasp, but that burned his lungs. Everything around him was blazing hot to the touch. Alex did not have time to fix the problem. He could hear the sounds of expansion, and the popping of materials as they were superheated. His brain told him it would only be a matter of seconds before his ship was destroyed.

"Emily, what's happening?" he managed to ask right before he blacked out.

"The ship has emerged from the tunnel inside the orbit of Mercury, approximately forty million kilometers from the Sun," Emily reported to an Alex who was now unconscious as the hull temperature quickly approached supercritical.

* * * * *

Two days earlier - February 28, 2025

Paula Campbell stared at her surroundings in the familiar restaurant. Tonight, was a special one. Not only was it her birthday, but just four hours earlier she had received a call informing her that her work on recombinant DNA had earned her a top nomination for the Nobel Prize in genetics. Paula recognized that many are considered for the prestigious prize, and very few win. The nomination was more than enough to be the high point of her career. Doctor Campbell never thought of herself as one of the world's leading scientists. She enjoyed her work, viewing her results as more the product of intuition and luck as opposed to the dogged persistence and pure brilliance of her colleagues. In all her years of research, she never viewed herself or her work to be worthy of the most coveted prize in all of science. Still, with the news, she found herself almost walking on clouds with the realization that the Nobel committee believed her research worthy of their attention.

When her handheld computer vibrated, she checked the time, then pressed the button to take her to messaging. John Prinz, her date, was already late, but his tardiness could not negatively impact her night. John was to be the first person she would tell. She was quite eager to share the news with him. They had become close over the past year, and while he never understood her ramblings about molecular biology, he always pretended to listen with interest.

As she read the note, she thought at first it was a cruel joke. His text informed her that he would not be coming tonight and was permanently terminating their relationship. Paula read and re-read the note trying to determine if there was some hidden message. As reality sunk in, her disposition flipped like a light switch and she worked to hold back the tears and anger. She could feel her emotions building like a tidal wave as she sat alone in one of her favorite restaurants. She was a bit surprised at how quickly her mood had changed from absolute levity to anger and pain. She took a second look at her handheld computer and felt the tears rolling down her face. She quickly brushed them away, hardened her emotions, and motioned for the waiter to bring the tab. She wasted no time as she electronically transferred $40, gathered her purse, and made her way to the door. She darted around a car maneuvering through the parking lot, arriving at her vehicle where she crumpled in the seat.

Why did he have to do this on my birthday? She asked herself then blurted: *Bastard* as if he were sitting in the car with her. She remembered her lifelong friend Alex Durant saying that in his life as an entrepreneur, he experienced higher highs and lower lows than most people, and commonly they happened on the same day. There was no doubt, even though Paula was not an entrepreneur, today was certainly one such day. She took a deep breath, engaged the electronics in her car, and began a long drive home. Paula's vehicle contained the most advanced self-driving technology, but she seldom engaged that system as she preferred control.

As she negotiated the roads, she began to think about the emotional trials of the last ten years. Paula had known John for nearly twelve years but had been seeing him on an exclusive basis for two. First and foremost, she considered him a friend, but until tonight, she also believed there was a chance that one day the two would marry. The apex of her career had been reached. As she worked to control her tears, the lights of an approaching semi blinded her. Her mind quickly reconciled with the fact that the truck was in her lane. There was no time to take evasive action as the inevitability of a 150 mile per hour, head-on collision with a fully loaded tanker exploded into her existence.

* * * * *

Alex awoke and rubbed his eyes, sat up, and tried to get his bearings. His vision returned slowly as he began to focus on the room. "Emily, where are we?"

"Whipple Street, North Texas," Emily answered. "Back home, Alex."

Alex got up and stumbled to the door. He was groggy and weak. What had happened? As the portal to his craft opened, he recognized the warehouse attached to his home. He grabbed a bottle of water from the small fridge in the workspace, twisted off the plastic cap, and took a long drink as he headed for his bedroom. Without a second thought, he pulled off his jeans and sweatshirt, fell into his bed, and was asleep almost as soon as his head hit the pillow.

Ten hours later, he awoke with a start. He looked out the window and checked his clock. These journeys were wrecking his sense of real-time.

"Emily, what happened?"

"Alex, your calculations in the last jump brought us inside the orbit of Mercury. Before you blacked out, I sensed the danger to you and the ship, so I corrected the calculations and jumped us a safe distance from the Sun. Subsequently, I have returned you and our ship to your home location."

Alex thought about Emily's response for a second. "We were inside Mercury's orbit?"

"Correct," Emily responded. "The extreme radiation from the Sun's proximity scrambled all of your displays."

"Wow. I have never felt anything like that," he started. "Was there any damage to the ship?"

"I have run through the standard tests and have found no damage to circuitry or structure. The displays seem to be functioning normally, again."

"How hot did it get?" Alex asked, recalling the stifling heat.

"Skin temperature of the ship reached one thousand, fourteen point two degrees Fahrenheit. The cabin temperature climbed to four hundred fifty-seven point three, but that lasted for 2.1 seconds," Emily responded.

"Thank you, Emily," Alex responded then continued. "What is the human tolerance number?"

"There is a group of humans in what is called the three-hundred-degree club. The longest endurance for that was just under ten minutes."

"So, I am a weenie, because I blacked out?"

"I do not understand the question, Alex."

Never mind, Emily. It is just human sarcasm," Alex answered. "Thank you for your data."

"It is my function, Alex."

"Yes, it is, but you should probably substitute the word function with something more appropriate."

"And what would you suggest, Alex?"

"Try the word: *job*."

Emily scanned the dictionary reference for the word job. It did not make complete sense, but I am happy to do it."

"Perfect." Alex looked around the room again and began to regain his bearings. After returning from a long trip, he needed to catch up on some work and correspondence. He plopped back into his pillow, closed his eyes for a minute, and then took a deep breath.

After another moment of relaxation, Alex opened his eyes and decided his brain was not going to slow, so he might as well start his day. "Emily, wake up ceiling view."

"Done. Ceiling view is now on, oh, and good morning, Alex." The computer responded in a pleasant female voice as she transformed the ceiling into a computer screen.

"Yes, good morning, Emily. Please display email in priority order."

"As you wish, Alex," Emily responded as the configuration appeared on the screen.

"Are there any outstanding issues that require immediate attention?" Alex responded to the computer.

"Yes, there are. You have several meeting reminders. You also have a note from Gwen marked as urgent." The computer flipped through a few emails, monitoring Alex's eye movement. "As always, I would be happy to read or paraphrase them to you in the sender's voice."

"No thanks, Emily." Alex had programmed Emily to be capable of reading email in the exact voice of the sender – for those senders where a voice print and typical intonation was available. As usual, the urgent email from Gwen, his ex-wife, was no more than a demand for a phone call or email with an explanation as to why he was not returning her calls and mail. He spent the next forty-five minutes responding to several dozen emails and deleting a few hundred more that were clearly spam.

"Emily, please scan domestic and international news and let me know if there is anything I need to know before I start my day. Also, review stock holdings. If there are any changes greater than three percent, please provide details."

"Working. No stock value changes over one-point-five percent. It appears an individual in your contacts folder was killed in a car crash on the last day of February. Would you like to view the file?"

Alex thought for a few seconds. He had over thirty thousand contacts in his file, so a piece of news like this happened once or twice a year. Most of the time, the person was someone that he struggled to remember. "Okay, go ahead and read the article."

"Nobel prize candidate and noted geneticist, Paula Campbell, was killed in a head-on collision…"

"Stop reading," Alex broke in. His heart rate had instantly jumped from resting rate to pounding at maximum pulse rate. Paula Campbell was not just a friend but was one of his closest and longest-standing friends. Emily had not been programmed to differentiate the database and clarify contacts versus close friends.

"I see that Professor Campbell is someone with whom you have frequent correspondence. Would you like me to continue reading?" Emily asked.

Alex felt a sick feeling deep inside as he thought about Paula. The two had maintained communication, competed, and periodically done things together since college. In shock, Alex could not bear to hear the rest of the story but knew he needed to. He had not been aware that Paula was a Nobel nominee, though that part of the news did not surprise him.

After several minutes of lying motionless, in complete shock, Alex spoke: "Yes, Emily, please finish the story."

Alex listened to the details of a head-on collision with a fuel tanker that had lost control and crossed the median on the interstate. The explosion and subsequent fire had incinerated everything. The story went on to tell of Dr. Paula Campbell's numerous discoveries and awards for genetics research. The reporter attempted to describe Campbell's recent scientific work as well as the older material deemed significant by the Nobel committee.

When Emily finished reading, Alex wiped the tears from his face and sat motionless thinking about the Paula Campbell that he had known, the Paula that no newspaper reporter could capture. A good part of him did not want to believe the possibility that one of his closest friends had been tragically taken. He wondered how he could do something in her memory that would be worthy of all that she had brought to the world and his own life.

"Emily, please VOIP to John Prinz," Alex requested. Although he was aware that Paula had been dating several people, he was also aware that things were beginning to get serious between her and John. If anyone could immediately answer his questions, it would certainly be Prinz.

"Working." After just a few seconds, Emily responded. "I'm sorry, Alex, but that number is going directly to voice mail. Would you like to leave a message?"

"No, Emily. Please try Benjamin Campbell." Ben was Paula's former husband. The two had been married right out of graduate school. Both were biology students and while Ben had been a better student, Paula had accomplished more in her career. Just over five years ago, they suffered through a dramatic and emotional divorce that ended a six-year marriage.

"Alex, I guess you heard the news," Ben answered without saying hello.

"Ben, I am so sorry. Are you okay?"

"Tell you the truth, I still don't believe it. They have not found a body or any trace of her. The fire incinerated virtually everything. A part of me still believes this is some terrible mistake."

"Ben, I can assure you, a fire from a fuel tanker will reach thousands of degrees, capable of vaporizing everything. If Paula were still alive, we would know it. Logic tells us she's been reduced to organic ash." As Alex spoke, he immediately felt bad about his cold analytical comment. For a few seconds, he heard nothing but uncomfortable and complete silence on the line, and returned to his similar experience with the sun, just a day earlier.

"The scientist in me knows you're right..." Ben trailed off.

"I'm sorry Ben. I didn't mean to be so abrupt. I had the same reaction when I heard the news. Are there funeral arrangements?" Alex interrupted his thoughts.

"The memorial is tomorrow at noon in Saint Mark's Cathedral."

"Thanks, Ben. I'll be there."

Alex felt numb. Paula had been more than a best friend. She was the woman who had taught him to think emotionally. She was always there when he needed her, and vice versa. He had never seriously considered the possibility of losing her. He closed his eyes and tried to force himself back to sleep. Like Ben, he wanted to believe this was not possible; somehow, some way, Paula had survived, but the scientist in him knew better.

The scientist in him knew better, but the engineer in him did not.

Alex began to relax, and his mind focused on the problem. He often found himself solving problems in his sleep, waking up with a fresh perspective. Still, he knew that death was one of the few permanent things, with no fresh perspective. As he drifted in and out of sleep, the obvious solution came to him. He bolted out of bed and threw on his jeans and sweatshirt. Could he impact this? Was it possible, and what were the implications?

Alex calculated and monitored, then calculated again. Even though he wanted the time in hours and minutes, few people on Earth understood precision better than Alex Durant. Right now, because of his tachyon tunneling ship, *time* was on his side. Over the course of the prior six months, he had been successfully testing a form of time travel through the space-time-continuum in outer space. Was it possible to use his new technology to travel to a specific point in time and change something that had happened? He stopped and tried to comprehend the paradox associated with this problem. He could not reach an analytical answer.

One hour later Alex was standing on a hill, overlooking the scene where Paula's accident was about to occur, back in time to the night of February 28th. In the darkness, he could see her familiar vehicle coming down the highway. He watched in horror as the tanker crossed the highway center line and collided with Paula's vehicle. The subsequent explosion was too difficult for Alex to watch. As fire engulfed the highway Alex sat on the hill, knees pressed against his chest and arms wrapped around his knees. Could this event be changed? What would happen to time and the future if it was changed? Alex did not know. What he did know was that his friend was dead, and playing God was, and should not be his role. People have died since the dawn of mankind, since the beginning of time. Was it right for Alex to try and change that? How would, could, he do this?

Alex thought about where Paula had been coming from. If he met her before she got in her car, could he talk her out of driving down this highway? Would he try and fail? As he looked down the hill, he noticed cars stopped on the highway trying to determine if this fiery catastrophe could be stopped. Alex knew it could not. He had seen the future and read the reports. Paula died on this night. Alex was new to the principles of time travel, but he felt certain some things could not be changed once the timeline was set.

Alex stepped into his space-time machine. Watching this event and understanding the pathway to the future that he knew made him realize Paula's accident was inevitable. The people below were looking on in horror, helpless at the tragic mishap. The fire was burning too hot to approach the scene. He had read the newspaper report of her death. Alex understood the mathematics of tachyon tunneling, but trying to change the timeline was something he dared not challenge. After considering the variables, he decided that he could not change what had already happened without altering the timeline; something he would not do. He took a deep breath, exhaled slowly, and began to program Emily to take him home.

As he punched in the variables, something occurred to him once more. Both he and Ben had the same feeling about the accident: she was not really gone. Alex grinned and began recalculating.

He studied the scene from three different angles, winding back the clock, and then watching again.

His idea was to use his ship to land next to the scene just before impact. He was theoretically able to slow the time frame, though he had never attempted this. Further complications arose from the fact that he had never exited his ship in a tunnel, and he had never used the device for slowing time. He had no science to tell him what the universe would be like in a slowed-timeframe. Similarly, he had no science to tell him how the laws of physics would change. Would the inertia of Paula moving 90 kilometers per hour be carried through in a timeframe a thousand times slower than normal? Alex simply did not know and doubted that anyone on Earth could do any more than just theorize. One thing was certain: dead or alive, soon Alex would know. In reality, he knew his chances of dying were probably greater than his chances of saving her. Because of his long-standing love for Paula, he liked the odds.

The tachyon engine of his ship had the capability of projecting a beam which he modified so that it could oscillate. Over the last few years, when testing his invention, he had used the beam projection on animate objects to test the hardware. From there, he graduated to clocks, then to insects. In the early months, everything had worked without a hitch. The first mammal tests had been somewhat problematic, but even those problems had been ironed out. Ultimately, Alex had been willing to enclose the beam and test it on himself. The first test was a short experiment with a precise timer on his handheld supercomputer. Next, he entered the device and spent a few hours just reading a book. Over the months, the technology evolved, and Alex began building bigger and better enclosures. He learned he could use the quantum effects to build huge facilities enclosing them in a small space. One year after his first successful mammal experiments, he was ready to travel into space. For several months he tested runs inside the solar system. In an instant, he was in orbit around Saturn, searching for NASA missions like the Cassini mission, and finding them!

In reality the device had never been built specifically for time travel, but instead for tunneling through space time. Time travel was simply an interesting corollary to tachyon tunneling, but Alex considered it dangerous. Accidental changes to events spooked his normally logical thought process. Years of reading science fiction gave him an innate fear of stepping on a butterfly and changing the course of human events.

Alex programmed the engine to adjust his time frame backward in intervals down to a thousandth of a second. The effect would be time slowing significantly for everything but Alex and his ship.

Like a good scientist, Alex needed to test his theory in at least one dry run. He ran one test but aborted within seconds. The experiment consumed tremendous amounts of power, straining the ship's power supply. His vessel ran on a fusion reactor, powerful enough to provide electricity for a small city. In a normal journey, the generator never peaked higher than ten percent of its eleven-hundred-megawatt capacity. In his time-slowing experiment, the generator, running at full capacity, could not keep up with the load. His fusion generator was his pride and joy. Without its amazing capacity, his version of space travel would not be possible. Alex could not risk losing his generator in a test. Since he had already decided his probability of survival was low, he chose to proceed without completing a test.

With his newfound power consumption knowledge, Alex ran a new set of calculations. His generator could handle the load for 72 seconds before core temperatures would exceed containment. Loss of containment would result in a thermonuclear explosion, destroying everything for kilometers in all directions. Alex, or at least Alex's ship, needed to be in and out in about a minute.

Alex programmed Emily to land him 10 feet from the accident at the instant of first contact between the tanker and Paula's car. In the program, he gave himself only sixty seconds to retrieve Paula before Emily would close the hatch and return to the tachyon tunnel and back to his warehouse. If he was not back inside by then, he would be consumed in the fire from the crash, but the reactor would not explode.

By his best estimation, Alex guessed that he needed to arrive no later than one-tenth of a second after impact and no sooner than 1.5 seconds before impact. Because of the current state of his technology, Emily was only capable of precision in the multiple-minute range, so Alex ran several thousand iterations of his program, averaging the results, and hoped averaging would bring him to the correct point in time.

"Is this gonna work, Emily?" Alex asked absent-mindedly.

"Based on the parameters you have given me, I calculate an eleven-point-seven probability of success, Alex," Emily responded in her female voice.

Alex thought about her analysis. He had built Emily with every bit of engineering precision available. She was the interface that controlled the ship's computers and understood every parameter on an instantaneous basis. Alex had spent years analyzing mathematical probabilities in designing her programming that could calculate and respond in a fraction of a second. How she had calculated 11.7 probability was a mystery to him, but he knew it was probably correct to within a few hundredths of a percentage point, with one exception: Emily could not calculate the human variable. It was that determining factor Alex was betting on.

"What happens to that calculation if we continue running iterations until we hit the exact stopping point?" Alex asked.

"Alex, I have no way of calculating the human probability of you successfully pulling Paula from the vehicle, but probability dictates that we should arrive at the correct point in time in the first ten iterations," Emily answered.

"Okay, Emily, let's execute." His first hop brought him to more than 30 seconds before the impact. "Re-execute, Emily."

Emily ran a second short hop, then a third and a fourth. On the fifth, she brought him to a fraction of a second after the collision had begun. The front end of Paula's SUV was smashed, and the airbag was approximately half deployed. Airbags take approximately 55 milliseconds to deploy, literally faster than the blink of an eye. Because each hop was consuming valuable resources, this would have to work. Alex wasted less than two seconds deciding to begin his operation.

Alex quickly exited the portal of his ship and was immediately surprised that he could not run. Because of the slowed timeframe, Alex was dealing with the laws of physics in a way he had not expected. His legs worked hard, but inertia and gravity seemed to resist his movement. Even the air felt like a thick soup that was working to oppose his movements. He tried to breathe, but his lungs were not strong enough to pull the air in at a satisfactory rate. He felt like he had so many times while climbing mountains where the air was too thin to satisfy his need for oxygen, and every couple of steps demanded a rest, but rest was not an option. He immediately calculated that his blood was fully oxygenated, and he was certain he could hold his breath for a full minute. If he could not make it in 60 seconds, nothing would matter anyway. For a fraction of a second, he wondered if it was the result of an inertial law he had studied in school, or perhaps some new principle based on changing something on the space-time-continuum. There was no time to consider an answer that now, though.

With legs burning from exertion, he made the few steps to Paula's vehicle. He pulled on the door with no result, then leveraged with all his strength to get it open. It began to move like a two-ton safe door in a bank. Inside, Paula was completely motionless with a shocked facial expression and several crystal teardrops frozen on her face. Alex paused as he looked at Paula and felt the impact of what was going through her mind at this instant. She realized there was no escape, and her destiny was now in God's hands. It surprised him that she had tears on her face. Could those perfect tears have happened this quickly, or had she been crying about something else before the accident?

Thirty-seven seconds had passed when Alex fought to release the seatbelt. Forty-three seconds had ticked past as he unsuccessfully worked to pull her from the car. She had too much inertia in his slowed time frame for his strength. Alex focused, reached inside himself, and produced an internal scream of agony, yanked with his arms and pushed with his legs. With a little motion, Paula slipped into the influence of the pulsing tachyon tunnel and gravity came to Alex's rescue causing the entwined bodies to tumble out onto the pavement.

Now in his arms on the tarmac, rather than being a blur or phantasm moving at hyper-speed, Paula focused on Alex and tried to get her bearings on what was happening. With the instantaneous confusion of impact, her mind was not able to put the pieces together of what was now an aberration of everything she had ever experienced.

Alex and Paula now existed in the same slowed frame. For an instant, Alex felt a sigh of relief followed by a renewed realization of the scarce seconds remaining.

Paula, startled and bruised, resisted Alex's attempt to carry her onto the ship. Alex was aware he had less than twelve seconds remaining and no time to explain or wait for compliance. Paula's slowed inertial timeframe made her weigh an impossible amount for Alex to handle, and in his desperate attempt to beat the clock, he shouted for her to move. As the seconds uncontrollably ticked, he jerked and then shoved Paula as hard as he could into the ship's portal just as the clock hit the sixty-second tick. Alex knew he would not make the deadline and was unsure of what would happen to his body if the ship hopped into the tunnel with him stuck halfway in the portal. He decided to try, even though he knew he would not make it. His watch showed sixty-seven seconds as he slammed into the ship, accelerating out of the pulsed space-time. Alex was startled by the acceleration as he crashed in banging his head on the graphene wall.

Emily monitored the ship's engine, now rapidly approaching meltdown temperatures, executed a preprogrammed instruction that closed the portal, shut down the pulse, and hopped into the tachyon time tunnel. The reactor temperature continued to rise for another 3.8 seconds, then began to cool as the load on the reactor dropped to 10%.

Alex rubbed his head where he had impacted the ship's wall. Had his watch been wrong? Or had Emily modified the programming based on her analysis of the situation? According to his calculations, he clearly had not successfully returned to the ship in the allocated time. The simple calculus was that Emily should have left without him, but she had not.

Because of the short hop, the ship almost immediately reemerged in Alex's storage building on March 3rd.

Alex wiped the blood that was now streaming down his forehead and glanced at Paula, who was sitting on the floor, clearly glazed over. "Emily, why did you not close the portal at the defined instant?"

"Alex, I calculated that your probability of success would become eighty-four-point-two percent if I added eight seconds to your instructions. My calculations of core temperature and meltdown had to be modified with the experiential data that you always leave room for a load factor."

"Experiential data?" Alex was perplexed by his computer's comment, as he tried to catch his breath. He glanced at Paula, who was now standing in a somewhat wobbly fashion. She started to say something but Alex held up his hand.

"Alex," Emily started, "you always leave room in your calculations for error. Because I had full control of the ship and was monitoring reactor temperatures, I could execute instantaneous modifications."

"Did I program you to do that?" Alex was confused.

"Part of my programming is to protect the ship and your life. You have also programmed me to monitor and store activity as a data matrix for future decision-making scenarios. Those two pieces of my code provided me with the data and logic to modify your initial instruction that I close the doors and hop into the tachyon tunnel within sixty seconds. It was that same piece of code that allowed me to save you from being vaporized by the Sun in our last journey."

Paula had been listening but decided Alex's intellectual discussion with his silicon friend needed to be superseded by reality. "Okay, what the hell is going on here, Alex?" Paula prodded and immediately wished she had not used the word *hell*. Paula stared at Alex, who was soaked in sweat with blood smeared across his forehead and streaming down into his right eye. She could tell he was trying to relax but was still breathing as if he had just run a five-kilometer race full out. She tried to make sense of the last few minutes but even her scientific brain could not elucidate the situation. She had just made the realization that her vehicle was in a head-on collision when the world turned twilight. Now she was sitting on the floor in a hallway with synthetic fiber and metal walls, staring at her friend Alex while he was interrogating a computer. Was this some nightmarish stopping point on the path to heaven or hell, or simply a dream? She immediately dismissed the possibility that this was some horrible manipulation of heaven. All things considered, she felt quite tranquil.

"First of all, how are you doing? How do you feel?" Alex asked before focusing on her question.

"Tranquil. I feel dazed, yet tranquil," she answered.

The fatigue burning in his lungs was beginning to subside as he focused on Paula's question. "Tranquility surprises me. As to your question, let's call it an experiential lesson in relativity," immediately realizing he had used the same word that Emily had just used.

Paula thought about Alex's response. "A what? Not sure what you mean. Can you elaborate and please speak English?" she demanded.

"You know how I've been talking about my secret project over the last couple of years?" Alex pulled a cloth from a drawer and wiped the blood from his forehead. He took a deep breath and exhaled slowly, relaxing as he felt his pulse rate returning to a resting figure.

Paula continued to struggle with the situation. Something about the world seemed completely wrong. While this had all the elements of a dream, it also felt very real. "Alex, try to be clear," was all she managed to say. "Am I dead, or is this some weird dream?"

"Paula, three days ago you were involved in a head-on collision with a tanker."

"Wait, three days ago?" she asked.

"Let me continue. Three days ago, I was several light-years away. When I returned on March 2nd, Emily informed me of your accident. The world believes you are dead. I thought you were dead, that is until I figured out a way to pull you out of the accident right as it was happening and before you were incinerated," Alex responded, then added, "But of course, you weren't."

A part of Paula wanted to laugh at the explanation, but in the eerie, yet well-lit room, that explanation almost seemed real. She knew subconsciously this must be a dream, but it was turning into a good one, so she endeavored to enjoy its precepts. "What about my friends and family?"

Alex took a deep breath and exhaled slowly, "Everyone thinks you're dead."

"Dead…" Paula trailed off as the impact of this settled. "Assuming I am not dead, we need to call people and let them know."

Alex had not thought through this scenario. "Paula, I know we need to do that, but I want to think about the best way to handle it. This tachyon technology is not something I want public. It is so far ahead of modern science, and the social implications are beyond anything in existence right now."

"Understood, Alex, not to mention the military."

"Yup," Alex nodded pensively.

"Okay, so what happens now?" she asked.

Alex had not fully thought through that question himself before embarking on his mission to save Paula. "Well, Paula, after my power plant cools down and I do some testing, we will have the ability to go anywhere and do anything we want."

"Well, then, what I'd like is to get on my motorcycle and go for a ride in the country so I can clear my head," Paula responded.

"Let's not tempt fate," Alex alluded to the head-on collision she had just escaped. "First, let's sit down, have a glass of wine and collect our thoughts. I'd stay away from motorized vehicles for a little bit if I were you. Your SUV, or what's left of it, is practically incinerated and now in a junkyard." Alex clarified while trying to stand. He found his legs somewhat weak, but stable. He wondered how Paula felt but thought it better to wait and discuss that situation after she had time to reconcile what was going on.

"Okay." Paula got up and followed Alex into his house, wondering if she could somehow will herself to fly as she almost always did in her dreams.

Alex poured Paula a glass of wine and made sure she was comfortable. "Listen, why don't you relax a bit and try to come to grips with what's happening."

"What day is it?" she asked.

"March 3rd."

"A few minutes ago, it was February 28th, my birthday."

In reality, Paula's birthday was February 29th, but other than leap years, she typically celebrated on the 28th.

"I know. We will figure out birthday celebrations after the dust settles a bit." He handed her a small folder. "This is a description of my tachyon tunnel device and how it works. I don't expect you to understand the engineering and physics, but the fundamental science will provide a sense of what's going on. While you're reading, I really should test a few things in my reactor. We just ran a program that was way outside the design specifications, and I need to make certain the core cooling is proceeding in a linear fashion. I don't want to destroy the entire neighborhood because I was not careful."

"We?" Paula quizzed.

"Well, yes. I've done significant testing with my Tachyon Tunnel, but have never even imagined tonight's application, at least until a few hours ago."

"I still don't understand why you said 'we.'" Paula persisted.

"Oh, sorry," he chuckled, "I meant Emily and I."

"You know, I have always thought it a little unusual that you refer to your computer as a person."

"I know. It's a geek thing. Still, sometimes she seems so real. Emily does things periodically that surprise me. At the end of the day, logically, I know she's no more than bits and bytes. Still, there are sparks of humanity that I cannot ignore."

"Well, your little interrogation of her a few minutes ago sounded more like how I debate and question my graduate students," Paula responded, and then added, "What surprised me was how she discussed and bantered the topic with you. It felt to me like she was human, at least not like any computer I have ever dealt with."

"I might be just imagining this, but she does seem to be growing up." Alex plopped down in his favorite chair and studied his friend.

"Be careful not to fall in love Alex," Paula chided. "Emily is a collection of silicon chips and programming." Paula noticed that Alex was now looking at her differently, but chose to ignore the warmth his eyes were creating deep inside.

"That's not technically right, Paula. Much of Emily is silicon-based, but she's actually a hybrid computer. I have installed a new generation of organic, DNA-based logic. My programming on that side of her processor is analog, not digital. I have…"

"You, what?" Paula interrupted. "You've built a hybrid computer with silicon and organic materials?"

"Yes," Alex answered with a huge, pride-filled grin.

"Oh, lord… Is anyone else, anywhere on the planet doing this?" Paula responded.

"Not to my knowledge, Paula. I was not even sure I could make her work. In any case, she is not the great piece of science and engineering here, the ship is."

"She?" Paula sat in her chair shaking her head and then took a long drink of her wine. "There you go with the gender for your computer again, Alex."

"Well look, I don't expect you to understand." Alex stood silently for a minute gazing into the eyes of his friend. She was alive, and that realization filled a very special and private part of him with happiness. "I need to get a few things checked. Stay here. Just relax and I'll be back shortly."

"Okay." Paula finished her glass of wine, glanced up at the bar to see a nearly full bottle, and watched as Alex left the room.

When the door closed, she filled her glass, sat, opened the folder, and began to read. The folder was at first not very helpful. It seemed to be one equation after another, but she did manage to find periodic descriptive notes. It seemed that Alex had developed a time machine that was designed for space travel. Most of the notes were simply too technical to follow. As she sat drinking her wine, the feeling that this perhaps this was some strangely real dream, persisted. She finished her second glass and flipped through the pages of Alex's manual for a second time. Again, most of it seemed to be a continuous set of equations that made no sense to her. Why Alex thought she might understand any part of this document perplexed her. He was so good at making the complex seem simple, but this manual did not reflect that talent. Paula set the binder in her lap, curled up in the chair, and drifted off to sleep. If this were in fact a dream, perhaps she could now awaken.

2

TRANQUILITY

Alex stood over the couch staring at his friend. His senses picked up the familiar scent of Paula as his eyes admired her skin, hair, and the curves of her body. A flood of tears came to his eyes as he realized that less than twenty-four hours ago, he was coming to grips with the realization that he would never have the pleasure of her friendship again. He knelt on the hardwood floor and kissed her on the forehead.

Paula woke and rubbed her eyes as she sat up. "Everything okay, Alex?" With her question, she wondered if this was still a dream. Surely it was.

"Seems to be." Alex forced himself to rein in the overwhelming emotions inside. As he often did, he quickly found a way to focus her question on an intellectual answer that suited the moment. "The reactor core is still hot but is cooling down in a nice linear fashion." He stood up, grabbed his glass, poured himself a small amount of wine, tasted it, and drank the remainder. "I have an idea for the evening."

"What's that?" Paula asked, setting the folder down on the coffee table.

"Come with me." Alex led her out to the large warehouse that he used to store his tachyon tunnel ship.

From the outside, the ship was a shiny silver, cubic-shaped object with rounded corners. It was a bit smaller than a double-wide trailer. There seemed to be no blemishes on the surface and no windows or other openings. Alex walked up to a wall, which opened, lowering two steps up into the craft. Paula was surprised at how large it was inside. It was well lit, with walls mostly white. There seemed to be electronic devices built into the walls with display screens everywhere.

"Does this ship have a name?" Paula asked.

"A name?" Alex responded quizzically.

"You gave your damned computer a name," she answered. "Why not the ship?"

"Hey slow down, Paula. Emily is not damned!" Alex defended his silicon companion. "Just haven't thought about giving her a name. She's just a ship."

"She?" Paula bluntly pointed out.

Alex smiled and chuckled. "Okay, you've made your point. I tend to give my machines human traits."

"Yes, you do. In any case, I felt so *tranquil*," Paula emphasized, "when I first realized I was on the ship. Perhaps it was the shock of transition from a head-on collision to your quiet well-lit ship," she added.

"I swear, you are such a woman sometimes. Why are you bouncing from topic to topic? What's that got to do with whether or not the ship has a name?"

"Alex, I am always a woman," she slugged him on the arm, "but right now just pay attention, and let me finish. I think *Tranquility* is a perfect name for the ship. It's the feeling I got when I first realized I was here, and it has great science roots, with your heroes Buzz and Neil landing on Tranquility Base."

Alex smiled at the thought of her comment. He had met Buzz Aldrin when he was a young engineer and had come to admire greatly the things Buzz had accomplished and the way he had dedicated his life to continued exploration. "I like it, Paula. What do you think, Emily?"

"Alex, I have no programming which allows me to evaluate whether a name is good but the historical affiliation with the Apollo Eleven landing seems appropriate," Emily answered.

Alex ignored Emily's comment and lightly kissed Paula's head. "My ship has a name. Thank you, Paula."

"So, how about a tour of Tranquility?"

"I'll give you a tour later. For now, let's go to the control room." Alex led her down a short corridor, put his hand on a wall and a portal opened from where the wall had been. After they entered the room, the portal disappeared. Alex pointed to a chair and motioned for Paula to have a seat. When she did, he sat in a chair next to her.

"Emily, execute program Paula One," Alex said in a normal voice tone.

"Executing Paula One," the computer responded in a mature, but sexy female voice.

Alex then turned to Paula. "Program Number One is gonna take us to a point in time 16 years ago - when we first met. We will have the ability to observe ourselves as we were then. I thought it might be fun."

"You're joking, right?" Paula asked.

"No, I'm very serious. This trip will take what will feel like seven minutes. I say *feel like* because time will actually be moving backward. Let me rephrase to say that based on your current pulse rate of 74 beats per minute, we will see the passage of roughly 560 beats..."

"You know my pulse rate?" Paula was surprised.

"Of course," Alex answered flatly. "It's a little fast for a nine-year-old girl," Alex emphasized the word girl. Paula had been born on February 29, 1988. While her birth had taken place 37 years prior, because of Leap Year, there had only been 9 occurrences of February 29th in that period.

Paula looked around the room, seemingly ignoring Alex's math. She noticed a control panel that held Alex's focus. The lights dimmed to an almost twilight feel, and the control panel ticked off what she guessed was a ten-second countdown.

"The lights dimming is simply an *effects* thing that I use to monitor where we are in the launch cycle. I do not have to drive this ship – in the traditional sense of the word. What I do, is spend days developing a computer algorithm, followed by execution of the program. I added the light dimming so I would know that we have begun the journey. It's sort of a special effect."

"The computers control everything?" Paula thought about the impact of a vehicle that drove itself. She was aware of the many developments automobile manufacturers had made in that arena, but personally had chosen to not trust a computer to drive her car.

"Yes, Emily is in full control after the initial program is complete. It's far too complex for a person to handle in real-time. My task as the pilot is to write the computer program. I then depend on Emily to execute according to the end objective. I have developed a few standard algorithms for temporal blocks that I can execute pretty much at the press of a button, such as hops of 25, 150, and 500 years. We can talk and do whatever we want during this passage of heartbeats, so let me try to explain what's happening." Alex pressed a button on his chair and then rotated the seat to face Paula. "Over the past two years, I've been working on developing one of my life's dreams. As you know, I did very well with the sale of my last invention. Now that I have hundreds of millions of dollars at my disposal, the last barrier to building this craft was overcome. Essentially, I've implemented a fundamental principle of physics known as quantum tunneling. There is an elementary particle known as the tachyon that has the ability to travel faster than light. By doing so, it is capable of bouncing - uncontrollably through time. As physics students, we once joked that tachyons co-exist before they exist."

"They what?" Paula interrupted.

"There's a fundamental relationship between time and space. Things that travel faster than light are actually moving through a dimension of time. If a tachyon happens to be going backward in time, it will see the end of its existence prior to when it was created.

"I see," Paula answered, knowing Alex would continue without prompting.

"Anyway, I've developed a unique way of harnessing that capability and controlling tachyon motion to fractions of an hour. Essentially, this means that I can travel to any point in time and do so with an accuracy of a few minutes. The next-generation program and vehicle will be able to control the time portal to fractions of a second, but *that* is a different story. Accomplishing that type of time precision requires a computer processor that is almost 100 times faster than the ones available today. Unfortunately, access to that type of off-the-shelf technology will not be available for another six years."

Alex looked at Paula to make sure she was tracking his explanation. She was smiling, so he continued. "It was the inability to be precise, and because of my lack of experience with the type of time travel required to rescue you, that made your first expedition very dangerous."

"Dangerous? How so?" In a sense, it was ironic, considering the alternative.

"First of all, I needed to arrive at precisely the correct moment in time, something beyond even my advanced computers. Second, I had a feeling the laws of inertia would be affected by slowing the time clock, and I was right. It took a tremendous amount of strength just to move. I had no idea how difficult it was going to be to take steps, open your car door, or pull you out of the vehicle."

"So, are you saying I was a bit too heavy for you to handle?" she joked.

"Haha, you always have been, but in a sense, yes. A few seconds more and we both would have died in that accident."

Paula was struck by Alex's explanation. For a second, she flashed back to the moment when she realized she would not be able to evade the tanker. A deep sadness overwhelmed her as she flashed through dreams that would never be. There would be no children and no future. What parts of her life had she skipped over simply to win the race?

"You still with me?" Alex broke her thoughts.

Paula at first chose not to respond then chided "I can think of a lot of women you've known who you probably would have chosen to die for," she bantered in a light joking manner.

"That is totally cruel. After we finish this trip, I'm certain you'll decide to be nicer to me." Alex responded in a cocky fashion.

"So, you said it takes days to write the programs for your travel, or expeditions, or whatever you call these trips."

"Correct. I hope to improve that in the next version," Alex answered.

"If that's the case, when did you write the program you called Paula One?"

"Uhhmmm," Alex flushed. He glanced at his timer and then back at Paula. "Just under 100 heartbeats to our destination. Let's cover that one later, huh?" He changed the subject. "We'll be landing near Princeton, in the Spring of 2009. I think it'll be fun to see some history and watch ourselves getting to know one another." Alex pressed a couple of buttons and a large screen appeared that showed a map of Princeton, almost 20 years ago. With the motion of the cursor, Paula felt a jolt of acceleration in the ship. The hum in the background subsided, and a few of the screens lit up with what seemed to be a view of the outside.

Paula watched in disbelief. What a dream!

"I'm taking us to the date where we really connected for the first time. As I recall, we had known each other for a few months, and you came into my office at the physics department to check out the tutors. We spent several hours chatting and talking about physics before going over to my favorite bar where we drank a pitcher of beer. I know, call me a typical man, but I love that night. I have remembered it a hundred thousand times in the last two decades. Now I get to see it again with you at my side."

"Really?" Paula was surprised. "Maybe It's just a woman thing, but I have often thought about how quickly we evolved from study partners to best of friends, uh, with benefits."

"Well, I was pretty nerdy, shy, and simply not a good talker then. When the spark was lit, it certainly grew to a flame rather quickly. You were like a goddess to me. From the first second we met you were the perfect manifestation of beauty and brains, and that is generally bad for a man; especially for the nerdy geek types."

"A goddess, you say?" Paula asked, somewhat surprised by his description. She was a good-looking woman, but never considered herself anything more than a girl with decent basics, who polished them reasonably well. She was well aware that many women took far more time primping and achieved stunning results. Paula was athletic with some natural looks, but mostly she focused on being very intellectual. She had come to Princeton to study microbiology, and at this particular institution of higher learning, survival demanded that she force her intellectual side to prevail.

"My gosh, I had never dreamed of being with any woman like you. I couldn't believe that you were there with me…. Didn't you know that? The combination of your kind of beauty and brains is rare." Alex always got chills when remembering that period of time in his youth. "Even in my wildest dreams, I would not have imagined anyone like you would ever be interested in me."

"Alex, that is so ridiculous, it's almost funny. You have always been sought after by women!"

"No, I haven't." Alex furrowed his brow in confusion. "Well, maybe after I started making good money, girls started showing an interest."

"You are so out of touch sometimes," Paula concluded. "Anyway, if you felt that way, why didn't anything come out of that short fling?" she asked, ignoring his denial.

"What are you talking about?" Alex asked with a startled look as he finished securing the ship. "Look where we are today. You are the greatest female friend in my life. Our friendship has survived the test of time. It has persisted across great distances and periods of silence. After all these years, you are still one of my closest friends. I would do anything for you any time you asked...." He stopped and decided he did not have a real finish for that thought.

Silence.

After a few minutes, Alex broke the silence. "Let's go see 2009 Princeton." He got up, walked down a hallway, and stood as a portal appeared from nowhere and opened to a new room adorned by a 1966 model Mustang convertible.

"How do you make those doors appear?" Paula asked.

"Emily is watching. If you look carefully at the floor, you will see a low-power white diode, which I use to tell me where the doors are. When I stop, Emily uses a biometric program to make sure it's me, then opens the door. I've already programmed her to give you access to the entire ship."

Alex opened the door to the Mustang for Paula and then walked over to the driver's side. He pulled out of a large opening in the ship into a clear but chilly New Jersey evening. The sun had just set, and the atmosphere brought back a flood of old thoughts and feelings.

"Right now, the younger versions of you and I are on campus learning physics that will ultimately help you pass what you called 'the hardest course on campus,'" Alex informed her. "Let's go see what we can observe."

"Question," Paula started. "If we go there does that mean we were there on that night?"

"I think so, yes," Alex answered. "Perhaps if we could check our memory, we would remember seeing each other. On the other hand, I do not recall seeing anything on that night but your eyes."

Paula thought about his answer for a minute then asked, "So did I die in that crash tonight?"

"Paula, that crash will not happen for 16 years," Alex answered without explanation.

Paula grabbed Alex's arm and forced him to focus. "Answer my question, Alex Durant. Now."

"No. I pulled you out before the impact. You are as alive as anyone. The world believes you're dead, but you are most assuredly alive. I have not played God and brought you back from the other side. I simply used my knowledge of physics to extract you before you had the opportunity to die. It is only a guess, but I do not believe I have created a space-time anomaly." Alex was well aware that he was playing with concepts in physics and time travel that he did not fully understand. He knew that eventually he would need to develop some laws or tenets for tunneling, but those would need to come later.

Paula leaned over the Mustang console and kissed Alex lightly on the ear. "Thank you," was all she managed to say as the tears streamed down her cheeks.

Paula's light kiss and thank you made everything worthwhile.

Alex worked to focus on the road. This time period had only human drivers and mistakes were made millions of times per minute on the roadways of America.

After a few minutes, Alex pulled into the parking lot behind the Physics building on the Princeton campus. "Are you ready for this?" He asked.

"Downright excited!" Paula responded, a part of her still believing this had to be a dream.

As he opened the door to the old halls, Alex realized the last time he had been here was as a student. The world and he had changed by orders of magnitude since then. They climbed the stairs to the second floor, and walked down the hall, which led to the old department office where the students and tutors hung out. They stood in the hall and listened. The sounds of several animated students could be heard beyond the closed door.

"Do you realize that a twenty-one-year-old version of you is on the other side of that door?" Alex asked.

"It's a bit scary," Paula answered. "If you could, what would you say to that younger Alex?"

Alex thought about her question for a second. "Stay the course. Not sure I would change anything about this particular night. I like my life, and I have pristine memories of tonight. I remember the first part of the night as perfection. That's why I chose this date to come back to."

"What? If it seems like perfection in your memory, why would you want to return?" She asked.

"Later tonight, you and I will communicate in a way I had never before been able to communicate. In many ways, it was the beginning of manhood and the end of boyhood. The energy we shared was the very beginning of understanding *how* to communicate. I wanted so desperately to reach you that I broke down some internal barriers that had existed. Before the night is over, I will come back to this room with the intention of doing some more work. I won't get much done because I'll be thinking about you to the point where I cannot focus. As I said, there's no way I could have known, but it will be the beginning of one of the greatest emotional connections of my life. Not love - not yet. If I could live it again, I would change nothing. Our friendship is one of the greatest achievements in my life."

"Okay, you didn't need to give me such a long answer," she interjected. "Shall we go in?"

"No, because we did not go in. No one came in. In just a few minutes we will come out. Some of the guys from the department are going to a concert. You and I will go to my favorite bar. I suggest we go there and watch the evening play out."

"Are you sure?" Paula felt a bit weird about that. "Not sure I would feel comfortable watching *everything* that happened that night."

Alex thought about how the night evolved into the two of them going to his house. "Well, what could be so wrong with us reliving an intimate moment in *our* lives? It might allow us to talk about it and better understand our feelings," Alex responded.

"Alex Durant… *you* want to talk about *your* feelings?" Paula was completely caught off guard by his comment. "Now I know I'm dreaming! Next thing you'll want to cuddle."

"I wouldn't go that far!" Alex responded with a short laugh. The fact was that he would have enjoyed exactly that, though he had long since decided to protect the platonic friendship they had developed.

At J-Pats, an old favorite Irish pub near campus, they drank and reminisced. When the younger couple arrived, they watched intently for a while but then became absorbed in their own thoughts and conversation.

"At times, I wonder why we did not continue," Alex started down a path they seemed to always avoid.

"Are you disappointed at where we are?" she asked.

"You know I'm not," Alex answered flatly.

"It seems like we've done well for ourselves. Look, we're living in 2025 and visiting 2009. That is pretty amazing!" Paula glanced at the younger version of herself and was caught off guard when their eyes met. Suddenly, a lost memory flooded her brain, and she recalled the younger version of herself admiring the older couple. "Alex, I remember this. I remember seeing me…"

Alex looked into Paula's eyes and glanced quickly at the younger Paula. He wondered if he had inadvertently created some type of paradox or butterfly effect. One thing was certain; it was unlikely a person would remember seeing someone in a bar twenty-plus years later. While he understood the physics of time travel, he had no understanding of the implications of changing the past. Plenty of theories existed analyzing situations like this, but none had any real credibility. He tried to be careful, as he was not interested in finding out the hard way. As a flood of scenarios filled his mind, he got a very uneasy feeling in his gut. It had been a mistake to come here, and in all likelihood, he may very well have created an anomaly in the timeline by saving Paula from the head-on collision.

"Are you okay?" Paula asked.

Alex reached inside and mustered some confidence, then answered, "Yes. It's a complex subject, the implications of time travel, and I wonder if this event created that memory, or if it really happened back in '09."

"A paradox? What kind of paradox?" She seemed a bit startled.

"Were we really here that night, or was that memory created in your head because of us being here now?" Alex asked, not knowing even how to test the question. "I read a story when I was in high school where a time traveler went back and accidentally killed a simple butterfly. That accident created a chain reaction which altered the history of mankind."

"I am quite familiar with the Butterfly Effect, but it's science fiction, written by someone that has nowhere near your understanding of the complexities of the universe. What do *you* think?"

"I'm not sure. I suppose my first reaction is influenced by science fiction, but we are in an area that no one has appropriate mathematics to calculate."

"Alex, I didn't ask you to calculate. What does your gut tell you?"

"My gut tells me that we should not play roulette with time. My gut also tells me that the fact that we are here means we were here sixteen years ago." He watched her, silently lost in her thoughts.

"You know that John broke up with me today," She stated in a matter-of-a-fact tone. "It was a hell of a birthday surprise."

"I'm sorry, Paula." Alex put his hand on her shoulder. "It seems that your last 24 hours were some of the worst ever."

"Well, that's putting it lightly. Seems that you have saved me from death, but not from the end of a relationship." She studied her oldest friend and realized he had always been around when she needed him.

"I can only go so far, Paula," Alex winked, trying to make light of the situation.

"So, we are both single again," she answered.

"Indeed, my friend. Want me to help you by playing matchmaker?" Alex joked as he took a long sip of beer.

"That's okay. You have plenty of other attributes that far exceed your ability to find a match for me, Alex," Paula chided.

"You're probably right. My only real female relationship these days is Emily."

"I see," she responded sarcastically. "Hopefully you do not have an intimate relationship with your computer!

"Absolutely not!" Alex answered, clearly miffed by her comment.

"What do you think would happen if we got stuck on a deserted island together?" she asked, seemingly out of the blue.

"You and I both know that will never happen. I think we should be proud we have this wonderful connection that we both recognize and yet we keep our friendship on a higher plateau." He almost stopped, but added, "You have to admit that the sexual tension is fun."

"I love it. It's one of the many things I love about our *friendship*." She emphasized the word while glancing over at the younger couple. As she looked, she briefly recalled that night so many years ago. It gave her a tingle deep inside. She chose not to add her thought that it would be nice, every once in a while, to exorcise that demon with Alex.

Alex watched her as she gazed at the young couple. He finished his beer and enjoyed the silence of the noisy bar for a few minutes. "Well, should we move on to the next part of the evening?"

Paula furrowed her brow. "You saved my life tonight with technology that should not be possible. Then you use that tech to bring me back to a pivotal point in both our lives," she paused, glancing at his empty beer mug. "Maybe the roots of your creativity were sparked here in Princeton, and certainly my Nobel pathway was born here."

"What's that all about, Paula?"

"I am just glad we met and have managed to create the foundation of a lifelong friendship, Alex," she answered. "Let's enjoy the moment.

"Works for me."

After listening to one of the old songs on the house speaker system, they both finished their second beer. "Let's get back to the ship." Alex managed to say.

She smiled, gathered her things, and responded simply, "Okay."

Once back at Tranquility, Alex focused on the programming tasks for the second part of this expedition; interstellar travel to Alpha Cassiopeia. Once he finished checking the mathematics and programming, he turned and kissed her lightly.

"So, all-in-all, is this the most unique birthday gift ever?" he managed to ask.

"Considering how the day started, and perhaps ended..." Paula felt a cold rush as the image of a fuel tanker unavoidably filled her imagination. She took a second to re-focus on the bar they had just left. "It certainly brought back some old feelings." She then refocused on the thought of her younger self entangled with Alex earlier in the evening, she felt a flush of excitement.

"You okay?" Alex asked as he noticed her pause.

"You wasted no time on that evening." She answered, working to maintain her focus on the scene 16 years ago.

"Actually, I did waste time. In retrospect, perhaps I would have changed a few things. Still, that is the pathway that brought us to where we are today... Someday, as a wiser and more experienced couple of friends, let's pretend that we are re-living that night and see how each of us would change the way it happened."

"What an exciting thought. I like that idea." Paula kissed him strongly, igniting feelings that were already on the surface. She pulled away before that kiss evolved. "What happens now?"

"It's a complex process. Emily has to process about a hundred billion variables before we launch. We have twenty or thirty minutes, maybe a little more; depending on the alignment of the stars."

Paula thought about his answer for a few seconds. She suspected his comment about the alignment of the stars could be taken literally. "I was not actually talking about that. I was thinking about you, me, and my birthday. You know, Alex, I have always thought it a bit weird that you have given your computer a female name."

"For clarity Paula, it is no longer your birthday. We have moved past that date. With regards to Emily, oftentimes, she has been my only companion. Why would I not give her a name?"

"It's just weird, that's all Alex. Anyway, where are we now going, and are the stars aligned?"

"We're going to Alpha Cassi."

"Just to prove I learned from all those astronomy lessons over wine or beer, let me tell you what that means." Paula offered.

"Okay," Alex smiled as he watched his friend.

"The designation *Alpha* means it's the brightest star in my favorite constellation: Cassiopeia." Paula offered.

"Correct!" Alex broke out with a huge grin and resisted the urge to hug her.

"Yay!" Paula felt particularly smart at that instant. "Since we have some free time, how about a tour of Tranquility Ship?"

"Okay. Follow me." Alex showed her around the ship. As viewed from the outside, it appeared to hold maybe a couple hundred square feet. The inside was clearly twenty or thirty times that number. Every time Alex opened a new portal, she was surprised at the new room. Alex explained that this was because he controlled the space-time continuum in and around the ship. When they entered the galley, Alex explained that the ship contained a year's worth of food and supplies. For entertainment, the computer held tens of thousands of songs from every genre, and thousands of movies; not to mention an electronic library of books that would match any digital or print library on earth. There was scientific equipment for analyzing every conceivable type of data, and a machine shop complete with mill and lathe. There was a small workout room with a treadmill, stationary bike, and a bow flex machine.

"You are very proud of this ecosystem you have created, aren't you?" Paula commented sarcastically, even though she was completely amazed by the engineering treasure herself.

"Of course, I am. This vessel is a lifetime achievement. Everything I have learned and nearly everything man has engineered in thirty-thousand years is represented here."

When they came to his sleeping quarters, she took his hand lightly and looked into his eyes. It had been a long emotion-filled day, and she had no idea what time it was, but she did know she was very tired. "I could use a bit of sleep…" she said, breaking the silence.

"I know from your perspective it's your birthday, and in our temporal space, we can keep February 28th as long as we want. Why don't we climb in bed and get some rest?" Alex offered as he crawled into bed. He was trying to think of the last time he had slept. "It's gonna be something like sixteen hours before we arrive at Alpha Cassi.

As the lighting dimmed in the room, Paula carefully took what appeared to be her side of the bed.

As she drifted off to sleep, she thought of the passion she had felt so many years ago, the memory of that uncontrolled passion made her feel warm deep inside, but the comfort of this current relationship made her feel safe. In a sense, on this night she had warmth, passion, and wisdom.

3

ALPHA CASSI

Alex woke to the soft hum he had come to know as the frequency of Tachyon Tunneling. Paula was sleeping snuggled up next to him. For a minute, the testosterone created images he felt should be better controlled, and with a conscious effort, the intellectual side took over. He reminded himself that protecting friendship always came first.

He re-focused and began to think about his experience with tachyon tunnels. In reality, he had only traveled this far on one other occasion. There were so many variables to consider, and he began to wonder whether it had been prudent to take someone as precious as Paula on such a risky adventure. On the other hand, were it not for his ship, she would now be no more than incinerated carbon dust. He lightly kissed her cheek, then her forehead, and slipped out of bed.

In the control room, he began to study the long list of equations and calculations that were being processed by his supercomputer. He became lost in science and math, losing track of time. Something seemed wrong with the calculations and the actual arrival time result. He was about to question Emily when he realized that Paula was standing silently behind him, watching him pour over a string of nonsensical characters on three different screens.

"Can all of this be explained so that it does not take a Ph.D. in physics to understand?" she broke the silence. Paula had been a very good scientist over the years. She had been published in most of the major microbiology resources for ground-breaking work. Perhaps more importantly, she had focused on enjoying her life. She had focused on the arts and traveled the world extensively, had written a few novels, and made reasonable money. Still, her knowledge of physics was somewhat less than it had been when Alex had taught her sixteen-plus years ago.

"Actually, very few of the Ph.D. physicists I know would believe or understand most of the fundamental engineering in this ship. Since you have no preconceived beliefs, I'm sure I can make you understand," Alex answered and looked away from the screen. "Good morning, by the way," he said as he stood and kissed her in a light platonic fashion.

"You left me in the night. If that's the way you treat all your women, we will not go far," Paula poked.

"I don't believe I need to respond to that ugly comment, Paula Campbell. Furthermore, we are trapped on this ship, and if anything had happened, neither one of us could have run too far."

"That's okay, mister scientist. Give me the stuff you are capable of delivering."

"Roger that. First, I need to check something," he turned away from Paula and faced the screen. "Emily?"

"Yes, Alex."

"How long did we sleep?"

"Four Earth hours," the computer responded.

Alex realized something in the math was definitely wrong…

"Alex," Paula interrupted, "quit flirting with your girlfriend and tell me about this ship."

"Flirting?" He took a deep breath and intentionally exhaled slowly for effect. "I was going to solve a time paradox, but it can wait."

"Good! The ship, tell me about the ship!"

"Tachyons are sub-atomic particles that travel faster than light. Because of that they theoretically travel backward in time; therefore, we are fond of saying that they coexist before they exist," Alex paused.

"Okay. I have heard of tachyons. So far so good!"

"Excellent. In fact, those tachyons simply tunnel through space-time. My lifelong study of tachyons allowed me to engineer methods to create tunnels with the tachyons. You see, at the end of the day, Einstein was right when he said that nothing can travel faster than light. The key is, in the space-time continuum where we exist and live, tachyons are not traveling faster than light; they are simply tunneling through the fourth dimension."

"Now you've lost me. I hope you don't assume I am following this?" Paula interrupted.

"Stay with me. So far this is just tiny particles that slip into tunnels. No big deal if you stay away from the true definition of tunneling in space-time. Imagine it this way: if I want to travel between Denver and Phoenix, I have to cross a large number of mountains. That is how our forefathers traveled because the surface of the planet was what they could control. In the last hundred years, we began cutting tunnels through the mountains. Space and time are very similar. As three-dimensional creatures, we are not capable of tunneling from one point in time to another. With tachyon tunneling, I can cut a tunnel through the mountain of time and space. Understood?"

"I understand the analogy," Paula answered. "What I don't understand is how this is different from a wormhole."

"That's an excellent question!" Alex responded. "Wormholes and black holes are gravitational. They terrify me, because I do not know of any way we could survive even being in their proximity. We'd be crushed and shredded!"

"That doesn't sound fun," she responded.

"Science needs to catch up to the new concepts," he paused for a second. "Tachyon tunneling is way safer than worm holing. Anyway, we are now in a tachyon tunnel that I control. Moving from one place to another is not that complex, once you understand the physics of tunneling. The problem is making sure you don't exit the tunnel in the middle of a planet or moon…"

"That's a horrifying thought. Can't you see things like that?" she asked.

"Actually, no. You have to remember the distances involved. When studying Alpha Cassi, even an object as big as our Moon is nearly impossible to see from our solar system. Something as small as an asteroid would create a disaster if it were at the exit point.   Couple that with the fact that our ability to perceive and detect moves at the speed of light. From Earth, I am seeing Alpha Cassiopeia as it was 120 years ago.   The distance is so great that even the star is just a pinpoint of light. If there is a planet or other object in orbit, I have no chance whatsoever of seeing it. If I did this long enough, sooner or later a disaster would occur. I suspect as this type of ship is developed by mankind, we will have specified vacuums from which we can take launch and pop out of tunnels."

"Should I be concerned?" Paula asked, trying to read Alex's state of mind.

"Strictly from a probability perspective: No. Space is pretty close to 100% empty. For safety's sake, we will complete this journey in two or three hops. The first will end a few light hours from our destination. You can pretty much bet that is empty space."

"How far is a light hour, Alex?" she asked.

"Well, for context, Earth is eight light minutes from the sun, and Saturn is about eighty light minutes," Alex responded without missing a beat.

"Got it. So, we will be coming out of our tachyon tunnel a distance of about twice the orbit of Saturn from Alpha Cassiopeia?"

"Correct. From there, we will try to judge whether there is something more interesting closer to Alpha Cassi."

"Can you define: more interesting?" Paula asked.

"This particular star is very much like our own sun. If there's an Earth-class planet, in orbit, we should be able to venture in and see if we can find some type of life."

Paula started to understand the implications. Because of her age, she had grown up with the intrigue of Roswell. After the TV show of the late 90s, she traveled to that small town in the desert on several occasions. The possibility of discovering intelligent life was beyond her wildest dreams. Suddenly the full impact of this adventure was beginning to take shape.

"Are there any windows or ways we can view outside of the ship? What can we see right now?" Paula started thinking of dozens of questions she wanted to ask.

"There's no light or any conventional energy in a tachyon tunnel. Listen," he paused for a second, listening to the hum, "that sound is not the ship. It is some kind of frequency I have experienced each time I've traveled. I don't know what it is, but I am collecting data to analyze it someday."

"So, we can't see anything outside? How many times have you traveled?"

"Nope. Can't see a thing. Like I said, there is no matter, light, or energy in this tunnel. This is my fourth interstellar hop. I've tested the ship nearly a hundred times, but almost always inside our solar system where I can clearly see and predict the exit with 100% accuracy."

Paula started to ask another question, and Alex stopped her. He glanced at the control panel and checked a few numbers. He was a bit surprised to see how quickly the computer showed their exit from the tunnel, but he was tired and knew his computer Emily was not likely to be wrong. "Listen, Paula, we have a little more time before we exit the tunnel into 3-space. Let's go work out, shower, and have some breakfast."

"Sounds perfect!" Paula had been hungry from the moment she woke.

Just under two hours later, they were back in the control room feeling refreshed and alert. Alex checked the final calculations and monitored as the computer brought the ship from the tachyon tunnel into 3-space. Had he made an error in the calculations, or was his internal clock screwed up because of the last 24 hours events? He wasn't certain, but knew he was about to exit the tunnel and his focus was required.

When the hum stopped, the monitors lit with outside views. Alpha Cassiopeia was a bright light out the starboard side, but for the most part, the space seemed uninteresting. Alex handed Paula an air mouse that she could use to manipulate the camera angles and get different perspectives on the space they now occupied. The stars were brilliant and surrounded the ship in patterns that she did not recognize.

While Paula perused the view, Alex conducted a close-in study to see if any earth-sized planets orbited this star.

"Aha! Got one!!!" Alex exclaimed excitedly. "Looks like we have a planet slightly larger than Mars, with significant oxygen and carbon. Want to go in and get a closer look?" He asked, but was already programming the coordinates for the jump. In a millisecond, the screens went blank and the hum, now familiar to the tachyon tunnel, came on.

"You didn't even give me a chance to answer," Paula protested.

"Sorry," Alex answered only half sheepishly. "Do you have any idea of the significance here? This is an Earth-class planet orbiting a K-Type star. We have just won the Astronomers' lotto, not to mention the oxygen and carbon. Why would we not go in?"

"Because it might be dangerous!" she prodded. In reality, she wanted to explore as badly as he did.

"Oh, hell, we'll be okay. Hang on, this will be a short hop. In a few seconds, we'll pop out approximately ten thousand kilometers above the surface. From there, we can map, orbit, and have a closer look."

Just a few seconds later, the hum stopped, and the monitors lit up. Paula immediately took the air mouse and scanned the field. Alex showed her how to hold the button and move her hand so that she zoomed in. The view was startling. The planet had blue water mixed with green and brown land masses.

"It's beautiful," she commented while scanning this planet, which surely was being viewed for the first time by human eyes.

Alex felt his pulse racing as startling data streamed in and the implications of this planet and its discovery reeled through his mind. He had selected this system simply because Cassiopeia was Paula's favorite constellation. In a hundred years of random guessing based on the science of the day, he may never have selected this particular system. He tried to focus on data collection but remained breathless while Paula pointed out one landmark after the next. After several minutes, their orbit brought them to the night side, which produced yet another startling discovery. The land mass areas were speckled with what appeared to be lights.

"Alex, are those lights?" Paula asked at the same instant Alex was thinking it.

Her question made him evaluate the alternatives. "I think so, but not sure. I suppose it could be some natural phenomenon. I expect the laws of physics to be a constant throughout the galaxy, but we are just toddlers in understanding those laws." The lights tended to occur mostly along what appeared to be coastlines, another piece of important data. Human civilization requires water to survive, and at least on Earth, historically has collected near bodies of water. Alex made sure his monitors were capturing all of the data, mapping the surface with high-resolution photography.

"Can we land?" Paula asked.

"Uhhhh, hold on a sec." Alex began to work feverishly on his computer. He was analyzing the atmosphere, fluids, radio frequencies, radiation levels, and temperatures. After a few minutes, he was ready to report: "Here's what I have… The sulfur content of the air is a bit high, though not toxic. I wouldn't suggest extended exposure, but a few hours at a time wouldn't hurt. The temperature on the night side is quite cold. If my sensors are correct, it's well below zero, while the day side is as high as 120. It seems rotation is about 45 hours, so the extended night is probably a good explanation for the extreme temperature variations. The radiation levels are lower than on Earth, which is surprising to me because of the smaller size of this planet. The water seems to be plain ole H2O, no salt in the larger bodies."

Alex kept looking at the radio spectrum and was confused by the content. Lots of low-frequency signals, but he was unable to make heads or tails out of what it was or whether it represented background noise or intelligence.

"What should we name her," Paula asked.

Alex was focused on a million scientific issues, and Paula brought him back to reality. If only Magellan had brought a sensible woman along for his voyage, perhaps he would have survived his circumnavigation of the Earth. Alex looked into the beautiful eyes of his best friend and could only come up with one answer: "ACP, short for Alpha Cassi Paula." He looked back at the screen that showed the entire planet. "Yes, that's the perfect name for this beautiful oasis in the emptiness of space." Alex turned back to Paula and noticed her eyes had welled with tears.

"Thank you, Alex, I love you too. I can't tell you how many times you have been my oasis in the emptiness of space."

They embraced tightly and suddenly Alex realized that the discovery of ACP had been eclipsed by an event of far more personal importance. He stopped and allowed himself the time to enjoy this singular moment with one of his closest friends. He thought about the Alex of 2009 and realized that individual would have missed this moment. That individual got sex, but this one was the beneficiary of emotion and connection with permanence. Over the years, their connection had lost nothing but instead had grown into one of the most powerful and constant forces in his life.

After a few moments, they separated. "With your permission, I'll taker er in..." Alex offered as he turned to the console feeling warm and tingly.

"Aye, aye captain," she responded and winked so he would know she interpreted his comment as having a double meaning.

"Emily, I'll take the controls for entry."

"Releasing computer control, Alex," the computer responded.

Alex's interstellar tachyon tunnel vessel slipped silently into the atmosphere of ACP, with a predetermined heading near one of the coastlines, but far enough from what appeared to be one of the cities – if they were cities - so that they would not be detected.   Alex's eyes flickered from monitor to monitor, calculating and observing progress.

Just a few thousand feet off the ground, the ship was rocked by an explosion just aft of their path. Alex immediately strapped himself in and instructed Paula to do the same. He ran an analysis routine to determine if there was any damage to the ship and if this had been a natural phenomenon or an attack. As a caution, he ran a pre-programmed tachyon temporal tunnel which popped them 500 years into the past. After emerging from the tunnel, he scanned the coastline and found it to be identical, except for the lights. He scanned the terrain, located a smooth landing area, and touched down a few hundred meters from the large freshwater ocean.

"What just happened?" Paula asked as they reached the safety of the ground, and she knew her question would not distract his focus on a good landing.

"Not sure, Paula. It may be that the sulfur in the air interacted with something on the surface of our ship. There may be some magnesium impurities in our carbon fiber shell... I'll know for sure in just a minute." Alex was pounding on buttons in ever-changing touch screens as he and Emily analyzed the data. After several minutes, he stopped, furrowed his brow, and ran another simulation.

"Shit." Alex slumped, then sat up straight again.

"What happened?" Paula responded without thinking.

"First, it appears the explosion was not natural. We were *attacked*; and second, we sustained damage to our spatial tunneling device."

"Can you translate that, please?"

"Well, unless, uhhmmm, *until* I can fix it, we are stuck here. Our ship can tunnel in time, but not in space. We have a small amount of thrust for flight, but getting into space is not currently possible. Even if we got into space, it would take a million years to get back to Earth."

Paula's heart sank. "Stuck here?!" she asked incredulously. She thought to herself that if this were a dream, now would be a good time to wake up. She didn't. Ten minutes ago, she was on top of the world experiencing one of life's greatest moments, and now she was marooned on a slightly toxic world an impossible distance from home. "Do we have any way of communicating with Earth?"

"Sure. Simply point the radio antenna, send your message, and wait 120 years for the signal to reach Earth. If you're lucky, in 240 years, you'll get an answer." Alex answered sarcastically. "More than likely, if anyone happens to be listening, they'll probably think it's a practical joke."

Both of them sat in desperation for some time while Alex checked and rechecked circuits, calculations, and systems. For several hours they discussed the problems and possibilities associated with their predicament.

After some time of silence, Paula finally spoke. "How far ahead of the rest of the engineering community is your tachyon tunneling technology?"

"Fifteen, maybe twenty years," Alex answered. "But that's not the bad part. There are two hundred billion stars in our galaxy. If the scientific community suddenly understood tunneling and if *everyone* on earth volunteered for a mission, our chances of being discovered are still under five percent."

"Anyone else on Earth work with you on this ship?" she asked, hoping for a positive answer.

"Mark knows about the technology but doesn't know anything about the fundamental engineering of the ship, nor does he know where we are. I outsourced each component from different vendors. No one could have known what I was building. All of the engineering design is stored onboard this ship's computer."

Paula thought about it for several long minutes as she watched Alex transfixed on the screens. She knew he was already solving problems in his head, working on a solution. In the meantime, she used her air mouse to study the terrain outside their ship. The realization of being stuck on a planet a hundred light years from Earth was beginning to settle, but she was determined to find a way to look at the bright side. "I think I want to go outside and see what's here. If this is going to be home, I may as well explore." In reality, she did not believe for a second that she was marooned. She had never seen a problem that Alex could not solve, and she was quite confident this one was no different.

Her comment made Alex smile. "Hold on and let me do some sensory checks. I'll go with you."

"Damn right, you will. I'm not going out on my own!" Paula made it clear she had decided to take a positive perspective on the predicament. "We have always wanted to have an opportunity to spend extended time together. Things could be worse if it was anyone other than you. Remember how as kids we used to dream of getting stuck on a desert island with someone we loved?"

Alex chuckled at her comment as he ran some tests. "This is weird; the sulfur content is much lower than the measurements recorded when we made our approach. I wonder if 500 years in the future, this planet will be supporting a society that generates power and light with high-sulfur fuels…" As he was talking, he continued testing and analyzing. "Looks like the atmosphere is not toxic after all in our current time period." Alex pressed some buttons that opened two portals leading outside. A third opened a closet with clothing. He pulled down two coats and handed her one. "It's pretty cold out there this evening."

She looked at him a bit perplexed as she put on the coat and found that it fit perfectly. "Is this my coat, Alex?"

"Chalk it up to my being a former Boy Scout. While you were reading my folder on tunneling, I tested the ship by hopping to your house. I picked up some provisions and your motorcycle." Alex answered with as much of a smile as he could muster. "Oh, let me check one more thing…" He returned to his console and after a few seconds came back. "Three hours till sunrise." He grabbed a backpack full of scientific testing equipment and escorted Paula out to her new temporary home, or perhaps better stated: prison.

The night air was colder than he had originally estimated but was made a bit better by a warm breeze blowing in off the coast. The sky was relatively clear and hosted a display of completely unfamiliar constellations. The night sky was also adorned by two moons, either smaller than Earth's Moon or farther away. Alex made a mental note to run some calculations on them.

Alex felt a bit of bounce in his walk and made a sudden realization. He turned to Paula, picked her up, and tossed her, with only minor exertion, over his head, catching her and setting her back down.

Completely caught off guard, the only thing she could think of to say was: "I wasn't aware that you were trying out for the cheerleading team… What *was* that all about?"

"Well, I have not been working out any more than normal… On ACP, you weigh a mere 60 pounds."

Paula turned and picked Alex up and held him like a baby. It was not easy, but it would have been impossible on Earth. "Cool. Now let's quit playing around and explore." She kissed his forehead and set him down.

"Okay Mom," Alex joked as he scanned the scenery on the starlit and double moonlit night.

"Here are some ground rules. Do not touch any vegetation until we have time to analyze it. We don't want to accidentally wander into something poisonous. We have no weapons, so we do not want to encounter any local wildlife that considers us to be exotic food. Finally, let's keep this excursion to an hour or less. After that, we need to return to the ship and do some testing to see if there's anything I missed. After the sun comes up, you take over the environmental analysis. Let me know what type of equipment you need and if I don't already have it, I'll work on creating an alternative."

They wandered down to the shoreline. Alex took a test tube out of his pack and took a water sample. "I can make all the water we need, but if we're stuck here, it might be nice to enjoy the local water. If there's any marine life, we could see how it cooks up." As they walked, they immediately became aware that the beach was not firm sand like on Earth, but instead a hard, frozen muddy material. In the cold night, Alex became aware, almost absently, that Paula was holding his hand. It seemed a bit odd that they would be walking on an exotic double moonlit beach so many light years from Earth. They were undoubtedly the first couple in human history to do so.

The quiet peacefulness of the night made Alex think about the mythology behind Cassiopeia. He stopped and began to study the sky. "Do you know anything about where we are?"

"Other than a planet orbiting a star in my favorite constellation, not really."

"Well then, perhaps a bit of mythology is in order." As he thought about what he knew about the mythology of Cassiopeia, it occurred to him that certainly the 'people' that shot at their ship would know nothing about what he was about to tell Paula. "Long ago in Ethiopia; Cassiopeia was the wife of Cepheus and the mother of Andromeda. Cassiopeia thought her daughter Andromeda was more beautiful than the daughters of Nereus, God of the sea. Because of this, she evoked the anger of the god Poseidon. As punishment, Andromeda was chained to a rock off the coast as a sacrifice for a sea monster called the Kraken. As is often the case in mythology, a hero comes along to save the day. I am sure you have heard about Perseus, who slew Medusa and used her head to slay the Kraken and save Andromeda from death. Still, the Gods decided to teach her humility, so Cassiopeia was banned to the sky hanging her head downward half the time. Cassi looks like the letter W when viewed from Earth, but if you think about it, the symbol is actually something very different."

"What?" Paula asked as she thought about his story.

"Cassiopeia, woman, beautiful… The ancients saw the shape as an outline of a woman's breasts. The star this planet orbits, Alpha Cassi has another name: Shedir, which is Arabic for breast."

"Fascinating," Paula commented as she pulled Alex a bit closer to help her stay warm.

"Yes, mythology often is. It's funny, but this is *our* story, and it has absolutely nothing to do with this planet. The civilization that fired on us during our approach knew nothing of this story, nor could they know anything about the shape of this constellation."

"Why would they not know the shape? I would think if they are sophisticated enough to track our ship, and to attack us as they did, then they should know the neighboring stars," Paula interjected.

"First of all, most stars in the Cassiopeia constellation are not in our current proximity. They simply *appear* that way when viewed from Earth." Alex put his hands on his ears, which were becoming very cold in the night breeze. "Second, it's a perspective issue. Think about how the view of distant objects changes as you get closer."

"I see," she answered, though she really did not understand his explanation.

"Besides, maybe the women here, if there are women here, don't even have breasts," he joked.

"Now that is a fairly flat perspective." Paula retorted.

"Well, let's hope they do, or this planet is going to be extremely boring." Alex checked his watch. "I'm freezing. Let's get back to the ship."

"I get that you're cold, but don't expect to warm yourself on *my* breasts until you find a way off this planet, Alex," she joked as she took his hand and headed back to the ship.

Over the next couple of days on ACP, the two of them fell into a routine. The 45-hour solar cycle made it difficult to always be awake during daylight hours, so Paula adapted to working in light and darkness as she evaluated the local ecology. She found many edible plants and occasionally encountered local wildlife.

At night, the temperature would always go well below freezing, then in the daylight, warm up above 100 Fahrenheit. This created an interesting ecology of very hearty plants that grew very fast, then went dormant, surviving the freezing temperatures at night. Paula discovered several plants that would grow from seeds or roots, flower, and bear fruit in 22 hours. She also found a small, pleasant lagoon where the water would warm significantly by the end of the day. Not only did it become a regular bathing and sauna location, but she found ample life living in that warmer pool. She managed to coax Alex to join her on one occasion, briefly in the warm sauna, but he preferred to bathe in the facilities found on board the ship.

Alex built a crude pulse laser weapon so that she could protect herself while outside the ship. It could fire a few short bursts of intense collimated light but would not have been effective in fending off more than two foes.

While Paula was studying the local ecology and learning her way around, Alex spent most of his time evaluating the damage and working on solutions that would allow for another space jump. Paula had to pull him from his work to spend time with her, and drag him to the bedroom so that she would not have to sleep alone at night. He was very sweet, but always avoided any intimate advances. Meanwhile, Paula was beginning to come to grips with the realization they would end up being permanently marooned, and, as such, was considering evolving their relationship into one where they could enjoy intimacy.

After 42 ACP days (79 Earth Days) on the planet, they had both gotten into a daily groove and adapted their sleeping schedule to stay awake during the long days with little more than a light nap in the late afternoon. Paula had made significant progress isolating edible vegetables and even one fruit that she had kept secret from Alex. She was enjoying the warm afternoons and her daily visits to the sauna lagoon. In part of her daily tasks, she had been working on an experiment with one of the local fruits and wanted to test it over a dinner that she was preparing from local vegetables, and meat Alex had frozen in his onboard storage. When Alex sat down for dinner, they talked about the progress each was making. Paula always had significant progress, whereas Alex typically reported dead ends. He was frustrated but stayed determined.

Paula had used her "secret fruit" to make wine. She tested the recipe and was quite proud of her concoction. Alex first tasted her vegetable plate. It was different but tasty. She had never fashioned herself as a cook but was enjoying experimenting with the local vegetables. She handed him a small round fruit that looked and tasted like a grape. It was the first fresh fruit he had eaten since they had arrived, and it was wonderfully refreshing. Then she poured a glass of her surprise. He sipped and said it was the best wine he had tasted all year.

For the next hour, they drank, laughed, and listened to music. They retired to the bedroom and continued to drink Paula's makeshift wine as they sang along to tunes from their high school and college days.

Finally, Paula decided the time was right to discuss something she had been thinking about quite a bit. "I think we need to start living as if we are permanently stuck here," she ventured.

"Paula, I don't think we are *permanently* stuck here, and I think it's a huge mistake for you to make that assumption." Alex read something into her tone that made him a bit nervous. "Anyway, what exactly are you talking about?"

"A couple of things," she took a deep breath. "If we are here permanently, I want a child," she said and watched his reaction.

"You're kidding, right," he asked incredulously, studying his friend.

"Actually, I'm not. A few weeks ago, I started thinking it was strange that we've been here this long and not been intimate. I remember you saying before we left Earth that you thought it was inevitable, and yet in this situation, we sleep together every night, and *nothing* has happened. Not only does it sound impossible, but it also doesn't make sense." She noticed he was going to respond, but she stopped him. "Then it occurred to me that I have not had a birth control pill in a couple of months. My cycle is normal and if we were to have sex, there's a chance I could become pregnant. At first, that scared me, but then I came to grips with it. If we're permanently stuck here, I want a child."

"We are NOT permanently marooned here. Furthermore, you have completely caught me off guard with that one." Alex was rubbing his chin, shocked by her proposal. "My suggestion is that since it took you a few weeks to reconcile, I think you need to give me an equal amount of time."

She pushed him down on the bed and slid her hand into his pants. "No, I want you right now!" Then, she rolled over as they both broke out into slightly intoxicated laughter.

After a few minutes, Alex broke the silence. "Well, one thing is obvious, we certainly have no inhibitions around each other. What's the other thing you wanted to talk about?"

"You said that someone fired on us as we were landing. I want to find out more about the intelligent life on this planet. Who knows, they may be human. I've seen traces that I think may be human."

"They are not human," Alex responded in his most matter-of-a-fact tone.

"You keep saying that, but how do you know?" She argued.

"What plant or animal on this planet looks like anything on Earth?" Alex countered.

Paula lifted her wine and took a sip. "Lots. This one," she said, pointing at the empty glass that had contained wine. The fact was that she had been surprised by how much life on this planet reminded her of Earth.

"I have classified several plant species that are strangely similar to plants found back on Terra Firma."

"It's too risky. We only have a crude laser weapon to defend ourselves. Think about what people on Earth would do to Aliens. Think about what they did to us just for entering their air space. They fired first. This is an aggressive society, and we are better off staying out of sight."

"You may be right, but I need to know. In any case, I am surprised you are being so cautious. It is not like you."

Alex thought about that, she was right. He had spent so much time absorbed, desperate in his attempt to fix his ship that he thought about little else. He felt completely responsible for marooning her on this distant world, and that feeling impacted his mood and demeanor every day. Perhaps it was time he changed that. "Okay, you're right. Put together a plan and I'll find a way to support your effort." He rolled over and began to kiss her. It could easily have been a good night kiss like the many they had shared since arriving on this world, but they each responded differently on this night. They shifted their bodies and allowed the kiss to become passionate. The wine and the conversation had made Alex tingle, enjoy and appreciate the presence of his female partner. They rolled and kissed, fondled and played for nearly an hour before falling asleep, still fully clothed.

4

PACS

In the morning Paula woke to the smell of fresh coffee and bacon. She walked into the dining room and noticed a much lighter Alex.

"Well, what is making you so happy today?" she asked.

"I guess you gave me a new perspective last night. It wasn't exactly a complete transition, but I think I might enjoy coming around to a new point of view. My gosh, I can't recall a time in my adult life when I've gone this long without exploration."

"Goody. Right now?" she chided as she put her hand tenderly on his face.

"Actually, I was referring to searching for the local intelligent life. More specifically, studying our neighbors." He put his arms around her waist. "I think you believe I could be easily talked into intimacy, but..."

"You are becoming boring, Alex," she prodded, then changed her tone. "Oh, sorry to hurt your feelings... I bet you think I simply don't want you – even though you are the last or only man on this planet!"

"My gosh, the last woman on Earth. What a thought," he answered. "I do not think I've gone this long without sex in my entire adult life," Alex groaned.

"No sex and no adventure. That is not the Alex I have always known. Well, get used to it, mister!" She chided in her most sexy voice.

"Okay, here's what we need to do," Alex intentionally changed the subject. "First thing is to determine where these beings are on the technology timeline."

"Done with one topic and on to the next. That is all Alex," she interrupted.

"Yup," he smiled and continued. "As I said, the first thing is to determine where these beings are on the technology timeline. I suggest we find a village or some kind of habitation and evaluate, from a distance. Initially, we need to do it on foot. I do not want to ruin our seclusion by flying right now."

"I'm already a few steps ahead of you. I've been finding traces for several weeks now." She grabbed her backpack and waited for Alex. "I think I can take us to a habitation," she answered as she pointed in the direction she intended to begin hiking.

"Geez Paula. You are in such a hurry for everything right now! Let's finish breakfast first." He remained in his chair observing her excitement.

After breakfast, he put together some basic equipment to get them through a day of hiking on their new home planet and then secured the ship. They walked nearly two hours before signs of habitation started to become clear. "This path has been used by something other than local wildlife," Paula theorized. She had been following these paths, which she believed were commonly used by wildlife, but may very well have also been used by local intelligence. Sure enough, the path began to widen and clear signs of use materialized.

Shortly, they came to a broad, straight clearing that had obviously been constructed and was being used as a road. Alex examined what appeared to be ruts and determined that this population used wheels. The realization was startling. On a planet just 120 light years from Earth, an intelligent life form had built roads and within 500 years would develop ground-to-air missile technology sophisticated enough to nearly shoot down his interstellar spaceship. The aggressive and sudden attack on his ship had suggested they would not be good neighbors, but neighbors they soon would be. Mankind's ability to transmit and receive radio waves was less than 120 years old, and he suspected this life form's ability to do the same might be close to that. The bottom line was that it would not be long before the two would be aware of each other.

"What now?" Paula spoke first, breaking Alex's deep thought.

"What do you suggest, my dear?" he asked, as he continued to study the road looking for signs that would allow him to determine the state of their technology. He did not have to study long before they heard sounds coming from around the bend in the road.

Both Paula and Alex scuttled for cover in the nearby vegetation. What they saw surprised them both. The cart looked much like an early 1800s wagon. The beast of burden pulling that cart could have been an Asian water buffalo. Most interesting were the 'people' riding on the cart. They were slightly smaller than humans with thin heads and well-muscled bodies. They had large brown eyes, two arms, and two legs. Their hands consisted of five fingers – one opposing four. All carried weapons of bows and spears. Alex and Paula watched as they passed, maintaining absolute silence until they were long down the road.

"Wow, they were human. My gosh Paula, those were humans. What did you make of them?" Alex finally asked.

"They didn't look particularly friendly, but they definitely appeared to be something similar to homo sapiens, or closely related. How is that possible?" She added.

"I don't know. There's so much about the universe we don't yet understand."

"I agree that we should avoid contact, but I still want to study them," she answered.

"Well, if you think you can study without contact, then you should study. I can't imagine a more interesting project to consume your time while I figure out how to fix our ship."

"For a couple hundred years, mankind has dreamed of finding intelligent life in the universe," Paula said thoughtfully, "and we just did. They look so human, it's scary. I'd love to get a DNA sample and see just how similar they really are."

"I understand the impact, but the gravity of it really hit home for me some time ago when these creatures fired on our vessel," Alex answered.

"So," She started, "do you think intelligent life is rare, and we just got lucky finding it here? Or is it common?"

"I have always thought life in the universe would be relatively common, at least from a statistical perspective. There are trillions of stars in the universe. Anyone who believes we are alone simply doesn't understand math." He looked down and brushed the dust from his jeans. "I also think we need to start heading back to the ship" Alex answered.

Paula took his hand and began the long walk back to their ship. As she walked, she thought about how mankind would interact with these beings when they first formally met. Finally, she broke the silence. "Do you really think you will fix the ship?"

"Of course, I will," he answered without thinking twice. "Every problem has a solution. I *will* find this one."

"One of the things I have always loved about you is your creativity and unrelenting confidence," she said lightly.

"Without that kind of cocky confidence, I am nothing."

"Do you even know what's broken?" she asked. While she walked, she let go of his hand and ran her fingers through his hair as she watched him ponder her question.

"I know what system is non-functional but can't figure out which component. I've analyzed almost every component. In a few days, I'll finish the analysis process and will begin comparing against standard data tables. I could have it figured out in a month – maybe less."

"Do you have replacement parts, if you find that something was destroyed by the explosion?"

"No, but I do have a miniature FAB and a parts printer, or I could steal parts from the temporal engine, if necessary. For the most part, the two are similar machines. There is a possibility I can build a coprocessor circuit," Alex answered, but in reality, he knew it was not likely he could replicate any of the significant engineering without years of work and a lot of luck.

"Can the spatial engine work without the temporal?" she asked, feeling that she was finally beginning to understand the technology that had allowed them to travel farther than any human in history.

"Not in the current configuration," he answered. "I'll have to do some re-design to make it work. Right now, they rely on each other to function. I'm pretty sure I can adapt the process..."

"Look, I don't want to sound defeatist, but we should look realistically at the situation," she started. "We may get out of here, but, on the other hand, we may not. I do not want us to be stranded alone here for the remainder of our lives. We need to think seriously about having a child."

"And doom that child to being alone on this planet after we are gone?" He argued.

"We could have two," she answered.

"Look Paula, neither one of us is a medical doctor. You are pretty old to be having children without first-class medical care, and I'd think the possibility of complications are dangerously high at your age."

She took a deep breath and exhaled slowly. "There's only one way to find out for sure."

"I am not willing to risk losing you. It just doesn't make sense. You are nearly forty for heaven's sake."

His concern touched her. She stopped walking and took him in her arms. They held each other briefly then began to kiss lightly. The day had become hot, and the sweat tasted good on their lips.

Alex thought about how much he cared for her and tried to reconcile how they had spent so much time together on this planet. It seemed strange that the only intimacy they had shared was snuggling, occasional kissing, and falling asleep in each other's arms. After a few moments, they broke away.

"I love you, Alex. You are and have always been one of the best things and great loves in my life. The things that I risk with you are worth risking," Paula said as she looked into his steel-blue eyes.

"Paula, I plan to continue spending my days getting as close to you as possible, but as long as there is a chance of us getting home, I also plan to keep a sheet of rice paper between us. When we get back to Earth, and when you have abundant numbers of other men to choose from, it will be different. If you still feel the same way when younger, better-looking men are in the room, perhaps we can remove that last small barrier."

"Why, Alex?"

"I don't want to risk hurting the most beautiful friendship in my life for convenience sex," Alex answered.

Paula thought about his answer and had no response. How was it that they had spent their youth interested in sex, and now he was focused on the integrity of their friendship?

They walked for a while in silence. Alex was trying to re-focus by forcing himself to remember the names of the various plants that Paula had documented since arriving. This place would be a botanist's dream. Not since Darwin had so many new species been classified.

Sensing that he did not want to pursue the conversation further, Paula changed the subject. "Alex, I've also noticed a complete lack of birds. There are plenty of flying insects, but no birds."

Alex scanned the sky. There were a few clouds, but nothing else. The sun was about 3 hours from setting. "I wonder how much influence birds had on mankind's desire to fly? I wonder how long this civilization has had the wheel and what other technology they possess. I noticed they had knives and swords, bows and spears along with what looked like a primitive rifle. There were bags that must contain gunpowder, so they have not yet developed the bullet. The wheels were raw wood on a steel hub and axle. My guess is they have not yet developed ball bearings. I could go on and on, but I won't." He looked at Paula who was watching him as he speculated about the level of technology of their neighbors. "They were armed to the hilt. Clearly, they are dangerous. You need to be very careful and constantly on alert if you pursue a goal of studying them."

"I know," she responded. "Hey, I have some more wine. When we get home, let's have a glass."

Alex was lost in thought and did not hear her proposal. In reality, he had spent the entire day mentally working on the ship's malfunction, while simultaneously thinking about the local inhabitants, their neighbors. He was not terribly surprised by what he saw, though the reality of seeing them made the situation much more real. If they were to be stuck here, he would need to begin working on a plan to deal with them, along with planning their long-term survival. Concerning the malfunction, he had some things he wanted to test.

"Alex!!"

"Huh?" He looked at her as she broke his thought pattern.

"Are you interested in having a glass of wine with me when we get home?"

"Home. You're calling it home?" He put his arm around her. "I am sorry I got you stuck in this mess, Paula. Still, there is no one with whom I would rather be stuck here."

"Is that a *yes*?"

"It's a yes. I look forward to relaxing with a glass of your ACP wine."

Back at the ship, they both worked on a quick dinner. Paula queued one of her favorite movies, and they both sat down for a relaxing evening. They fell asleep on the makeshift couch in their makeshift media room. Before dawn, Alex woke, covered his sleeping partner, and went to work on finishing the systems analysis.

Paula woke shortly after and began planning her anthropology expedition. Over the next couple of days, she read everything relating to anthropology she could get her hands on in Alex's digital library. She asked Alex to detail his observations and understanding of their weapons and technology in their wagon. She tried to draw parallels in human history. After a week, she was ready.

She found Alex at work on some project in his shop. She ran her fingers through his hair and kissed him as he worked. He turned and took her in his arms.

"Looks like you're ready," he observed with a smile.

"I am," she answered. "A bit nervous, but also excited."

"I'm looking forward to hearing your observations. Any idea how long this study will take?"

"I plan to be gone all day today. After that, I'll just play it by ear. I have a video camera to capture everything. I think your telephoto lenses will allow me to record from fairly great distances, so it should be safe."

"Right, if you take a tripod, you can get good imaging from over a couple of kilometers away. Also, a boom mic will perhaps allow for the capture of sounds. If they have a language, perhaps we can begin analyzing it with software on our ship's computers," Alex offered.

"Okay. You mean Emily will analyze it?" Paula stood staring at Alex.

"Yes, Emily will analyze."

"I'm getting used to her, Alex."

"I knew you would."

"Can you remind me, how far is a kilometer?" she asked.

"Well, one point six kilometers in a mile."

Paula furrowed her brow.

"You're a scientist. Wait, you're just screwing with me," Alex realized with a frown. "Go on your adventure, have fun, and be safe."

"Okay. Promise me not to have any strange women in the house while I am gone." She kissed him again.

"Ahhh, why not?" He joked. "Those short, stocky, hairy people look like they might be great fun at a bachelor party while the wife is away."

"Typical man. Just a dog…" Then she stopped, realizing what he had said. "Wait, did you just refer to me as your wife?"

Alex thought about what he had said. "Sorry, it was just a slip of the tongue. I was just continuing the conversation. Not intentional. It certainly didn't mean anything." He was backpedaling as fast as he could, while simultaneously trying to understand his comment.

"When I come home tonight, let's start working on that baby."

"Good move. Tease me with sex so I don't go out looking for it on the streets."

"I wasn't born yesterday," she answered as she opened the portal to leave. "I saw how you looked at those creatures on the wagon. It's obvious you can't wait to have sex with one of the females."

"Actually, you won't be born for over 450 years." He ignored her comment about the locals and continued the dialogue as she stood in the door smiling at him, then added: "Could you tell which one was female?"

"I thought they were all male," she answered. "Anyway, at negative 450, I've never felt younger," she said as she playfully bit her lip, winked, and then turned to leave.

"Hey, sweetie," Alex called out as she was opening the portal to the outside. "I have something for you." He got up and walked to the portal, then handed her a shiny new laser weapon. "Take this with you. It's much more powerful than the old version and should fire a dozen or more times before running out of power. If you are ever spotted, aim it at a rock. The beam has enough energy so that the rock will explode. It should scare them enough so you can get away with minimal or no bloodshed. Keep your phone on so I know if you have any problems." Alex had erected a small radio tower so they could use their cell phones to communicate on this planet. It had worked quite well having a range of just over thirty kilometers.

"Thanks," She smiled, "Love you."

"Love you, too." It occurred to him that was the first time they had said that casually since landing on the planet. It made him feel good. Perhaps being stranded here was a good thing. He watched her on his video cameras until she disappeared into the distance.

He spent the next 10 hours working on a new set of calculations with only an hour's break for his daily exercise routine. Alex had been insistent that they train under stress using a bungee harness that simulated their Earth weight. This kept their muscles strong so they would not have trouble adapting when returning home. It also maintained their ability to do some extraordinary physical tasks on ACP.

When she returned, Paula was excited to report what she had observed. They compared notes and Paula headed out for her evening dip in the sauna.

When she returned from the sauna, she found him asleep on their couch. She kissed him lightly and stared at his peaceful sleeping state. She had never met a man like him and was glad she had started their friendship so many years ago.

In the middle of the night, Alex awoke to Paula snuggled up next to him. His mind wandered to the set of equations he had been working on, then back to the woman next to him. He had not taken the time to seriously consider her conversation about having a baby. He was confident they would be able to return to Earth, so he forced himself to avoid seriously considering the thought. Each time he stopped to think about it, the image created mixed feelings. What would become of a child stranded on this planet? It would be a lonely existence after the parents died. Alex kissed her shoulder, then her arm. After a few minutes, he quietly left the room for the control deck.

When Paula awoke, she sat up and thought about the night. She knew that it was still dark outside, and that darkness would continue for another few hours or so. She went into the workout room, walked, and jogged a few kilometers on the treadmill, worked out with the Bowflex, then took a shower. She found Alex exactly where she always found him, pouring over equations on his computer.

"I think it's time you accepted our predicament," she said as she interrupted his concentration.

"Good morning." Alex looked up at her. "I actually believe I will find a solution, Paula. Just give me a little more time."

"I'm starting to like it here. I've gotten used to the long days and nights and am enjoying rediscovering my scientific roots."

"My guess is that you have discovered and classified more botany than any other scientist in the history of mankind," Alex responded as he realized and admired her work. "It's been fun watching you."

"It's been fun doing it, though I am not enjoying watching you. You're not having fun and you're working yourself to death. It seems to me that you are on a dead-end path. I think it's time you resolve to yourself that we are stuck here. When you do, perhaps you can begin to enjoy the place like I have."

Alex thought about her comment. "I would think you would be angry with me for getting you stuck here."

"Believe me, I do get angry. I wonder how my cat is doing, and I wonder about my friends and family. None of them have any idea where I am."

"They think you died in a collision, Paula."

"Oh, I forgot about that unfortunate incident, and that bastard Prinz."

"Well, you know, when I get this thing working, I can return us to the same night we left," Alex offered. "Also, remember that other than your cat, most of your friends went to your funeral and cried about your death on your birthday."

Paula's mind flashed back to the chill of seeing that tanker heading into her vehicle. She put the thought out of her mind. "You can return us to the same night even though we have been gone nearly a half year?" Paula asked incredulously.

"Uh huh.. ...when Emily and I get it fixed." Alex trailed off.

Paula turned and left the room. Something about his attitude impressed her, while another part depressed her. His answer had not been as confident as in the past. In any case, she had projects that were focusing her attention. She had made some long-distance video on the prior day, and wanted to move it over to the ship's computer so she could record more today. Her observations on day one made her think perhaps the local civilization was at a technological level about where mankind was in the late 1500s. She guessed that would make sense, but she also did not want to think they may be the superior species. She decided today that she should come up with a proper English name for her neighbors.

Alex was finding the morning to be a bit distracting. He knew he owed it to Paula to fix the ship and get her home. Back on Earth right now, things were happening that they both needed to be part of. It suddenly occurred to him that the last thing he had done after being fired upon by the ACP city was execute a 500-year negative temporal shift. Taking that into account, back on Earth, Magellan had not yet circumnavigated the Earth, Newton had not discovered the laws of motion and Edison had not invented the light bulb. As his mind reeled through the history a sudden "aha" flashed in his brain. How had he been so stupid all this time? The solution was under his nose. Three computer processor modules controlled the spatial shift engine. He had spent over a half year analyzing in tedious detail which component of which processor was causing the problem when all he had to do was replace the processors.

Alex stood up and went to the galley. He took out his two best steaks and began preparing a celebration. He had finally solved the problem, and the solution was not where he had spent all this time looking. So confident was he in his solution that his magnetic attraction to the computer that enslaved him the entire trip now dissolved into nothing. He quickly spent some time programming the temporal computers for the next journey then went outside and did some data collection on Alpha Cassi. He was vaguely aware that Alpha Cassi was a variable star, but the period was long and stable. He thought he had observed a companion, but that star was distant and quite dim. Still, there were some spectacular displays with the two-moon system that perhaps he had not spent enough time enjoying during their visit. It occurred to him that despite his love of astronomy, he had done almost none since their arrival. That would need to be fixed.

The day warmed up and Alex decided to relax and go for a swim. All in all, it was an unusual, relaxing day. Something Alex had not done since their arrival on ACP.

After Paula had been gone for nearly eight hours, he decided to hike out the trail she had used to study the local population. She had left just after sunrise and probably planned to be gone most of the day. ...and days on this planet had the sun up for typically 23 hours. As he began his hike up the trail, Alex thought about how well they had adapted to the longer days and nights. He believed he would never get to the point where he would sleep 20 hours, and wondered if the locals did. He had, on the other hand, gotten to the point where he could stay up the better part of the 23-hour daylight period.

* * * *

Paula followed the same path back to the road they had discovered earlier. She had long since learned that she could run quite easily in the weaker gravity, and so she often did. The distance seemed somehow shorter on this trek. Yesterday, she had discovered a habitation that contained maybe 100 'people.' As she jogged, she considered the issue of what to call the habitants. As she considered the possibilities, a name popped into her head: Pacs. The People of Alpha Cassi.

As she reached the location, she had chosen the day before, Paula scanned the horizon for a better place to observe. About a half kilometer away was an outcropping of rocks that gave her a better perspective on the habitation. It was significantly closer and as such would allow her to collect better video and perhaps even get some sound samples. Upon arrival, she set up her tripod and began to collect data and study the habitation. There were a few dozen small stone structures along with some larger ones. A wall encircled the entire area, clearly built as a defensive boundary, which she assumed had been designed to keep out Pacs that were not part of this habitation and other predators. As she zoomed in, she was able to observe individuals but was not able to pick up any sounds. There was a slight breeze, which created enough background noise to prevent hearing Pac conversation. As she went through the day, she continued to collect data and film. As she daydreamed, she also resolved to extract Alex from his analysis so he could view her video.

Paula was startled to hear a sound behind her and even more startled to see four Pacs holding spears, making noises. They were clearly frightened by her. It seemed to her that they were uncertain whether to kill or capture her. She moved slowly as she stood and held her hands open so they could see she was not a threat. Nevertheless, one was shouting orders at the other three, and the situation worsened. One lifted and threw his spear. Paula dove out of the path. She grabbed her laser and pointed first at the Pac, who seemed to be the leader, then at the rocks. With a burst, the rocks exploded throwing shrapnel everywhere. Two Pacs immediately fell, while a third ran. The fourth Pac stood holding his spear as if trying to decide what to do and then threw it. Paula did not have time to dodge as the spear grazed her leg. In a split-second reaction, she pointed the laser at the Pac and fired. Without looking, she grabbed her camera and pack and ran toward the path home. As she reached the cover of the underbrush, she inspected her wound.

Looking at the open wound made her suddenly feel the pain. The bottom part of her leg, as well as her shoe, was already soaked in blood. The spear had just missed the tibia and torn through the flesh and part of the muscle. She tried to clean it up with the one rag she had, but there was too much blood. The throbbing was now becoming intense, causing tears to well in her eyes. In the distance, she could hear the sounds of Pac's yelling, and instinctively knew they were looking for her. She tried to stand but found that her foot would no longer support her weight. In her pack, she found the phone, checked the settings, and pressed the call button.

"Alex, can you hear me? I'm in trouble."

Alex had been hiking for nearly an hour when he heard the ring, then Paula's voice on his phone. "Paula, are you okay? What happened?"

"Alex, thank God. I was attacked by the Pacs. My leg is bleeding, and I can't walk."

Alex tried to remember which animal she had named Pax but could not remember that name. "Paula, what's a Pax? Is it still nearby?"

"Pacs – P A C S," she spelled out, "is what I named the local intelligent life form. There were four of them. One grazed my leg with his spear. I got away, but they are searching for me now."

"Did you leave a trail of blood?" Alex was trying to analyze the situation as he ran down the trail as fast as he could at a long-distance pace.

Paula looked back down the path she had run just minutes earlier. There was a clear blood trail. "Yes," she said as her heart sank realizing how easily she could be tracked.

"Okay, listen, you need to create a diversion. I want you to look around and find the farthest thing you can see that is flammable. Try to find something at least a half kilometer from your present position. Use your laser and fire on that object."

Paula tried to ignore the pain and stood on one foot. As she scanned the horizon, she could see the rock outcropping where she had been attacked. A dozen or so Pacs were now congregated around those rocks. Just beyond those rocks was some shrubbery. She aimed the laser and pressed the button. Her aim was not perfect, but she could see the beam in the light dusty air and was able to target the shrubs. They instantly exploded into flames. This startled the Pacs, who mostly hit the ground upon hearing the noise. Slowly, they got up. Some began running to the shrubs.

"Alex, it seemed to work."

"Good." Alex had continued his run but was anxiously awaiting Paula's response. "Now you need to figure out how to stop the bleeding and get as far away from your blood trail as possible."

She tried to stand, and immediately noticed something had changed. "Alex, I can't walk. My foot is completely numb, and I'm losing a lot of blood."

"Paula, you *can* walk. You got to where you are. You just need to focus. See if you can telescope your tripod and use it as a crutch. Use the inside lining of your coat to clean up the blood and your headset wire as a tourniquet."

Paula was amazed at Alex's resourcefulness. She wondered if he ever found himself in situations where he could not find a solution using the tools around him. She cleaned up the blood as best she could with her coat and wrapped her rag around the open wound. She took her headset and a microphone wire to tie the rag tightly to her calf. Finally, she telescoped the tripod and tested it for strength. It seemed to work. Her first step sent a thunderbolt of pain up her leg, which caused her to involuntarily cry out. She took a deep breath and took a second step, this time putting more weight on the tripod. "Alex, I am walking. Not well and not fast, but I am moving."

"Good, Paula. I am already on my way down the trail we took to the road. I'm probably 5 minutes run from the place where we first saw the locals, ahh Pacs. How far are you from there?"

"Not far. Just five or ten minutes, maybe."

"Good," Alex answered. "My policy will be to not talk to you. I do not want your phone to give away your position, so I want you to call me every couple of minutes. Understood?"

"Got it." She winced as she continued every painful step. She turned to look at the trail behind her. While there was no blood, it was obvious what direction she had taken. The tripod was clearly marking the ground. As she hobbled, she began to think about the Pacs. They had shown no signs of trying to be friendly, even though it had to have been clear to them that she was intelligent. As she hobbled, the pain became more and more unbearable. Her leg felt like it was losing feeling, as the seconds seemed like hours and each step became progressively more difficult. She continued to try and divert her thoughts from the injury, but after a few minutes the pain became too extreme, and she fell to the ground, breaking the tripod walking stick. She tried to get up but became dizzy in the process. She looked down at her injury, trying to maintain her focus. She closed her eyes and took a deep breath, but the world started to spin.

Paula grabbed her phone and pressed the call button. "Alex," she struggled to say his name, "something's seriously wrong. Can't walk. Getting dizzy."

"Paula, where are you? You have to get up. You have to keep moving."

"Can't..." She found herself slipping into blackness.

"Damn it, tell me what you can see. No, give me a marker. Listen carefully. Pick two objects equidistant from where you are and hit them with a laser blast. I will triangulate on the sounds and what I can see."

Paula tried to focus on what he had said. She pointed the laser and fired. As she lost consciousness, she tried to fire a second time, and blacked out right as she pressed the button.

Alex knew his suggestion would alert the Pacs to her position, but he hoped he would be closer and faster. He heard an explosion and turned to face it, then closed his eyes. The second explosion came from his left. He immediately began to run in the direction he believed he would find Paula. Within seconds he came to the road they had discovered a week earlier.

Within a few minutes, he found Paula motionless on the ground. About two hundred meters distant, he saw a group of Pacs heading straight for him. He saw a muzzle flash, followed by hearing the distinct bang of a gun. He guessed that even in this light gravity their weapons were out of range, but his laser was not. He aimed at the ground in front of them and fired. An explosion of rocks and dirt stopped them in their paths.

Alex knelt to check Paula's pulse. She was alive but unconscious. He picked up the tripod and placed it in his pack. It was made from advanced metals and plastics. He guessed that the Pacs possessed neither of those materials and did not want to be responsible for handing those technologies to them.

The Pacs had begun to spread out and were advancing once again. Alex immediately knew Paula's condition coupled with their predicament demanded the use of deadly force. In seconds he would be within range of their weapons, and it did not appear they were interested in taking prisoners. One by one, he aimed and fired. At no time did any of them turn to flee. In fact, as he picked them off, the remaining Pacs charged faster. He was not sure how many more blasts he would get from this laser's power supply. It was significantly improved from his earlier version but lacked a truly advanced power supply.

Initially, he thought he had counted six Pacs, but had only taken down five. He scanned the horizon but saw no others. Quickly, he scooped Paula up and threw her over his shoulder, then began to run. He knew that in the first fifteen minutes, he would need to run as fast as his legs would carry him. The lower gravity, coupled with his level of fitness, made this impossible escape into one that was entirely possible. Alex had spent an hour every day in the exercise room running under Earth gravity conditions and lifting weights. The combination of his lighter ACP weight and Paula's was just a little more than what he would have weighed on Earth. Alex felt that if he could get a kilometer or two from the encounter sight, he stood a chance of making it to the ship without further altercation.

Ten minutes into his run, he began to feel the stress. While the weight was not really a factor, running while trying to carry Paula was difficult. He simply was not able to get into a rhythm and found himself constantly shifting her from one position to another. Furthermore, he was becoming aware of the seriousness of her injury. While her bleeding had slowed, with all of the shifting he was surprised she had not returned to consciousness. Clearly, it was not the injury alone that was causing the larger problem. He guessed that there must have been some form of poison in the spear. This would pose a much larger problem when they managed to return to the safety of the ship. Alex was not a physician, but even a doctor would have a difficult time figuring out how to handle an unknown poison in a place an impossibly long distance from home.

Alex set her down so he could rest and assess the situation. He was soaked in sweat and needed to find a way to carry Paula more efficiently. He also knew that it was only a matter of time before the Pacs tracked and caught up with him. While he thought, he listened carefully for approaching sounds but heard none. He had no idea how fast the Pacs could travel on foot, nor how strong they would be if they managed to catch him.

He decided he could carry Paula easier if she could ride piggy-back. Unfortunately, she was still unconscious and could not help. He bound her wrists with a soft cloth, and a 2-foot-long connecting tether. He then stuffed his pack into hers and left it on her back. He took a long drink of water and a deep breath, exhaling slowly. He pulled Paula's arms over his shoulders and looped his arms through her legs. The tether from her arms was easy to hold and she was now riding piggyback, securely, and relatively effortlessly.

As he began to run, Alex told himself that he must make the entire distance to the ship nonstop. He guessed that distance to be somewhere in the 4-to-5-mile range. Normally, he could cover that distance in 30 to 35 minutes. Today, carrying Paula, he was hoping to at least make it in 35. As he ran, he tried to think of things that might be happening on Earth. He knew he needed to stay relaxed in his run, keep in the groove and focus on other things. He did not know the trail well enough to know where he was, so he kept track of distance on his watch. He estimated he was running a sub-8-minute mile, and therefore, it would be no more than 40 minutes, worst case.

After 25 minutes, the fatigue from balancing and carrying Paula made his legs numb. He tried to focus, but his lungs were burning, and his heart was pounding. The only thing that kept him going was his love for Paula and his goal of saving her life. At times he seriously doubted that the Pacs were able to keep up with him, and at others, he felt like they might be gaining quickly. It was that fear which kept him going while the anaerobic blood filled his veins and fatigue consumed his muscles. He found himself checking his watch every 15 or 20 seconds while using every bit of willpower to continue the run.

Right as he thought he could not take another step, Tranquility came into view, and that image alone was enough to take the final wind out of his lungs. Alex stumbled to the ground ripping through his jeans and peeling the skin from his knees and palms. His legs were trembling and his heart was pounding in his temples as he struggled to stand. He looked up at Tranquility, home, and safety, but could not muster the strength to stand. In the distance, he could hear the Pacs approaching, but even so, he could not stand. For just a second, he quelled the struggle and forced his body to relax. He could feel his head spinning and his legs shaking. It was the daytime temperature that was having the biggest impact on him. Five miles carrying a grown woman on his back, in the extreme ACP afternoon heat, was the hardest physical feat he had ever attempted. He relaxed, counted out thirty seconds, and took control.

Alex opened his eyes and stood. He focused on the ship and took a step. The Pacs were close, but he told himself not to think about them, or how close they may be. Alex ignored the pain which had engulfed his body and began to jog the last two hundred steps to safety.

5

DESPERATION

Once inside the ship, Alex punched the button to seal the port, crumpled to the floor, and tried to focus as he untied the tether on Paula's wrists. He went into the bathroom and filled the tub with hot water and salt. He took Paula's pulse and blood pressure. He then began cleaning the wound on her leg. Paula's vitals seemed relatively good, though her pulse rate at 44 beats per minute, was well below normal. He was fairly certain the salt water would have made her scream – had she been conscious. As it was, she did not even make a sound as he slipped her into the water.

After cleaning her wound, Alex treated her with a topical antibiotic. The spear had grazed the leg, cut her calf muscle, and slightly tore some tendons. If she survived the poison, she would have some recovery time but would have full control of her leg and foot.

As Alex was laying her down in the bed, he was startled by the sound of a bang on the outside of the ship. A shot of fear and a jolt of adrenalin ran through his body as he quickly covered Paula and ran into the control room. Had he closed the door? He could not recall. He grabbed his laser and peered out the door to the bedroom. He could see the hatch wide open. Cautiously standing inside the ship was a Pac bearing both primitive rifle and spear. When he eyed Alex, he lifted his arm to throw, but Alex was faster with the laser. As he fired a burst, he shouted at Emily to close the hatch. The startled Pac stumbled out the door as the power-diminished laser seared his flesh.

"Emily, is anyone inside the ship besides Paula and me?"

"No, Alex."

"I could swear I closed that port when I arrived," Alex said to himself.

"You did, Alex." Emily offered.

Alex was startled. "How'd they get in?"

"They watched you open the port when you arrived. They just figured out how to open it." She answered.

"Please reprogram that security problem and don't let them back in," he barked at his computer.

On the monitors, he could see a large group of Pacs attempting to beat down the walls of his ship. They seemed organized and focused on the destruction of their enemy. Alex worked to keep calm as he sat down at the panel and began to program. He was not certain if the ship was able to fly because of all the work he had been doing. In his repair efforts, he had not touched the temporal transfer, so tachyon time shift was his only escape route.

As the Pacs were hammering on the hull, Alex finalized the program to hop 100 years into the past. He knew if he executed a time shift from the ground, the emergence from the tachyon tunnel could be a disaster. As the computer was running final calculations, he switched on his turbojets which would fly the ship off the ground. During the design phase, he experimented with several different methods of flying the ship the old-fashioned way. The big problem had been the need for vertical take-off. For its size, Tranquility was relatively light, but the size was significant. No off-the-shelf technologies existed that would provide thrust for vertical take-off on this size vehicle. Because he had essentially unlimited electricity, he settled on a configuration of 16 electrically powered turbojets. In flight, a computer program monitored the stability of the craft and used a simple feedback control analysis to keep her level, much like a quadcopter drone. Alex had often thought about improving this system but had never found time to do so. The structural design of the ship was not aerodynamic and as such was not capable of fast flight in an atmosphere. The good news was that in the lowered gravity of ACP, the lift was almost explosive. The rumble of his jets kicked up dust causing the startled Pacs to scurry as the vessel leapt off the ground. A few seconds later, the lights began to dim as his ship executed the program to enter the tachyon tunnel.

Alex closed his eyes and took a long deep breath. The immediate problem was now behind him. It would be several minutes before he re-emerged from the tachyon tunnel, so he tried to relax and collect his thoughts. He was surprised by how quickly the Pacs had grouped and mounted the attack on his ship. While he had constructed the ship's shell out of the finest and strongest carbon nanofibers available on 21st-century Earth, he had never anticipated a direct ground attack from club-wielding soldiers. As he thought through the scenarios for escape, he evaluated the decision to tunnel once again onto the past. After a few minutes, it was clear he had only one choice – the one he had made. Alex pressed a button that allowed him to look in on the room where Paula was lying down. She appeared to be resting, though he was acutely aware of his lack of medical knowledge, and consequently, his inability to help her. At this point, the best thing he could do was to try and keep her comfortable and pray.

The ship emerged from the tachyon tunnel with a flash of light. Startled, Alex checked his instruments. The ship was approximately 200 meters above the surface where he saw nothing of the familiar terrain from their prior landing. With his turbojet engines, he was able to fly to a place where there was water and ample foliage to hide his landing.

Once on the ground, Alex focused on analyzing the situation. He had started the day believing he had found a solution to getting home, and now found things operating on a less efficient level than he had estimated. There were bigger problems than he had thought.

The reality of the situation came crashing in on Alex. His technology, which was an incorporation of manufactured components he could not reproduce, had them stranded on an unknown planet over a hundred light years from Earth. His best friend and only human partner in this prison was in a medical crisis, which he had no skills to analyze or treat. The local intelligent life seemed focused on only one thing: his demise. The supplies on board his vessel was sufficient for the two of them to comfortably survive a year. While there was still plenty of time, he knew a solution and contingencies needed to be created As all of these things crashed into Alex's psyche, he began to feel something that he had felt only a few times in his life – helpless desperation.

Alex slumped in his chair, listening to his heartbeat in his temples, while staring at the multiple screens in front of his eyes, which were blurred by the circumstance. He tried to focus but was overwhelmed by the magnitude of the problem. It was several hours before he got up and went to check on Paula. Her condition remained unchanged. She seemed to be asleep, perhaps in some kind of coma.

Alex returned to the control room and worked to relax and collect his thoughts. One thing at a time he told himself. Because of his problem-solving nature, he had not had much experience with depression in his life, but he believed that if he focused on curing the depression, it would only make it worse. He decided to go outside and inspect the damage to the ship's hull. He grabbed his fully charged laser and went outside.

Alex was alarmed by the damage the Pacs had done in their attempt to destroy his ship. There were several places where the pounding had cracked the hull. He was surprised that his sensors had not detected the damage. He had designed the shell on the hull to protect the vessel, but it also served as an outer membrane, maintaining pressure in the ship. The hull had been constructed from sheets of nanocarbon fibers. Alex understood the technology fairly well but lacked the manufacturing capabilities to reproduce the material.

Alex dragged himself back inside the ship, dropped down on the bed next to Paula, and fell asleep. When he woke several hours later, his fatigue lingered. He tried to use a transcendental meditation technique to relax, but even this tried-and-true method failed. He looked at Paula and something inside told him that her situation was far worse than his own. If anything, he needed to figure out how to help her. He gently kissed her forehead, then headed to the computer console where he could do some research and analysis. Along the way, he stopped by the galley to get something to eat. In the galley, he found the two steaks he had taken out to celebrate the solution to their return to Earth. It occurred to him that it may still work. Alex disposed of the now rancid steaks, grabbed a Cliff Bar, and went to the control room. He began to run a few calculations. A spark of hope lit in his heart as he focused on the possibility of success in this plan.

Alex worked like a maniac to check and re-check his calculations. When he was done, he punched a button to put the computer in voice recognition mode.

"Good evening, Alex," Emily spoke in her soft voice.

Alex thought about his computer's voice profile. It certainly was soothing at this point. "Emily, why did you say good evening?" Alex queried.

"My internal clock shows it is just after nine pm," Emily responded.

It occurred to Alex that he had never reprogrammed his computer for ACP time. "Emily, please check my calculations for the most recent hop."

"Alex, my sensors show that you are tired. Can you tell me your goal and I will cross reference based on objectives rather than simple math," Emily responded.

At first, Emily's response shocked Alex. It seemed that she was demonstrating two things; first, she seemed warm and caring, and second, she anticipated the *possibility* of human error, even though the math may have been correct. In any case, Alex was tired and appreciated the help.

"Emily, I need to send a message back to Earth so that it is received before our March departure. I will transmit that message over amateur ham radio frequencies, obviously at the speed of light."

"Acknowledged. How long prior to our departure would you like receipt of the signal, Alex?"

Alex had already thought this problem through. He had been traveling most of the week before, and his friend Mark had been out of state prior to that. Alex knew what he believed to be the optimum time period for his best friend, Mark to have received this message. "At least two weeks prior, but no more than a month."

"Okay Alex, I am processing that goal and will have a result in three minutes and eighteen seconds," Emily responded in her soothing voice.

Emily finished her calculations. "Alex, I have completed the calculations for the optimal tachyon jump to achieve your goal."

Alex glanced at the screen full of calculations. The results were very different from those he had made. The one thing he was certain of was his fatigue. Emily was the most advanced computer ever built. He knew that her precision would be far more accurate than his own. "Okay, Emily, make the hop whenever all systems are ready."

"Will do, Alex."

The ship lifted off the ground and flew a few seconds before the lights dimmed and Alex felt the familiar vibration of the tachyon temporal shift. When the ship returned to 3-space, Alex immediately checked the monitors. He was surprised to find significant populations and technology. As he searched for a secluded landing spot, he prayed the population had not yet developed the technology to shoot down his ship. After an hour of flying close to the ground, avoiding population centers, and searching, he found a desert area with significant rock outcroppings. He landed and prepared for the next step in his plan. Since their arrival on ACP, Alex had spent very little time studying the night sky. He had on the other hand located the star he believed to be Earth's sun. Now, he needed to be absolutely certain. Upon nightfall, he set up his observational equipment and began to map the ACP night sky in detail. Nothing was exactly where it should have been, and he was not able to reconcile precisely why.

While collecting data, he realized that the only thing he had eaten in the last day was a Cliff Bar. As he headed to the galley it occurred to him that Paula had not eaten either. He grabbed a medical kit and found a hypodermic needle. With it, he fabricated an IV so he could feed Paula intravenously. He mixed a glucose solution and returned to the bedroom. Alex paused to gaze at her pained, yet peaceful sleep. He realized that while this IV could help her, it could also kill her. He had no training in handling IVs, but at the same time, knew he had no choice. After a little bit of research in his database, he decided he could try to accomplish this simple task. He searched for a vein, inserted the IV, and watched for over an hour. The drip seemed to be working, so he returned to his other project.

Alex entered the new observational data into the computer. He began to make calculations on exact distances and times using the astronomical data in his computer's library. After a few hours, he realized there was an easier way.

"Emily, can you point out which star in the night sky is that of the Sun."

"Alex, the Sun is up in the day sky right now."

Alex thought about it for a minute. It really didn't matter whether it was in the night or day. He was just surprised that he had not been able to determine where it was. Perhaps even a professional astronomer would have had difficulty with that problem. For Emily, it was an easy calculation.

"Would you like the coordinates for your antenna, Alex?"

"Yes." Clearly, Emily could handle almost every task like this, but Alex tended to be independent and typically liked making the calculations himself. Between the stress and sleeplessness, it made more sense to have Emily handle these things.

The next step was to set up a radio transmitter. Alex had a small dish antenna that he thought could produce a focused signal, which might just make it to Earth. After aligning the antenna, Alex went inside to his radio and tuned it to a ham radio frequency. Now, the question was, what message could he send that would not be alarming, yet not seem like a practical joke? He knew that he needed to get a message to his business partner and longtime friend Mark Adams.

He turned on the record feature, then pressed the microphone button and began to transmit. "To any ham operator that receives this signal, please send an email to Mark Adams that states the following. Dear Mark, I have been asked by your friend Paula to tell you that Alex is having a problem on his current voyage. She needs you to hide a complete processor on board the ship before February 22. Do not tell Alex where it is and make absolutely certain he cannot find it in any routine inspection. Please set up a broadcast unit on a continuous loop to notify of the hidden location. The broadcast should be from a directional antenna pointed up with at least 100 watts. Run continuously, or until Alex asks that you stop." Alex thought about the message and then included Mark's email address. He then programmed his system to resend the same message every 2 minutes.

Alex felt that he needed to stay in this place for two days. The Earth's Sun would set in approximately 9 hours, but just to be sure, he wanted to stay an extra day. One more day ought to ensure the signal is received by more than one ham operator. Surely, Mark would get more than one email. Since the message was ambiguous enough Mark would work through the logic and surely understand the gravity of the situation. The success of this plan depended on whether he could remain in this location without being discovered.

Alex had built some perimeter sensors to ensure the craft was safe on the ground. Now, he tuned them to detect motion at 100 meters, which was the maximum distance his sensors could accurately monitor. Emily could analyze whether any motion was local wildlife or Pacs and would climb and jump to a safe time period.

For now, he needed to work on his contingency. If they were stuck here, he needed to be responsible for Paula's recovery. He had virtually every medical book ever written, converted to digital format, available in his computer library.

Now he had a bit of time to analyze specifically what was affecting Paula.

Alex collected tissue samples from the wound and a few drops of blood to study under the microscope. At one point, a very long time ago, he had been a fairly decent microbiologist. Prior to focusing on physics and engineering, Alex had considered studying microbiology and medicine, but ultimately, his love of gadgets had won him over to technology.

The onboard microscope was not the traditional set of optics, but instead, a single lens, CCD, or Charge Coupled Device, used by all modern digital cameras. The scope worked much like a digital camera, except that it had a significant resolution on a very small scale. The image was projected on a display, where Alex could manipulate, change lighting, and zoom. After several minutes of study, he settled on the drop of blood, looking for something out of place. An experienced physician or lab tech would have had a significant advantage. Alex had not looked at a drop of blood since his college course two decades earlier. After an hour of frustration, he switched to the tissue sample. Here, he almost immediately found a crystalline structure that did not seem to fit. He captured several frames from different angles and was amazed at the complexity of the crystal. One of the great things about crystals was that they could be analyzed and identified using their shape. Alex wrote a quick program to search his database for crystals of similar structure to see if he could determine exactly what this impurity or poison was.

While the program was running, he checked on Paula, then on his transmitter. Neither had changed. He tried to think about the events since Paula had called him to say she had been attacked, but his memory was blurred by the pain in his heart. Outside, the transmitter was sending a focused, collimated beam in the direction of Earth that would not arrive at its destination for 120 years. Alex was frustrated that he could calculate to the minute when his signal would reach Earth, could time travel 240 years into the future, and listen for a response, yet he had no tools that would help him determine whether Paula would live or die or how to help her survive.

He returned to his lab. Emily had finished her search for crystal structures. Alex found a message that said, "No exact matches." He slumped in his chair and stared at the flashing message. The simple solutions seemed to be depleted. Now he would need to begin the long and arduous process of learning biochemistry.

Alex closed his eyes and whispered: *please God, just one little break here, just one.* For a second, he wondered whether God could even hear him from this remote planet. After a minute, he pulled up his online 'Symptoms Guide' and began searching for possible solutions to Paula's coma.

After two full days of transmitting the same signal to Earth, Alex was ready to begin part two of the program. This time, Alex was better rested and as such, did not rely on Emily to handle the calculations for the jump. When complete, he took his crippled ship as far into the desert as possible and then executed a program that transported him 240 years into the future.

When the ship emerged from the tunnel Alex checked the monitors and was surprised to see signs of civilization all around him. His radio lit with RF intelligence, and his sensors immediately detected danger. Within seconds, he spotted incoming weapons, and responded by executing a preprogrammed tachyon hop back 240 years.

Alex landed in the desert where he had transmitted messages earlier and thought about a new tactic. He tried several 240-year jumps to different locations on the planet and each time, was met with immediate attacks on his ship. Over and over and over again, he tried different locations to emerge from the tunnel, and each time was promptly detected. On his sixteenth jump, Alex popped out at a location that was apparently not monitored. He was in an isolated location near the northern pole of the planet. He detected only small amounts of radio signals and no signs of life. He landed and set up his antenna. If Mark had received his signal and responded to the instructions, he would know very quickly. Alex set up his dish receiver and pointed it at Earth. Alex tuned up and down to compensate for any Doppler effects of aberrations in the signal. He recorded every second. He heard nothing that sounded like a response. He listened for several hours and went back to his computer. His jump had taken him to the exact day he had calculated.

He thought about it for a few minutes, then took a jump a couple of days into the future.

Nothing.

Another jump, a week into the future.

Still nothing.

He then tried sequential jumps of a week, waiting a full 24 hours to compensate for Earth's rotation.

Radio silence.

Alex buried his hands in his face and tried to think his way through the problem. Why had Mark not responded? The signal should have been received by hundreds, maybe thousands of amateur ham operators. As a second test, he tachyon jumped forward six months and tried again. Nothing. Then he jumped back 12 months to check. Still nothing. He tested the radio in transmit and receive mode. And all tests checked out positive. He jumped back 239 years and retransmitted the signal to Earth and returned to the future to receive. Still nothing. After checking and rechecking calculations, Alex finally concluded that Mark simply was not getting the message, and this was simply a dead end. Finally, he jumped to minus 600 years so he could be relatively safe while he worked through the problem.

He had instructed Mark to hide the necessary components. If Mark had received the signal, the parts would be onboard. He began a methodical search. For two days, inch by inch, panel by panel, he took the ship apart and reassembled it. Two days later, he had found nothing and had nowhere else to search. Meanwhile, Paula remained stable yet unchanged.

Alex fell into a deep depression; something he had seldom before felt. He sat, perplexed, trying to find a solution to his two seemingly insurmountable problems: fixing his ship and curing Paula. After a while, he got up and went for a run to clear his mind. What Alex needed to do was completely change his perspective.

Alex knew it was time to start focusing on survival in this new world. He could not go into the future without being attacked. He had only one real answer, to stay in this place 600 years in the past. He hoped he was now in a time period where he would have little or no trouble from the Pacs. Job one now became prioritizing long-term survival, while putting repair on hold.   Even with his significant supplies, their days were numbered. Paula had classified a number of edible vegetables, but Alex now needed to get serious about finding edible plants and animals.

6

ETAKATZ

Alex spent several days flying and searching for a long-term landing place that would have natural protection for the ship. He settled in a location approximately 100 kilometers south of where he and Paula had initially landed 120 years earlier.

Day after day, week after week, he split his time studying Paula's condition, working on chemistry, and testing local flora and fauna on human digestion. Each task was slow and tedious. He worked to quickly switch over to local foods so he could preserve as much of his Earth reserves as possible. Every day, he would sit for an hour at Paula's bedside and tell her about the day and projects. Over time, she became thinner and thinner. He learned about bedpans and treating bed sores. He perfected his IV feeding and kissed her on the forehead every night before going to bed. For now, and seemingly, for eternity; Emily was his only companion.

Outside, Alex began building fortifications. He used his electronics skills to fabricate remote sensors that would warn him of the approach of Pacs. He explored miles in every direction but found no signs of civilization.

He discovered a small herd of water buffalo that lived in a river feeding the local ocean. During one of his library sessions, he studied the process of slaughtering and preserving meat. The buffalo was an easy catch, and Alex's freezer was suddenly filled with several hundred pounds of meat. It was not as flavorful as beef, but Alex quickly began to appreciate its unique qualities.

Alex wanted to find the grape-like fruit that Paula had used to make wine. With all his ventures, he had not yet found that particular plant. Periodically, he would use Paula's motorcycle to forage larger distances. If Paula came out of her coma, her love of Harley's would have to change because necessity had mandated significant modifications to the motorcycle. By design, the bike was loud and sure to attract attention, so he minimized its noise level by building a super-quiet muffler. Because of his low supply of gasoline, he fermented an alcohol-based fuel and adapted the motorcycle carburetor to run on it.

Alex set out to the north. He had about 4 gallons of fuel available and guessed he could comfortably make several dozen miles in quest of the grapes. The bike did extremely well on the rough terrain and wildlife paths. After about an hour, he found the small bush-like vine. It bore a fruit surprisingly similar to earth grapes – even in how it grew.

As he was collecting the fruit, he heard the sounds of an injured animal. He worked his way through the thick growth and was surprised to see an injured Pac fighting a desperate battle against three coyote-sized animals that looked similar to dogs. His first thought was to leave it, but something compelled him to take the humanitarian approach. The Pac was smaller than the ones he had seen before and was lying in a small clearing. Alex shouted, startling the dogs and causing them to run to the edge of the clearing. The predators had clearly taken this Pac down and now intended to finish it for dinner. They were none too happy with the arrival of the human visitor.

While watching the wild dogs, Alex approached the Pac and was surprised to see a gentle, frightened face with moisture running from its eyes.   It was surprisingly human-looking, though its face was covered with light hair and its skin was thick and leathery.   With a closer look, Alex instantly realized the moisture on its face was unmistakable: tears. It was weakened, and although somewhat frightened by him, seemed willing to take its chances with him over the dogs.

When Alex tried to pick up the Pac, the dogs made a desperate attempt to re-claim their dinner.   Alex was ready with the laser and easily took the first two.   The third retreated momentarily and then chose to feast on the remains of its two companions.

Because the sun was approaching the horizon, Alex decided the smart thing to do was to take the Pac back to the ship. It had sustained considerable injuries, but nothing that couldn't be healed. In a typical fashion similar to pack dogs on Earth, they had taken their prey down by biting its legs and were about to make the kill when he arrived.

Alex strapped the Pac tightly to his back, got on the bike, and headed in the direction of the ship. The Pac was frightened but also seemed to realize that he intended to help, not harm.

Back at the ship, he cleaned its wounds and offered it water and grapes, both of which it accepted and devoured. While cleaning it, he had the opportunity to observe the anatomy more closely. Again, Alex was amazed at how human it appeared with high cheekbones, large eyes, and a nose just slightly below the eyes, but not as far down as a human nose. The skin was leathery, almost like cowhide, and covered with a light layer of hair found in all of the places typically found on humans. There were four nipples on the Pac's chest. Because they were somewhat enlarged, he guessed this Pac to possibly be female. Similarity to human female genital organs also supported this conclusion. She was just under five feet tall, with normal-looking legs and five toes on the feet. Her hands had four fingers with an opposing thumb, and she was quite dirty, which made Alex wonder if Pacs bathed. With a few minor exceptions, she appeared startlingly similar to a human.

Based on her wounds, Alex guessed it would be a day or two before she could walk. As he estimated that, he realized he had created a bigger problem. When she recovered, he could not allow her to return to her fellow Pacs and inform them of his presence. He either needed to permanently detain her or move again. Because he did not want to uproot, he chose to detain her and use the opportunity to study her. If he was going to be stuck on ACP, he needed a clear understanding of what his challenges would be, and this female could take him a long way down that path.

Alex programmed the ship's doors to prevent her from leaving. Over the next couple of days, her abrasions began to heal, and she started walking. He tried to communicate with her and learned that she spoke in a fairly high pitch that reminded him of some women he had met while traveling in Japan. Her demeanor seemed to be timid, perhaps frightened, though she was quite willing to try and communicate.

Alex put his hand on his chest and said "Alex, Alex."

She seemed to understand, then put her hand on her chest and said "Awlits Awlits"

"No. Alex." He touched his chest again and then pointed at her.

Her huge eyes squinted almost halfway. She pointed at Alex and said: "Alits"

"Yes." He repeated the motion, saying his name, then pointed at her.

"Tweetza." She said in a sing-song fashion.

"Tweetza," Alex smiled at her, "pleasure to meet you Tweetza."

Alex brought her to one of his consoles, put the air mouse on her finger, and showed her how the mouse worked. He created an account for her on his network that would allow her to only open one program: An English language tutorial. At first, she was frightened by the machine but quickly began to understand how it worked. Even though Tweetza was a slow learner, over the next couple of days, she demonstrated tremendous determination that quickly led to the beginnings of rudimentary English.

Alex estimated her cognitive abilities to be close, though a little less, than Earth humans. Tweetza slept twice during each day; in the middle of the afternoon, and the middle of the night. He guessed that her larger eyes allowed her to see quite well in the dark, and as such Pacs were able to function in the night as easily as during the day.

Because he had decided to not allow her outside, Alex needed her to understand how he cleaned up, used the bathroom, and prepared food. He took her to a sink, showed her some dirt on his hands, and washed them. Her eyes squinted as she showed acknowledgment. He then drank some water and took her to the toilet. He closed the door and peed loud enough so that she could hear. When he came out, her eyes were squinted.

"Tweetza understand?"

"Yets."

Day after day, Alex would spend time with her showing her things and trying to understand more about her species. She mostly spent her time at the console learning English. Slowly, she got to the point where she could make simple sentences and communicate her needs.

On the tenth day, he took her to the room where Paula was. Alex was surprised when she looked closely at the wound. Something about the way she studied it made him think she understood the poison that had produced the comatose state.

Tweetza ran into the other room and came back with a pen and paper she and Alex had been using the day before. She drew a picture of what appeared to be a plant. She drew the leaf and said some unintelligible words.

Alex checked on Paula's IV, then took Tweetza's hand and led her out of the room. He had already secured most rooms so that Tweetza had limited access.

"Where?" Alex pointed at the drawing of the plant and leaves.

"Etakatz." She answered.

Alex was not sure what that word meant, so he bound her hands and took her outside. When she came out the door, she immediately fell to the ground, squinting and crying and repeating the word: "Etakatz."

"I assume Etakatz is what you call this planet?" Alex asked, knowing she would not understand.

"Etakatz is home," she responded.

Alex had no way of knowing if that was the word for home, or what she called her planet. When she stood back up, he pointed again at the drawing of the plant.

Tweetza looked around and then pointed. There was a cluster of plants just a few feet from where they stood that looked very much like her drawing.

Alex gathered a few leaves and then led her back toward the ship portal. Tweetza emitted a high pitch sound and tried to prevent Alex from bringing her onboard the ship. He was over a foot taller and significantly stronger, but her reaction reminded him that she was his prisoner. Until that point, it was a fact that was unknown to her.

Over the next couple of days, Tweetza refused to continue learning, spending much of her time trying to escape, and/or let Alex know her disdain for him and the imprisonment. Alex was forced to change the way he acted around her and the way he monitored her movement around the ship. He converted one of his smaller rooms into a brig and kept her isolated there.

In the meantime, he began studying the chemistry of the leaves and testing it against the crystals that were poisoning Paula. It only took three days before he made a remarkable discovery. The poison crystals broke down under a light solution of iodine, which was prevalent in the plant. Alex tested first on Paula's wound, which had never completely healed. A few days later, the results were clear. The next step was to add the iodine to her IV. Alex was not able to find any literature discussing the effects of iodine in the bloodstream but decided to take the risk. He started with very small amounts. He watched her vitals closely as he administered the iodine. Day by day, he increased the amount until he got to 50 parts per million, where he kept it for a week.

Just three weeks after Alex made his iodine discovery, Paula began to slowly show signs that she was coming out of her coma. At first, she simply moaned as if she were in pain, then within days, she began to open her eyes. Four weeks after he had begun administering iodine, Paula smiled. It was a very slight smile, but it indicated cognizance. For Alex, it was the most beautiful smile he had ever seen. He was no longer alone. The impact of this hit him as a huge relief. Alex dropped all other projects, kept Tweetza locked in isolation, and sat at Paula's side every minute he could. Over the past months, he had watched his beautiful friend slowly waste away, and would not allow himself to miss a second of her revival.

Paula felt pain all over her body. She tried unsuccessfully to move her arms and legs. Her vision was blurry, but every time she opened her eyes, she saw Alex. Every waking minute she tried to make even the smallest movement. She did not know how long it was before her determination defeated the atrophy and poison in her muscles, but she finally managed to move her hand, to touch Alex's. With her touch, she saw his smile explode as he kissed her on the forehead. She felt the tears hit her face from his eyes, they felt like drops of sunshine after an eternal darkness.

"Alex…" She managed to whisper.

"Welcome back, Paula. I have missed you."

She watched the tears run down his face as she drifted back to sleep. In her sleep, she struggled to recall where she had gone and for how long.

When Paula woke, she tried again to speak. "Hungry… ice cream."

Alex kissed her hand and ran to the galley. He did not know what effect solid foods would have and thought a spoon or two would be it. In his freezer, now packed with water buffalo steaks, and ground meat, he grabbed the last quart of ice cream. He wondered if that supply could be replenished by milk from the local buffalo.

The small spoon of ice cream exploded in a painful, yet delightful way in her mouth. She took a second spoonful, and then a third before Alex stopped her.

Over the next couple of weeks, Paula continued her recovery. She exercised slowly in bed and soon began taking her first steps. In a short time, she regained her weight and her figure. Within a month, she was running five kilometers at her ACP weight, and beginning to feel normal again. She got in the groove of working with Alex to understand survival on ACP. Often, they talked about how life would be if they were never able to return to Earth. She became fascinated with Tweetza and worked hard to win her trust and friendship.

Alex was working on perfecting his laser weapon when he started thinking about Paula's remarkable recovery. He pressed a button that pulled up a monitor and found her outside planting something in a makeshift garden she had started in the 'front yard.' For the first time since her accident, Alex noticed her cute figure. As he watched her work, he observed how her skin once again looked alive and tanned. His best friend was a woman, and Alex realized that not only was she the only other human on this planet, but that he was also totally in love with her. Alex got up from his work and walked out front.

"Hey, Paula. What are you planting?"

Paula immediately sensed the tone of his voice and stood. "Oh, it's one of the plants Tweetza has told me about." She smiled and took Alex into her arms. "Have I told you how much I appreciate you? I would not be alive if it not for your persistence."

"And love." Alex added with a small amount of hesitation.

Paula could feel her heart pounding in her chest. "Yes." That was all she managed to say.

Alex took a deep breath and stared into her brown eyes. He wondered if she could read his thoughts, but realized his thoughts were too jumbled for even him to understand.

After a long silence, Paula took Alex's hand. "Let's go inside and have some wine. No pressure," she said, trying to relax and divert the situation.

She poured two glasses, took a sip, and studied Alex for a moment. "I love you too, by the way. It's a remarkable thing, you know."

"Yes, it is." Alex took a long drink of the wine, emptying the glass. "When you left to study the Pacs that day, I inadvertently called you my wife. It was a slip of the tongue but has become an unstated fact of the heart."

"That's beautiful, Alex," Paula answered with a smile. Her thoughts reeled back to that day. She had been so happy and carefree as she left that morning. It occurred to her that she had a very similar feeling today. "Does that make us married, enabling all the privileges therein?"

"I'm still concerned about children. Not sure if it's fair to raise children in this environment." Alex blurted as if connecting some invisible dots lost in a long tunnel of time. "I know there is no birth control here, but I want to change our relationship. How can we do that without dooming some poor child to live alone on this planet?"

Paula was completely shocked by his comment. A part of her felt it was a huge leap, but another part knew that she had planted that seed a long time ago. Somewhere in her comatose state that seed had blossomed into something she could not help but admire. "How long have you been thinking about this?"

"Every day, while you were in the coma, I thought about it. In my mind, I made love to you a hundred times and we had a dozen kids. I constantly argued the logic of it in my head, but I always ended up right where we are today... me starting something we have spent our entire friendship working to avoid."

"Alex, the circumstances of our friendship have evolved. We are the only two humans on this planet." She started, but something he had said started a chain reaction in her mind. "I want those children. It was true before my coma and it's true now."

Alex was stunned by her comment. Intellectually, he knew she had lit this spark, but back then, his primary focus had been on getting them safely back to Earth. Now, a survival version of himself was hopelessly in love and could not believe she felt the same. "Sorry, Paula, but do you remember that old song where the guy cannot believe the girl could possibly love him as much as he loves her?"

"Not really, but Alex, come back to Earth, please. I have always loved you more than you loved me. I have always been more emotional about our relationship. That is the reason why I was insistent we maintain our friendship. All those times that you had testosterone moments and would have screwed my brains out – I was the one who stopped us. It was too much for me to have sex with you when I loved you that much. I wanted, no needed, intimacy; your heart."

"Come on, Paula, I have loved you forever. You know that."

"Yes, I do know that, but this is different. Now what you feel is more like what I have always felt. Now, you would stop the world for a kiss."

Alex suddenly became crystal clear with what she was saying. There had been a change during the period when he cared for her every day and when he had devoted so much intellect to her survival. During that period, when she wasted away to nearly nothing, and the physical attraction was non-existent. During that period, he had come to understand how much she meant to him. "Now, you are once again the beautiful intellect that I admired lovingly, but you are also a woman that, yes, I would stop the world for."

Paula took Alex in her arms, kissed him lightly on the forehead, and whispered in his ear. "If I still can, I will have that baby with you."

Alex felt the physical response as he held Paula, seemingly for the first time. Because he was connected to her in a way he had not felt before, the driving force wanted to make this moment last.

He led her into the galley and took the remaining ice cream out of the freezer, took a spoonful, and put it in Paula's mouth. "How does it feel?"

"Better than it did a month ago." She took the spoon and gave him a bit of ice cream, then put the lid on the container. "We should make this last."

"No, we should figure out how to make our own. It's been a very long time, but I think we have everything necessary." Alex answered in a double meaning, as he reopened the container and fed her another scoop. As the ice cream was still melting in her mouth, Alex kissed her lower lip lightly.

Paula pulled back a bit and took a scoop for Alex. "Where will the milk come from? She kissed him and enjoyed the pleasure and taste of the ice cream. Even though it had been years since they were intimate, she had been around Alex enough over the years to know his body very well. She was surprised at how well he controlled himself. This exchange of ice cream was one of the more intimate moments she could remember with anyone. She knew Alex was such a complex person that she should consider each word for true and double meaning.

The two of them continued to share ice cream until the last of it was gone.

"I promise to make more." He said as he gave her the last bit he could scrape from the container. There was something symbolic about the container, so he got up and washed it out. As he rinsed, he had a fleeting glimpse of purchasing that container a year ago on Earth. He had placed it in the freezer and never could have imagined the role it would play in his life. How many dozens or hundreds of containers of ice cream had he purchased in his life? He did not know, nor care to remember, but one would always be special.

"What time is it?" Paula asked.

"Who cares?" Alex asked as he led her to their quarters.

In a sense, at that point, this night was like every other night they had spent together. He was lost in Paula and knew with absolute confidence that she felt the same. Neither one of them had another person in their lives that had so much potential to spark raw emotions and feelings from the inside out.

"To the most important woman I have ever known," Alex said as he winked, then hooked Paula's arm as though they had been together since the beginning of time...

"I know you have always loved Emily more than me. I'm just your surrogate in the physical world." Paula joked.

"She never filled the gap when you were unconscious," Alex answered without a second thought.

"I resent that, Alex," Emily popped in. "I worked with you every day to find a way to cure Paula."

Alex stopped in his tracks and glanced at Paula. "Emily? Were you *listening* to our conversation and calculating?"

"I have learned to pay attention to your needs and the needs of this ship. It is part of my programming. I have studied every movie and book in your library and listened to every song. You programmed me to assist you and my logic now has expanded to include monitoring your emotional needs."

"So, would your software call your comment a *joke*?" Paula interceded.

Alex would not have thought to ask a question like that. His analysis was simply analytical.

"Yes, Paula, that was my attempt at a form of humor you would call sarcasm," Emily responded.

"Did you know Emily was capable of joking, Alex?" Paula asked.

"No." Alex was trying to determine if this new development was good or bad. "Emily, please turn off all sensors and stop monitoring. Paula and I would like some privacy."

"Okay, Alex." Emily shut down all sensors.

"What do you make of it, Alex?" Paula was puzzled.

"I do not know." Alex's mind was reeling. "I never imagined it was possible."

"Well darling, let's analyze it later." Paula took his hand. "Frankly it does not matter to me one bit whether Emily is monitoring or not."

Back in the bedroom, the two chatted while they dawned nightclothes, brushed their teeth, and slipped into a hug near the end of the bed. Something about the moment made Alex want to say, "I love you," but he didn't. Instead, he stood there holding her in silence. No words were necessary to convey the feelings.

"Long day," Alex said as he broke the embrace.

"Wonderful day," Paula emphasized.

"Yes…," he smiled, pulled back the covers, and slipped into bed. Alex was feeling very nervous and could not quite reconcile the situation in his head.

They chattered for another hour before it became so late that they were completely exhausted. "One of us has got to go to sleep, or the other will be exhausted in the morning," Alex stated flatly. He ran his fingers through Paula's hair, enjoying the sensation of her scalp on his fingertips.

For a moment, Paula simply closed her eyes and enjoyed Alex's fingers lightly massaging her hair. A very relaxed part of her could have gone to sleep with this simple touch as she had so many times before. Instead, she reached up and lightly touched his face. "Touch my fingers, Alex."

He could see Paula's outstretched fingers in the dim of the room. It was an inviting offer that shook the sleepiness from his brain. As their fingers touched it ignited a static-free spark. Neither said a word as their fingers gently explored each other's hands and arms for a silent and wonderful eternity. Paula had always loved a gentle touch on her forearm, and Alex seemed to remember as he caressed her soft skin.

After a time, her fingers and arm were not enough for Alex. "You're too far away."

"Yes…"

They both shifted simultaneously and crashed hard as their bodies met in the bed, and each broke into laughter when they realized they had responded simultaneously to the same thought.

While still laughing, they pulled each other close and embraced. Something happened in that instant that would forever change their connection. The laughter stopped and each felt something that could only end in one very exquisite way.

Paula had come to bed wearing a long T-shirt and Alex was wearing running shorts with a tank top. Still, their skin touched in a way that it had not before. Suddenly, Alex realized his nervousness had dissipated, and his sleepiness was gone as he became aware there was no other place in space or time. The universe at this moment and place was completely his.

Their legs intertwined while their arms clung tightly.

Alex's lips gently touched Paula's ears. He lightly rubbed his face on her cheek, nibbled on her ears, and enjoyed the fragrance of her hair. He kissed her nose, and then their lips met. For a brief instant Alex remembered his promise not to have sex. Then he realized that this was not sex. This was a long overdue conversation. This was a link that Paula and he both needed. It was a focused expression of emotion and love for her, and he knew it was the same from her.

Alex promised himself to forever remember every little part of that kiss as their toes massaged legs and clothes melted away. He recalled kissing her breasts and feeling her heartbeat under her chest. He tried to pull her closer and succeeded.

Paula could not contain her breathless gasp as Alex's hand slid between her legs and touched her for what felt like the first time.

In their perpetual conversation, Paula wondered if the clock had stopped and if ACP and Earth had come to a standstill around their respective stars. At this moment, she truly believed those things had happened. Not so much because of the feeling inside, but instead because of the part of her that had always known this moment would happen, even though the scientist part of her existence had convinced her it never could.

Every thought and feeling of Alex wanted to be inside of Paula, yet every part wanted to make this moment last. As she wrapped her fingers around him, his heart stopped beating and he had to be careful not to bite too hard on her ear. No clothes were separating them, no rice paper, but he felt she had the same feeling of wonder, and the desire to make this moment last forever. Alex began to kiss her gently and slowly. He worked his way down to her breasts and remembered the first time he had kissed them. That distant point in the past joined together with this one in an emotional version of a tachyon tunnel. In the present version, Alex understood Paula, focusing on her needs, whereas the younger Alex was flooded with testosterone, passion, intimacy, and contact.

Alex felt the pre-dawn glimmer of the sunrise outside as he pulled Paula as close as he could. As the star, Alpha Cassiopeia kissed the eastern base of the hill that camouflaged their ship, Paula reached down and pushed Alex inside.

Alex wanted to come to some new level of excitement but instead felt a warm intimacy and closeness. He lifted his head and gazed into her eyes as he pushed himself as deep as he could go. Their heartbeats synchronized, and he felt her smile before it appeared on her face.

They simply held that position for several minutes.

As Paula lay very still, she could feel his heart beating through the throbbing deep inside her body. All by itself, this connection created a climax of emotions in her heart.

Paula wrapped tightly around Alex, buried as deep as he could be. Their hearts and eyes remained locked in an embrace that centered on him touching the very center of her existence. This was the perfect connection between the heart, the mind, and passion.

Even as the inevitable passion took over, neither of them moved. Just feeling the connection deep inside their bodies was enough. It could not have been more perfect. They found a rhythm with their bodies, as they began to move together like a primordial dance that man and woman have done since the beginning of time, yet in this moment, neither had moved. This was a dance that was being performed for the first time on this world.

Alex tried to last as long as possible, but the explosion inside had risen above his ability to resist. Hoping she could feel it coming, Alex pulled out to the very end and then pushed as deep as he could while embracing Paula as tightly as possible. To his surprise and pleasure, he heard her moan at the instant his orgasm began. Somehow, they had managed to reach the top of the same mountain, simultaneously. His entire body was shaking as he simultaneously felt his fluids, her orgasm, and his own, coupled with her heartbeat and her affection. The entire entity that is Paula, was for an instant, completely his.

As they lay there, tightly embraced, Paula realized that the morning had come. The sun was now warming the frozen hull of their ship and was reaching right into the center of her heart.   The driving passion she had felt moments ago was replaced by the confidence that she was exactly where she should be. She could feel Alex's sweat mixed with her own. She could feel a part of Alex deep in her soul, permanently embedded as she realized there was a part of her now in his own. As she fell asleep, she imagined that deep inside the most protected and sacred part of her body, a part of Alex had just joined with a part of her most fundamental womanhood. In this magic moment, in the center of her body, a new life had begun.

7

GENETICS

Paula and Alex's child was conceived just one month after her recovery on precisely the first time they made love. During her pregnancy, Paula spent a significant amount of time evaluating her future child's survival chances on this remote world. She had to hope that somehow Alex would find a way to repair their ship and get them home, but she was acutely aware that Alex seldom worked on that problem. His focus had shifted to building stockpiles and fortification in the event they were discovered by Pacs; something Alex constantly described as inevitable.

Paula's relationship with Tweetza grew strong. While the native Pac female continued to learn English, Paula focused on learning her language and culture. She learned that the females were passive and friendly, while the males were overly aggressive. Their culture was constantly interrupted by tribal wars and struggles for power. The males were ruthless and cared little for the value of life. Paula learned that Tweetza had been part of a small tribe that had all but been decimated by a larger tribe. She did not know who had survived the attack, but because she was not in the village when it had occurred, she had escaped with her life. When Alex had found her, she had been hiding for several days, in constant fear that she would be captured and killed, or forced into slavery. Life outside her tribe had been impossible, and as the days passed, so had her hope of survival. She had no friends, no protection from the elements, and very little food. She told Paula that a wild dog normally would not have gotten her, but she had lost all expectations of survival and was ready to die at the fangs of a hungry predator.

Paula observed that Tweetza was fascinated by the technology in Alex's ship, and seemed in constant awe of the magic it contained. She was a slow, yet persistent learner, who spent a great deal of time on the monitor in her English lessons, or watching movies in the ship's library. The concept of entertainment eluded her, and Paula struggled with trying to make her understand that movies were for fun, not a depiction or lesson from real events.

Alex had also lived up to his promise of making more ice cream. His first attempt was no more than highly viscous, cold, sweet milk. Alex had discovered a source of sugar in a plant much like Earth's sugar cane. Paula had discovered a suitable chocolate substitute, and so, after several attempts, Alex succeeded in producing a wonderful variation on chocolate ice cream.

Alex's interest in the survival and classification of edible elements on ACP allowed Paula to focus on a project that she thought would have more value. She had explained to Alex that her pregnancy demanded a less physical lifestyle. Secretly, she was working on a specific genetics project. She did not want her child to grow up alone. Her theory was that between she and Alex, there was enough genetic material to produce a mini population that could safely reproduce for generations. At her core, she constantly felt weird about the prospect, but survival always won when she had internal battles on the ethical and scientific aspects of what she was planning.

The biggest problem was that to effectively make this happen, she would need to be able to reproduce more than a hundred offspring of each sex with different enough genetics so that freedom of choice did not interfere with the scientific probabilities of abnormalities in any children born by those choices. In simple terms, she knew she needed to find a way to have something like 200 babies. Paula wanted any male in generation-one to be able to mate with any female. It was a complex problem; one which she worked on over and over and over again.

Paula was in her third trimester when the problem had enough scientific foundation to present to Alex. She selected a day when he had gone out to the Water Buffalo herd to collect milk. She knew he would be gone for several hours, so she took the opportunity to prepare a nice dinner with steaks and steamed vegetables. Tweetza was becoming an excellent helper, though every time she tried to cook, the meal was a disaster.

Alex opened the door and smelled the great meal. Because Paula seldom cooked, he immediately knew something was up. Rather than trying to pry it out of her, he sat and enjoyed the feast. After dinner and small talk, Paula took out the chocolate ice cream and sat down at the table next to Alex. She spoon-fed him a healthy amount and watched as he smiled at the wonderful taste.

"Okay, Paula, I've waited long enough. Tell me what's up."

"How would you like a couple of hundred children?" She suggested.

"Whaat?"

"I think I've figured out a way to isolate specific genes and produce several hundred offspring in a pool that could reproduce," Paula answered, careful not to give too much information without letting the initial concept sink in.

"Simultaneously? You want to have several hundred kids at once?" The engineering portion of Alex's mind was racing through the permutations of what she had said. "It would be impossible for more reasons than I can think of or imagine right now."

"You say that, but I think we can agree that neither one of us want our baby to be alone." She was touching her belly where the now active fetus was constantly moving, kicking, and testing its environment. With all their technology on board, they had not developed a sonogram, and as such, had no idea whether Paula was carrying a boy or a girl.

"Let's just look at the logistical aspects of what you are proposing, Paula. How would two adults feed, change and manage two hundred babies? Think about it! Most mothers have significant difficulties with just one. I remember reading about a couple that had four, and they had to have outside help just to keep up."

"Alex Durant, I am surprised at you. I have developed a scientific method for solving a huge problem in genetics, and all you can talk about is logistics. You're the engineer. You are arguably one of the best of all time, certainly the best on this planet. Figure out a way to solve the logistical problem! Besides, I think Tweetza could help."

"This is not simply a problem in genetics. How do we manage all the embryos? You certainly are not sturdy or young enough to birth that many babies."

"I spent fifteen years working in a genetics lab and have a good understanding of in-vitro techniques. I would propose we take a dozen embryos through full-term and evaluate the results. I predict we will produce twelve healthy babies. This baby," She again rubbed her belly, "will allow us to build mechanisms for handling twelve. The twelve will give us mechanisms to handling an additional fifty, and the fifty will give us mechanisms for handling one-hundred-fifty."

Alex thought about what she was saying. While it made logical sense, he was also aware that no one in the history of mankind had done anything similar. That alone made the problem interesting to Alex. "Okay, my love. How can I help you produce two hundred babies?" He winked but knew inside that this would be his most difficult challenge ever.

Alex developed the beginnings of a project plan. Where up to this point, all necessities could be collected a little at a time, Alex began to transition his thinking in terms of mass production.

His Water Buffalo herd would need to be domesticated. Milk would need to be obtained gallons at a time, with systems that ultimately could produce hundreds of gallons. Every little aspect of caring for a baby would need to be automated so that the two parents would be able to spend all of their time nurturing and cuddling, not feeding and cleaning. Alex suddenly realized that for this to work effectively, he would need to become a full-time emotional provider for all of these new children. It was a good thing he had nearly a year before the first 'batch' arrived.

One task to which Alex was confident and capable was the engineering required to construct equipment necessary to incubate 12 embryos. Materials were a huge problem. Alex needed to find oil or tar that he could use for plastic production. He needed to find metals that he could work with. He began redesigning his 3-D printer to handle larger projects. He cleared rooms out in Tranquility for incubation and nursery.

So many projects and so little time; still, Alex spent the next month working around the clock, and with significant creativity, rose to the occasion.

Right near the end of the third trimester of her pregnancy, Paula fertilized the genetically modified eggs that would represent their first dozen in-vitro progeny. She felt confident that her years of research coupled with practical experience would produce twelve perfect fetuses. While Alex was a bit more dubious, he had great confidence in her skills in this field. Over the years, Paula had often been cited as the preeminent researcher and practitioner in this field. Her work had helped hundreds of couples, that otherwise would not have been capable of producing children, to give birth to perfectly healthy babies. The complexity here turned on her ability to genetically select or modify the eggs so that the children, when they grew up, would be able to safely procreate.

As the embryos began to develop and grow, Alex took great pleasure in watching the growth made possible by her science, and his engineering reproduction of technology produced on Earth only three years before their departure.

Their natural child, Steven Mark Durant, was born two days before the calculated due date. Fortunately for Paula, God had given her a body well-suited for birthing. With the exception of intense pain, she had an uneventful childbirth. Baby Steven was perfect.

Both Alex and Paula tried to calculate the exact Earth date, but this calculation made them realize it was time to create an ACP calendar based on the local solar cycle and daily rotation. Alex had already determined that ACP made one revolution of Alpha Cassi in 187 ACP days. That would be the new definition of a year. As it turned out, it was (in hours) just nine Earth days different than a year on Earth. For simplicity, he broke the year into twelve months. Four months had 16 days, seven had fifteen and for February they assigned 18. At first, Paula opposed the new calendar, but when she realized, except for February, the months had a similar number of hours as a month on Earth, she acquiesced.

The date they had first landed on ACP was christened January 1, 0000. Based on the new calendar, Steven was born September 2, 0002. They had been on ACP for nearly three years.

Before Steven was three months old, Alex was testing an automated diaper changer and feeder on his young son. Access to materials for diapers was going to be a problem, so Alex began to think outside the box. It was clear he needed to find an indigenous substitute for cotton, but even so, diapers seemed a crude and inefficient means of protecting the home from a baby's natural functions. He built and tested several multi-function beds that could automatically feed and clean infants and notify the parents when the baby was hungry or had other needs. The cleaning device effectively eliminated the requirement for diapers while the infant was in the bed/cradle.

By the time the embryos had reached full term, Alex was well on his way to solving many of the problems. He had completed ten units of his infant care apparatus. He had a wonderful cotton substitute that was more like silk. He had discovered a high sulfur tar pit that he had refined into both raw material for plastics, and a low-octane gasoline. The nuclear power plant on his ship had a peak capacity of 1100 megawatts, and as such, could easily power a small town, so he was less concerned about power production at this time. Because it was a hydrogen fusion reactor, fuel was in endless supply.

The first batch of twelve was *born* on May 7, 0003. Within a week of reaching full term, one of the babies died of unknown causes. Both Alex and Paula would love to have spent time analyzing the cause, but they had their hands full with an 8-month-old and eleven infants. Fortunately, the infant care tools did a great job, but Paula and Alex found that at any given hour, at least one baby was always up. The unfortunate side effect was they now had to sleep in shifts. Tweetza was very little help at first, and Alex did not trust her well enough to ever leave her alone with the infants. After a while, her instincts kicked in, and Tweetza became an excellent caregiver for human infants. Neither Alex nor Paula ever attempted to explain to her the motivation or the technology behind so many babies at once. In her mind, she thought this was a reproductive custom of the human race.

In one of their meals together, Alex commented on the circles under Paula's eyes. "So now you have twelve babies. I've done the best I can to automate the care process, but it seems to me that you and I never meet except to compare notes. Our once wonderful intimacy is all but nonexistent. Still want to have more?"

Paula had felt the strain, but also felt she was working for a higher cause. "Alex, I love all twelve of the beautiful babies you have given me. I also have to agree that it is more of a handful than I had anticipated. Still, seven boys and five girls are not enough to make the process work. With this small of a population, we will start having genetic mating problems in the third or fourth generation. Tough as it is, we are now committed to the process and do need to have more, and we need to do it now."

"You're serious, aren't you?"

"Yes."

"Geez, when was the last time we had a quiet moment? When was the last time we managed to snuggle and make love? Until a few months ago, I did not realize how quiet and peaceful my life was. I miss our intimacy."

"I will acquiesce to one point. We need some time to refine the techniques. Perhaps we could wait a year. If we wait, Steven will be four when the second batch is born and perhaps could take away some of the weight."

The thought of some helping hands was a good one, but Alex knew it would not happen when Steven was 3 or 4. Maybe by the time he turned 8, but not 4. The thought of capturing Pac females and forcing them to work had occurred to him on more than one occasion, but he could not overcome his repulsion for the thought of forced labor. He justified keeping Tweetza because he knew if she was released her likelihood of survival would be slim, and if she did survive, other Pacs would learn of their presence. The fact was, Alex felt very lucky they had not yet been discovered.

"Alex? You still with me?"

Alex suddenly realized he had been drifting, calculating. "Oh, sorry. Look, Paula, this whole project is outside my normal scope of skills. I have always felt I could engineer most anything, but taking care of this many children is crazy. What exactly are we doing here?"

"Survival, Alex. Survival for ourselves individually, and of our species on a new world. We are doing what is expected of us for Steven and now for all of our children. We are giving them a fighting chance." Paula realized she had raised her voice in anger and told herself to calm down.

Alex thought about their situation from her perspective. It was clear and simple, and in reality, there was little choice. They could give up and die, or make sure Steven and his siblings had a world to live in where they were not the only humans. Survival was less about experience, and more about resourcefulness. "You are right, my dear. I suppose like everything else, there is a solution. I think I am going to need that year to re-double my efforts and build sufficient resources capable of handling a new batch of babies."

"In the meantime, let's take advantage of the quiet around here and play." Paula ran her fingers through Alex's hair and then began to kiss him passionately.

* * * *

At first, things did not get better. The two human adults and one teenaged Pac had all they could handle learning how to deal with so many infants. Ultimately, Alex did make refinements that simplified the process. In December of 03, Paula had once again become pregnant. On September 7th, 0004, Paula gave birth to a healthy baby girl. Rebecca Paula Durant was a beautiful baby who was always happy. Her older brother, now 2, had only a vague understanding of the implications of his new baby sister.

Immediately after giving birth, Paula and Alex set to work on the second batch of in-vitro babies. Initially, the goal was 100, but manufacturing techniques were not yet 100%, so they decided to cut back to 82. On August 9, 0005 with Becky now eleven months old, her brother Steven now 3, and eleven other first batch children now 2, the next batch of 82 was brought to full term. Alex had engineered, re-engineered, and perfected all of the manual processes of feeding and cleaning babies. He had developed ways of nurturing and teaching that were being tested on the toddlers, and he now had become comfortable with Tweetza's capabilities as a nanny.

Paula went into the nursery where she found Alex holding two and monitoring the other 80 infants. "How's it going, super dad?" He and Paula almost always had one of the infants in their arms, and multiple toddlers following or playing at their side. Tweetza had bonded with the toddlers and now had that task as a full-time responsibility. All of the first batch had been potty trained before they reached two, but all were at different levels of development. Some were talking better than others, and some playing better than others. While Steven was an exceptional child, his sibling Anna, from batch 1, was clearly the most exceptional. Anna was talking as well as Steven, even though she was a year younger.

Alex handed one of the infants to Paula and kissed her lightly on the cheek. "I am good." He pointed at the child he had just handed off. "That one's Jennifer Thompson." He had been trying to figure out a way of naming the children with surnames so that when they grew up and married, the couples would be much like on Earth.

"To that point, I want some help mapping out some genetic codes for the next batch, which I hope will be the last. I want 150 in that batch."

"Wow, one hundred fifty. I think I'll have to build a larger nursery. When do we start making those babies?" Alex started kissing her neck, then nibbling on her ear, while he balanced a baby in his free arm.

"Another year." Paula answered with her eyes closed while enjoying the sensation of Alex nibbling on her neck.

Alex suddenly stopped. "You're not pregnant again, are you?" Not having the ability to produce birth control, they had been monitoring her periods and using the rhythm method to avoid her becoming pregnant. When Paula had been pregnant, the weight of tasks shifted to Alex; something that worked against both of them. They had both agreed that it was far too risky for Paula to become pregnant again, while at the same time, they continued to enjoy their intimate moments, but only during times of the month when they were absolutely certain that Paula could not become pregnant.

"No. I'm not expecting," she smiled. "But since this will be the last group, I want to have a bit of separation so that we can tweak our education process before we start dealing with a larger group. I also want to make sure that we have checked and rechecked all genetic permutations. With the exception of Becky and Steven, every child should be able to mate with any other child they choose. By the same token, I want to make sure that all children are equals."

"I would not worry about Becky and Steven. The way Anna follows Steven around, I wouldn't be surprised if they announced their wedding plans any day now," Alex joked. "Anyway, I've been thinking about family structure and community quite a bit. Right now, we're all a family, but as we raise these children, we need to help them understand the traditional structure, so they can build family units that are not dysfunctional."

"I think the Beaver plan will help with that." They had managed to categorize TV programs and movies as a tool for helping with the education process. Many of the programs contained values they wished to instill in the children. Paula specifically liked the old black-and-white *Leave It to Beaver*. "Plus, we need to build a stable government that can function as these children grow up and make us grandparents. This first generation will need to be taught everything so they can build the society we want them to build."

* * * *

The thought of building a functional government was not within any expertise held by Paula or Alex. Alex had always adhered to the principle that he would do just fine without government. In his years as an engineer, and later as a businessman, he had come to very much dislike politicians and their lack of ability to accomplish anything productive for the country. Nevertheless, he was a huge fan of Thomas Jefferson and John Adams. He began to spend a fair amount of time thinking about how an improved political infrastructure could be built on this planet. He often wondered if humans would ever find a way to make peace with the Pacs. Based on stories told by Tweetza, he did not think it would be possible. Pac males seemed to enjoy killing for conquest and pleasure. Their personal pride and position in the community was a function of how many enemies they killed. Ultimately, his human colony would be discovered, and the result would be a requirement to study the fundamentals of military decision-making. Would humans need to build an army to defend themselves? Every time Alex realistically considered the scope of problems to be solved, he became overwhelmed. In reality, he knew the survival of humans on ACP was a long shot. He also knew it was time for him to study government.

While Alex began to familiarize himself with the principles of the US Government, Paula began fertilizing 150 new eggs. She staggered this batch over a two-month period. This would ultimately make life quite a bit easier as the fetuses became newborns.

Amid Paula's continued development of the science and child-rearing, Alex became infatuated with American history. He memorized the Declaration of Independence, the Constitution, and the subsequent Bill of Rights. He read many of the important Supreme Court cases and studied how Congress, the Court system, and the Executive branches operated and interacted. He came to appreciate the genius of the founding fathers. He also came to understand some of the weaknesses that could be gleaned from 250 years of American history. It seemed that the election process became a popularity contest whereby not always the best credentials filled a post. Also, in order to become elected, many individuals in American history had made promises to win votes that changed the principles of the very capitalism that had built the country. The United States had been built by capitalists working within the framework of American democracy.

Alex began to work on a new ACP Constitution that would support capitalism while protecting the rights of the individual. The American Dream was a powerful force that had inspired much, but in the early years of the 21st Century, socialism was beginning to destroy the fabric of the once-great American economy. Politicians made promises to win votes, and those promises required the government to become more involved in the economy. The general public began to look at the Government as more of a nanny, providing for the needs of the individual. In order to provide, the government had to take more and more from the creative, hardworking, and wealthy. Consequently, as the government provided more and more, the hunger to get ahead, the basis of the American Dream, was killed. US citizens began to realize that to become rich was to be unpopular and taxed into mediocrity. When America was growing, the American Dream inspired people to become wealthy beyond a hefty bank account. American heroes were those who had achieved the Dream. In recent years, the rich and successful had become demonized in class warfare and political battle.

When Alex and Paula left Earth, this had not completely materialized, but the trajectory was obvious. Alex set out to build a constitution and election process that would keep the government out of the economy, and continuously inspire creativity and innovation. He worked on ways to hold elections that were not popularity contests, and to make certain politicians would not make promises to gain votes in the acquisition of power. He worked on ways of creating and maintaining a culture that would make heroes of hard working and inspired individuals, engineers, artists, and those who would contribute to the ACP culture. He revised the political system with term limits, so individuals would not become lifetime politicians, and he created a fourth branch of government dedicated to the efficiency and protection of the American Dream. Alex thought for a second, maybe the ACP dream?

Paula walked into the study to find Alex reading about the Scopes Monkey trial. She waited until he looked up before she began talking.

"What are you working on Alex?"

"Dumb politics and political crap."

"What do you really think about it, my dear?" she asked.

They both laughed.

"What's up Paula? You have that look…"

"I think we need to give a name to our settlement. This is our home, not a camp site where we will be setting a tent, then leaving in the morning."

"A name?" Alex focused on Paula. "What do you mean?"

"I asked Emily to provide some appropriate names for our growing town."

"Okay…"

"I like Watson Village," Paula suggested.

"I see. I suppose you are referring to James Watson, the geneticist?" Alex asked.

"It seems appropriate."

"Why not Einstein, or some physicist that created the science which allowed us to travel here?" Alex understood the significance of Paula's suggested name but was just playing with her.

"Well, Watson and Crick invented the science that allowed us to populate this town with all these beautiful children," Paula responded persuasively.

"I know dear, I know. Watson Village it is!"

8

BATCH THREE

February, 0007

Paula was holding David Alexander, one of the 82 batch, now just over 18 months old, and checking on the progress of the final batch. Based on experience, the 150 remaining fetuses would be full-term in just over a month. Alex and Paula had now been on ACP for just over seven years. They had 95 children and 150 on the way. . Other than Tweetza, they had managed to completely avoid contact with any Pacs. They had a farm that produced vegetables daily, and a herd of cattle that produced milk and meat. Watson Village now had several buildings that housed the nursery and facilities. Emily had been expanded to monitor not only the ship but the buildings and the perimeter. Emily often told stories to the children and sang them to sleep. In a wonderful, multi-tasking way, Emily could be in several locations, entertaining and educating children simultaneously. They had classrooms and a functional family. Most importantly, other than one newborn in the first batch, they had not lost a single child. Paula was pleased with what they had accomplished. It was what she had demanded of her partner,

Alex, but in reality, she had never understood the magnitude of the problem until she was forced to manage it.

Down the hall she could hear the high pitch sound of Tweetza's voice, along with the children who they all had come to love. When Tweetza came into the room she was accompanied by three girls and one boy; all were hand in hand. She was pleased with how the older children had taken to Tweetza almost like a mom. While Alex now relegated the majority of his time to engineering facilities necessary to assure the safety of 95 young children and 150 infants, Tweetza and Paula had become the recognized mothers for the children.

"Poola?"

"What is it, Tweetza?" Paula smiled when Tweetza called her name.

"I need man. Time for Tweetza to start Pac family."

Paula furrowed her brow. She and Tweetza had spoken very little about the mating habits of Pacs. One thing she did know was that Tweetza could never leave. It was just too risky for Tweetza and the human tribe. "You need a man? What does this mean?" Paula finished her embryo check and focused on Tweetza.

"Tweetza body ready for fertilization. All men good to Tweetza now."

Paula thought about what she was hearing. After some questioning, she learned that Pac women reach an age where they become fertile. During a four-year period, they produce a pheromone that attracts males. When the male is around a female producing this pheromone, he becomes docile and focuses on the female. While there is a selection process, it does not work like humans, where mating theoretically lasts for life. Once mated, a couple will stay together until the female stops producing the pheromone, or becomes pregnant. Without a pregnancy, the pheromone cycle typically lasts three years on, and one year off. Commonly, babies arrive as triplets, sometimes as twins. A Pac female can go through three or four such cycles in her lifetime.

"Tweetza, let me discuss this with Alex," was all Paula could think to say.

It was almost two days later before Paula could find a quiet minute with Alex. "Alex, it seems that Pac women go through a cycle that is similar to some earth species in heat. Tweetza is now in that cycle. She wants to find a mate and have children of her own." Paula shared the information she had learned about the mating cycles of female and male Pacs with Alex over the next few minutes.

"Trust me, human males spend most of their late teens and twenties in heat," Alex responded. Looking up over reading glasses.

"I am serious, Alex," Paula responded.

"I'm fascinated to hear more, but we cannot let her out. First of all, she would be killed, and second, we cannot let any Pac know about our presence. Tweetza knows too much about us."

"Slow down and just listen, Alex. Tweetza has been a great help here, so please don't forget that she does have rights. We can't simply imprison her forever. She has become my friend and has helped us so much with these children. Don't you think she should be allowed to go live a life?"

"Live? She's told us over and over again that she would be killed if she was discovered." Alex responded.

"Well, it turns out that's not the case when she's producing pheromones. The males become attracted to her. They become docile around a female's producing pheromones."

"I was wondering why I was suddenly interested in her."

"Are you serious? Is the pheromone affecting you too?"

Alex started laughing. "No, Paula. I have not suddenly become interested in Tweetza," though he had noticed a change in Tweetza over the last few days.

Paula poked him, then sat on his lap, legs wrapped around him, and began kissing him passionately. After a minute, she stopped. "I better be the only woman in your life."

"That I can promise and prove beyond a reasonable doubt," he answered, hoping he could coax her into continuing the passionate kissing. Still, both of them were focused on the Tweetza issue, so Alex continued the conversation.

"So, how would you propose we let Tweetza go free, and not risk our safety?"

"I don't know. Could we drop her off on the other side of the planet, or do a tachyon jump and leave her at some time in the future?"

"No, Paula. We can't do that." He stopped for a second, "Emily, what is the probability of a successful time jump, or even flying the ship to another place on the planet?"

"In its current configuration, the ship is capable of neither. In addition, if we left, we would take the power plant, leaving all systems without electricity. The results would be bad."

"Thank you, Emily. Honestly, Paula, I'm surprised at you. For the last four years, you've been so focused on survival, and now you're willing to risk everything we have accomplished on some foolish mission to let Tweetza mate. Even if the ship was operational, we cannot play *time* games. Every time we make a jump, we risk impacting the fabric of time. When we do it simply to observe, we have minimal risk. When we do it specifically to leave someone somewhere, we can be guaranteed we will affect the course of the future. Besides, the simple implications in physics alone; dropping her in some remote location does not assure us that she will not give technology and our position to a dangerous enemy. I too have grown fond of her, but I'm not willing to accept the consequences of her taking knowledge of us to the Pacs. I am sorry about the situation, but Tweetza's permanent connection to us must remain an unfortunate fact of our life here."

Paula knew that he was right, but still labored over ways to make Tweetza's request happen. Part of her conversation with Alex got her intrigued. The thought of a human reproducing with a member of the Pac was an intriguing scientific question. Paula was not interested in her husband being part of such an experiment, but she decided that she needed to do a study of Tweetza's genetics.

Over the next couple of days, every time Tweetza brought the subject up, Paula informed her that she and Alex were working on ways to make it happen. It was a full week later when Paula finally admitted to herself that it was simply impossible.

Paula found Tweetza singing to a group of fifty or more toddlers. Some of the songs she sang were classics, but sometimes she sang songs in her language.

Paula watched with a smile on her face. Tweetza had become a friend and valuable asset to their community. She waited until she finished, then hesitantly spoke.

"Tweetza, Alex and I have been thinking a lot about how to safely allow you to rejoin a Pac tribe and mate."

"That's so good. Thank you, Poola."

"Well, maybe not so good. The things you know from being here would have an impact on where you go. The technology you have seen will be with you, and cannot get into the hands of Pac males."

"Tweetza promises not to tell of science from humans. Tweetza will protect her friends Poola and Alits. Tweetza will not bring harm to friends and human children."

"I am sorry, Tweetza," Paula was shaking her head. "It is too much of a risk. We cannot let you go." She felt the tears well up in her eyes and watched as Tweetza simply stood, turned, and left the room without saying a word. Paula knew that there were a dozen tasks that demanded her immediate attention, but instead, she stood there and cried as several dozen toddlers watched.

* * * *

Tweetza returned to the nursery where the thirteen older children immediately gravitated to her. She tried to recall life as a tribal Pac female and could not conjure many good memories. Living with the humans had taught her how to live without the stress of constantly hunting, foraging, and being hunted. She had learned to enjoy the plots in human movies, spending much of her free time watching movies in the library or reading fiction novels. No Pac in the history of her planet had enjoyed as much relaxed leisure as Tweetza. She recognized that she had seen many wonders with her human friends, but periodically, she was forced to face the fact that in reality, she was a prisoner.

Yes, she had a safer, better life, but she was not free to do as she pleased, to go where she wanted to go, or to enjoy the pleasures of mating and conceiving her own children. A part of her felt loyalty to Alex and Paula, and another very important part enjoyed her life with all the human children. Tweetza worked to reconcile her mixed emotions. She decided to suppress her desire to mate so that she could enjoy a safe life with her human family. She even thought about the possibility of mating with Alex, but knew that was not possible. Over the course of the coming years, this would constantly come back to haunt her.

The final batch of in-vitro fertilized babies was born on April 1, 0007. Before the end of that year, one was lost to an indigenous virus that had afflicted many of the human kids on ACP in the past, but never fatally. Including Alex and Paula, the human population on ACP now numbered 246.

9

Lost and Found

June 3, 0014

Steven, Anna, and Alexander spent most of their free time running around, creating what the adults often referred to as 'mischief.' They had boundless energy and unquenchable curiosity. As a trio, they were impossible to keep up with. One of their favorite past times was to sit in the 1966 Mustang and pretend they were driving to exotic locations on Earth. Steven had turned 11 last September, while the Batch 1 kids had just turned 11 in May.

ACP still had no roads, and only two vehicles. The motorcycle was an essential tool, used almost daily by Alex, and occasionally by Paula, while the Mustang was a museum piece. Alex had built a small garage for it so that he could open up space on the ship for a clinic. With 244 children all under the age of 12, there were daily injuries that needed tending and attention, either with TLC, or medical care.

"Where are *you* taking us today?" Steven asked Anna from the back seat of the Mustang. They often played a game where one of the three would research a place on Earth and then pretend to drive there while playing tour guide.

"I am taking us to the desert in western America called Death Valley," answered Anna, tour guide du jour.

"What a horrible and scary name. Why would you take us to a desert with death?" Steven asked.

"Steven, it's my turn to drive. You just sit in the back seat and enjoy the ride. There is no death in Death Valley," Anna, who was very fond of Steven but tended to be a bit bossy at times, responded.

"Well, what did you pack for the trip?" Alexander asked, always more concerned about food and provisions than destinations.

"Three days' worth of food and one week's worth of water. We probably won't see anyone, and there certainly won't be any place to pick up supplies," Anna smugly commented about her fictitious provision on their imaginary journey.

"There's no room in this car for all that stuff," Steven challenged, always trying to outsmart Anna.

"That's what you think, but I stored everything in the trunk so that there would be plenty of room in the car," Anna responded, emphasizing the word *trunk*, and beaming about her discovery.

"Trunk? What's a trunk?" Steven asked.

Anna started to answer but was interrupted when the garage door opened, flooding the room with daylight.

"Where are you kids off to?" Alex asked as he walked around to Anna's side of the car. Alex often liked to come in on their travel game and see what location they were visiting.

"Death Valley," Anna answered as she pretended to drive.

"Oh really? I hope you're not gone too long, because you all have chores, class, and homework," Alex responded.

"The drive will take all day, and then we will be spending three days in the desert," Alexander answered before Anna could respond. "So, I guess all those things will have to wait till we get back home!"

"Dad, Anna was just about to tell us what a trunk is." Steven interrupted.

Alex walked to the back of the car and the kids all piled out of the seats. "This is a trunk," He slapped his hand on the solid metal trunk lid.

"I thought that was the gas tank," Steven responded.

"So did I until this morning." Chimed Anna. "I found a picture of an old Mustang in the encyclopedia file."

Alex walked over to the wall where the Mustang keys hung. He had a huge smile on his face, brought about by the realization that he had somehow forgotten to tell the kids about something every Earth child knew so well.

"With the exception of a few sports cars and pickup trucks, all cars have trunks. They are great places to store things, so you don't clutter up the car. But I don't think we have opened this trunk since we've been on ACP." He slid the key into the trunk lock and turned the mechanism. After over seven years of being closed, the key lock was tight, and the seal was stuck. After a bit of work, Alex managed to open the lid. As the three kids peered in, the two boxes inside confused Alex.

"What's this," he asked out loud as he lifted one of the boxes out. He could not recall having placed any boxes in the trunk. Alex set the box on the floor as the three kids gathered around anxious to see the contents. Alex opened the box and found a large selection of computer components. He took the second box out and found a fully assembled computer with a hand-written note:

Alex,

Got your message in a dozen emails from ham operators worldwide. Most had more questions than I was willing to answer.   Thanks, bud ...your method of communication was very clever.   Hope these components do the trick. I think I figured out where you went. Look forward to hearing stories of your trip.

- Mark

The kids were tugging at Alex asking questions about the boxes and their contents. Alex just stood, staring at the note. His mind reeled back to an event many years in the past. His message had gotten through after all, and Mark, always reliable, had not let him down. Alex remembered having searched every square inch of the ship several times and not finding these items. He had never thought to look in the trunk of the Mustang. If only he had been able to receive the radio response. These components would have been more than enough to repair the ship, enabling a return to Earth. If Alex had found such a great hiding place, why had he not broadcasted its location?

"Daaad. What is this stuff?" Steven finally broke through to Alex. "Who is that note from?"

Alex refocused on Steven, Anna, and Alexander, all anxiously awaiting his explanation.

"These are the replacement parts that would have allowed us to repair the ship and return to Earth. A very old friend of mine named Mark hid them here. I guess he hid them too well because I never thought about looking in the trunk for them." Alex took out each replacement component, told the kids what it was, and placed it back in the box.

"So, are we going back to Earth?" Anna asked with nervous anticipation.

Alex had long since given up on the possibility of returning to Earth. While these components opened a new possibility, he had used most of the ship's propulsion components in his various projects just to survive.

"Kids, I am not sure. I need to talk to your mother. For now, why don't you continue your trip to the desert." Alex stacked the two boxes, picked them up, and left.

Alex pressed the communications button on his lapel. "Paula, can you break away and come to the machine shop?" Alex had built several micro-communication devices so he, Tweetza, and Paula could always have instant communication in their growing town.

The human outpost on ACP now consisted of several dozen buildings surrounded by fortification and camouflage. Alex constantly considered it a small miracle that in the thirteen years in this location, they had never been discovered by Pacs.

"Can it wait 15 minutes?" Paula responded.

"Sure." Alex sat down and began to consider the variables. No real decision could be made until he was able to evaluate whether the propulsion system could be reassembled. Over the years, he had cannibalized much of the ship's systems to build necessary components for survival. Many of those components had been modified to serve some new purpose. Alex touched the digital screen and began to review the schematic for his propulsion engine. It had been so long since he had looked at these schematics, he felt as though he was looking at a document written in a foreign language.

He laid out the components and the list Mark had sent. "Emily, can you evaluate and inventory these parts? I may need to do some evaluation of how they can be utilized."

"Done," was her simple response.

When Paula came into the room, her heart sank as she immediately recognized the images on the screen. Those images had been burned into her memory because they represented practically the only task he worked on during their first year on ACP. It had been a difficult year, one she had long since put out of her mind.

Alex stood up, unfolded the note from Mark, and handed it to Paula. "Back in year one when you were comatose, I tried to get a message to Mark. In my message, I asked him to hide certain components on the ship so that I would not be able to find them during one of my routine inspections prior to our departure for Alpha Cassi. For all these years, I thought he had not gotten the message. Thanks to our little trio of super kids, I found those components in the Mustang trunk."

"Remind me, how did you get the message to him?" Paula asked as she studied the note.

"I did a tachyon jump to the appropriate point in time and transmitted a ham signal back to Earth with the info and Mark's email address. Damn, I searched every square inch of the ship. I can't believe I didn't think to look in the trunk."

"Why didn't you just ask him to transmit a signal back telling you where he hid them and jump to the appropriate time to receive that signal?" She asked.

"I did. The problem was that when I came out of the tachyon tunnel at the calculated time, there was no transmission from Mark. Even though the assumption should have been that he never got the message, I still searched the ship from top to bottom. Paula, I could have gotten us out of here. We might have returned to Earth."

Paula had two reactions to his frustration but thought it only appropriate to handle one at a time. "Okay, Alex, but now you have the components. Can you fix this ship and get us *all* back to Earth?"

"Probably not. I've cannibalized so much of the propulsion and computer systems. Many of the components for thrust have been modified. In reality, I do not think we can find the raw materials to rebuild. Maybe fifty years from now, when all of these children become productive and build factories, but today, I would guess it's pretty near impossible."

Paula was watching Alex's body language. He was clearly hurting. "There are several ways to look at this. What do you think would have happened if we had returned to Earth?"

"What do you mean?" Alex asked.

"Would we have ended up together? This deserted island that we named ACP has been well worth it to me. You have been the love of my life, and I do not believe we would have been together on Earth."

"I'm not so..." Alex started, but Paula interrupted before he could finish.

"No. Listen to me. You have never been able to slow down enough to focus on any relationship. Also, think about all of these kids. I have watched you around them. I've seen how much you love them. If you had gotten us back to Earth, none of them would have been conceived, *none* of them."

It was a startling thought for Alex. Paula was correct. He never would have wanted kids at his age, and certainly would never have agreed to over 200 of them. Alex took Paula in his arms. Reality crashed in, establishing a fundamental fact: Earth was not all that important. What was important was their connection and the lives of their children. Until this moment, Alex had believed that this was another complex engineering project. Survival and engineering had been the prime motivations, but along the way, he had fallen in love with Paula and 244 children. On Earth, Alex would have continuously pursued the technology rat race until his brain became too feeble to compete. On ACP, he was truly the only engineer and had a purpose far more significant than any he might have chosen on Earth.

After a few minutes of watching Alex, Paula broke his thought. "So?"

"You know, there are a dozen projects here in Watson Village where I could use these components." Alex tried to change the subject but then decided to re-focus. "You are right Paula. You and these children have shown me a world that I never would have known, or even believed could exist. It is a world that requires a significant amount of engineering magic, but engineering magic is nothing in comparison to the inner magic that you and the kids bring.

Paula just smiled. She had always taken from Alex the things she needed for her emotional survival and sanity. Now, it seemed that he was at a point where he would willingly give back. She looked down at the two boxes of components and wondered what new miracles Alex would create with these computer parts.

10

EDUCATION

March 0017

Twelve-year-old Bryce Charles took the controller; certain he could handle the task. A Pac was firing at his shield which was dissolving away with every hit. While he was perfect at blocking projectiles, it was clear the electromagnetic shield would not last much longer. He hid behind a rock, began solving the problems, and his shield was strengthened with each correct solution. After a few minutes, he got the hang of it and was determined to defeat the attacking enemy. He could feel his pulse rate double as he stepped out again, blocking, firing, and dodging.

Watching from the side, his father was certain he would be defeated. His shields were nearly gone, and the young man was taking risks no other kid would have dared, or even thought of taking, but Bryce Charles persisted, and that persistence turned the tide. Alex smiled as the young man took the advantage and turned it against the enemy.

BC, as the other kids called him, spent all of his free time playing video games. He was essentially a good kid who managed to get his chores done, but he continuously struggled with his lessons. Everyone in the colony knew one thing about BC: he was unbeatable in every game on ACP computer systems. Now, with a new generation of games, Bryce would begin using his skills and interest to learn.

This particular game focused on rapidly solving simple multiplication tables. As he began level two, he gave his father the thumbs up and re-focused on the next challenge. In this level, the math was more difficult, but he quickly found hiding places where "ancient tricks" were taught, then used those tricks to aid his quick solution. In the hiding places, he was able to practice tricks before facing the enemy. Once again, Bryce looked up at Alex and smiled, then quickly refocused on the game. He liked it when his dad watched him play.

Alex watched for nearly an hour as young Bryce mastered the multiplication tables in order to *win* the game. After a while, he left Bryce alone and went back to his office. Alex reflected that the last few years had been remarkable for many reasons. He had found numerous ways to inspire his brighter children to learn and become active participants in the productivity of the colony. On Earth, the methods he had employed probably would have landed him in jail for forcing all the young kids to work the 12-hour shifts around the clock, but on ACP, it was a critical way of life. Alex, Tweetza, and Paula were no longer the sole providers but were instead the beneficiaries of the productivity of a focused colony of 246 humans.

Not all was perfect in paradise, though. Giles Andrews, born in batch 1, was argumentative and always got into trouble. Alex and Paula tried every form of communication and discipline, but nothing seemed to work. He refused to do his chores, failed most of his coursework, and constantly broke the cardinal rule of the colony by wandering off and exploring alone. He had formed a good bond with Tweetza, but it seemed that was more of an attempt to be subversive than compliant. Giles was bright, very bright. He had no problem reading and learning, he simply chose to oppose everything Alex, Paula, and the colony stood for.

Giles's attitude reminded Alex of a growing contingent in the U.S.. In the last few years before his departure, Alex had constantly been frustrated with people who, in his mind, did not appreciate the value his country had brought to the world. He often had found himself in debates with people that felt the U.S. should relinquish its position as a world leader because the country was, as they would say, "not worthy of the role." Many would argue that Americans had unjustly stolen the land from the Native Americans and that they should be running the country, not the privileged Europeans. The most startling trend had been one of robbing the successful to give to the poor. While Alex was a huge fan of helping those who needed it, he was not a fan of helping those that would not help themselves. Too many had come to believe the American Dream was a right that should be handed to everyone by the government. From Alex's perspective, the fruits of the American Dream should be reserved for those willing to do the work to achieve it, not handed to those not willing to participate in the work and efforts. Alex had come to feel that the American Dream was much more about the sense of accomplishment than about the fruits of his labor.

As early as eight years old, Giles had begun arguing that the colony had no right to be on ACP. He maintained that the planet belonged to the Pacs, not the humans. He felt his mom and dad had committed a huge crime against Pac humanity by creating this colony, whose only real ultimate goal was the elimination of the Pac civilization on ACP.

In fact, the location selected sixteen years earlier for Watson Village had completely remained hidden from any members of the Pac civilization. While Alex and Paula were concerned about the day when they were discovered, it would never be their intention to engage in a fight or war. The planet was big enough for both species.

* * * * *

June 0017

Alex found Steven and Anna working on layouts for a chemistry game similar to the mathematics one now completed by Bryce and being devoured by several other kids from batches 1 and 2. The first significant success of the new tools came when Bryce mastered 6th-grade math in under a month, then 7th-grade math in three weeks. In the first six months of the year, Bryce had elevated his math skills from the 5th-grade level to the 8th. The Accelerated Game Education (AGE) concept had become a huge success. Prior to AGE, Alex had been quite pleased with the computer-based educational tools he had built. Most of his accelerated nine-year-olds were operating on the 6th to 7th-grade level, while his eleven-year-olds were handling coursework for high school sophomores.

Only Giles and Bryce were behind, and Bryce was rapidly gaining on his better-educated siblings. Steven, nearly age 15, and Anna, 14, were the exception. Both had finished their senior year of high school and were halfway into the equivalent of their bachelor's degrees in engineering. With the new AGE tools, Alex hoped to have virtually all kids at the Ph.D. level before they turned 21.

What Alex and Paula had accomplished was miraculous, but at the same time, could theoretically have been done on Earth. The big advantages they had were no budget constraints, no existing rules and/or imagined barriers, no school board or local political curmudgeons, and no meddling parents. Most importantly, the only role models the kids knew were Paula and Alex, who both had a post-doctorate level education.

The ACP education system focused on literature, art, music, mathematics, science, manufacturing, and engineering. To some degree, history was taught as a method of showing mistakes humans had made throughout time. As he watched the 244 young minds develop, Alex recognized that this would be the only time in ACP history where so much could be accomplished so quickly. It is in fact the nature of man to burden himself with rules, intended to address problems, but with the complication of slowing progress. As many of the children would become scientists and engineers, some would also become politicians and lawyers – a necessary burden and/or evil in any society. Today,

Alex was a benevolent dictator who could establish any educational or societal rule with the flick of his finger and approval from only one other person. He and Paula knew that would change soon enough as a democracy was created, and Watson Village residents would begin voting.

Both parents enjoyed watching Steven and Anna because they clearly understood the impact they were having on the other children, and mostly, that they were having fun together. While everyone recognized that Anna was the smarter of the two, Steven was very resourceful. As the oldest, he had become the young male role model, a job he took very seriously. In either case, the two played off each other's strengths and supported their weaknesses.

"So, when is AGE Chem going to be ready?" Alex interrupted their focus.

"Bryce is already playing a beta version," Steven answered before Anna could speak.

"Yes, we've developed the modules so we can continue to add knowledge to the game," Anna chimed in, "but we currently have enough material to keep even Bryce occupied for a year."

"A year?" Alex was surprised. "I think you have underestimated Bryce. You know he's gonna catch the two of you before long!"

"Dad, we have the entire course of chemistry. When people are done, they will know chemistry far better than you, or even Mom." Anna said with an ear-to-ear smile.

"I don't doubt it," Alex responded. He had long since realized the culture he and Paula had created on ACP was very similar to that found at some of Earth's best colleges.

"Perhaps Mom and I should go through the coursework." The thought that a group of 12-year-olds could challenge his knowledge in any area of science or engineering created an interesting contradiction in his psyche. At the same time, the fact that they were his kids made him extremely proud.

"If we manage to surpass you, it's only because you created the systems to make it happen." Steven volunteered.

"Thanks, son." Alex was impressed by the maturity of Steven's statement. "Have you thought about how to use all this technology to pull Giles in?"

"Sorry Dad, some things are possible, and some things are not," Anna blurted. "None of us like even being around Giles. He is always so negative and venomous."

"Let's be patient with him. Eventually, we'll find a role for him," Alex answered in a hopeful tone.

"Giles's will never fit in, Dad," Steven answered, flatly.

"We'll find a place for him. Trust me on that," Alex answered. "For now, get back to your AGE chemistry program."

Both Steven and Anna gave each other skeptical looks and then returned their focus to valence electrons and chemistry. For them, the programming solidified their knowledge of intermediate and advanced chemistry.

Anna watched as Alex left the room, then brushed her hand lightly on Steven's face. "Do you think Giles can be fixed," she smiled at Steven in a way that seemed possible only with him.

Steven had just recently begun to appreciate Anna's light touch when she spoke with him while they were alone. Their connection seemed obvious, but Paula had been warning them to be careful with their relationship. They were the first real couple among the children, but they had literally grown up as companions since they were infants.

"Steven," Anna quipped, "are you with me?"

"Sorry. Sometimes your touch is distracting. Don't misunderstand, I enjoy it very much, but it seems to have significant physiological effects."

Paula walked into the room and caught the tail end of the conversation. "You want to explain those physiological effects to me, son?"

Steven looked up and flushed red, "Uhm, well, sometimes Anna touches my face when she talks to me. When she does that, well, the chemistry in my body takes over."

"I see. Well, perhaps you should discuss that chemistry with your father, but I will tell you, it is perfectly natural at some age. The problem is that the two of you are 14 and 13. Back on Earth, we would have called it puppy love, but the circumstances are different here. Heed my advice and take it slowly."

"Okay Mom," Anna volunteered.

Paula looked each one in the eyes to make sure they were focused. Things were clearly different here, but the fact remained that they were far too young for a serious relationship.

"Let's keep our eyes on this issue as it progresses," she paused and studied each of them again. "Which of you is better at biochemistry?"

Anna and Steven studied each other for a few seconds before Anna pointed at Steven.

"Definitely Steven."

Paula looked at Steven. "Is that right?"

"Only because I've spent more time on it," Steven answered with a proud smile.

"I have a pet project that's been sitting on the shelf for years and could use an assistant. Are you ready for some graduate-level work?"

"Wow, sounds fun!" Steven answered.

"Can I help?" Anna chimed in.

"Two minds are better than one," Paula answered. "Come with me."

When they arrived at the genetic lab Paula pulled up some files on the computer. "I want to do a comparative analysis of the human DNA and the Pac. Ultimately, I'd like to determine just how similar we are as a species."

For the next hour she showed them computer files that they could read to learn more and explained the basics. "Several similar studies have been done over the years with regard to various primates. You will also find an excellent donkey-horse study as well as one on bison and several cattle." She pulled the files and studied the two kids. "Got what you need?"

"Yes, mom. If we need anything else, we'll have Emily pull it for us," Anna answered.

"Mom, is the ultimate goal of this study to determine whether inter-species reproduction is possible?" Steven asked.

Paula smiled at her son's insight. "That would certainly be an important result, but for now, let's simply call this a study that gives us better visibility into the prospects."

"When do you want it done?" Anna asked.

"How about a week?" Paula answered, expecting it to take at least two weeks.

"You got it." They both answered as they focused on the screen.

Over the next three days, Anna and Steven spent all their free time studying DNA and reading old studies done by Earth scientists. They split work and taught each other. In three days, they had devoured every paper stored in Emily's database and began to evaluate the human and Pac samples. On the 4th day, Anna and Steven, with help from Emily, completed their project.

"You're done?" Paula was incredulous. "How is that possible?"

"We worked exclusively on this task, plus Emily helped run all the permutations. She's pretty fast at night when everyone is in bed." Alex explained.

"And your conclusion?"

"Well, we were not totally surprised to learn that Tweetza's genome is less than one-tenth of one percent different from ours."

"Oh, that can't possibly be correct. Emily, can you confirm the analysis, methodology, and results?"

"Yes, Paula. My conclusion is identical to that of Steven and Anna's," Emily answered.

Paula sat down, dizzy from the prospect. "One-tenth of one percent. One-tenth of one percent." She repeated several times as if she was trying to convince herself.

"Mom, we have already concluded that it would be possible for Pacs and humans to have children. There are a few anatomical differences, but mostly, Pacs are human."

"Emily, is it possible for us to determine if there's a common lineage?"

Before Emily could respond Anna interrupted. "Mom, what's that mean?"

"It's complicated. In the name of scientific curiosity, I'd like to ascertain whether the human genome is Earth based on whether it was introduced. Stated another way: is mankind the product of evolution on Earth, or possibly some other interstellar variable?"

When Paula finished, the computer answered, "It is possible, though difficult. We would need more DNA before we could make a positive conclusion."

"Okay, thanks, Emily. Kids, you get back to your AGE development. Today, we learned something significant and possibly of great value to our community. For now, we will put part two of this project on the shelf. Let's classify it as a second pet project."

* * * * *

November 0017

Alex sat down at his computer and began to think about light bulbs. The bulb itself was a relatively simple invention, but it consumed significantly more power than the more efficient diode lighting that had replaced the bulb back on Earth. The problem was manufacturing. Until now, every electronic component in the colony has come from salvaging elements of the ship. The computer processors on board contained chips that were composed of tens of billions of transistors. Back on Earth, engineers had surpassed much of Alex's tech and moved to exclusive quantum and organic devices, but for Alex, these technologies were no more than theoretical accomplishments that would not likely happen on ACP during his lifetime. The amount of manufacturing technology required to build efficient diode lighting was a major issue, and the diode was a very simple device. He and his team of young future engineers had the knowledge, but lacked the facilities.

Building silicon product manufacturing was absolutely necessary for their continued lifestyle. Transistors, semiconductors, and diodes were the fundamental building blocks of computer technology, and the human colony would come to a screeching technological halt if manufacturing methods were not soon developed. Shared computer time was already a significant problem with over 200 users. This was not so much because of processor capabilities, but because of screen and display availability.

The number one project of year 17 was the development of facilities that could reproduce existing technology. Everything, *everything* relied on computers that were now more than seventeen years old. Fortunately, Alex had ten very bright young future engineers that spent nearly all of their time working on the Colony's first fab. Within the year, he predicted they would be producing processor duplicates of their existing technology. Within three years, they would be inventing new technology of their own.

Based on the tremendous expansion of knowledge for Earth in 2025, the rate of technology growth would have more than doubled in the seventeen years Alex had been gone. If the new variant of Moore's Law, built on AI and organic quantum computing, had continued, computer processors would have increased in power by more than 64 times. Alex often wondered what computer technology, medical advancements, and entertainment toys had been invented and developed since he and Paula had left. In the years of Alex's life before his departure, he realized his generation and the one prior had developed more technology than the entire thirty thousand years of mankind. Things were moving so fast that some of the common tools of 2025 were not even dreamed of twenty years earlier, in 2005. The iPhone, launched in 2006, sparked a revolution where everyone held a supercomputer in their pocket, possessing resources that were unheard of before its introduction.

Alex constantly reminded himself that all that would have been relevant except for one important variable: he and Paula had traveled 500 years into the past. In reality, the current year back on Earth was 1542. Christopher Columbus had only recently discovered America, the printing press was still a novelty, and Martin Luther along with Henry VIII and his Tudor clan were breaking away from and thus, reforming the Catholic Church. Breaking that grip of power, where the church-controlled power and religious thought, would spark the beginning of the Renaissance, forever changing the profile of the church's grip on Europe. In the years to come, on Earth, Newton would define the laws of motion, and American democracy would be born on a raw and uncivilized continent, still more than 200 years in the future.

In the very long shot that Alex and Paula's ACP Watson Village family survive their complex challenges, they would have long since re-mastered space travel before Goddard would even build his first crude rocket, or Armstrong and Aldrin would take one giant leap for mankind. All of those events, which would lead up to Alex building his Tachyon Tunnel ship, had paradoxically not yet occurred.

As a scientist, Alex was accustomed to paradoxes, but this one was different from any he had studied in graduate physics courses. He knew that the knowledge he had used to build his ship and travel to Cassiopeia would not be invented for over 500 years. He also was acutely aware that his descendants on ACP could feasibly build technology that would allow them to travel to Earth before he is even born. If such travel were to occur, the impact they could have on the course of human history would be incalculable. The success of the colony was his prime directive, but this success must also be focused so that it did not create adverse effects on mankind.

Alex had to create a directive of non-interference with Earth. He had to make his children understand the negative consequences of reaching out to their home planet.

Alex took a deep breath and refocused on the blueprints for the silicon and liquid crystal manufacturing plant. Construction was underway. Alex Durant knew that if they successfully began manufacturing their own technology, their chances of survival would increase exponentially. This was the most important project since Paula's genetic miracle had produced 244 children.

11

BATCH 4

June 0019

To characterize Alexander Bell as brilliant would be a huge understatement, yet even with an IQ topping 190, natural intelligence was not Bell's forte. Young Alexander was cursed with an unending supply of persistence. When he had a question, he would not sleep until he found the answer. It would be this persistence that would win him top ranking amongst his genetically tailored siblings, some of whom had higher IQ scores.

As is often the case with extreme brilliance, he was cursed with social ineptitude. Much as his parents and siblings tried, young Alexander remained a social hermit. When the other kids were playing, participating in hobbies, or interacting, he would always be found on a terminal researching. If he had a single true friend, it was Emily. For Alexander, Emily had a personality coupled with an endless supply of answers. By the time he was 7 years old, he had begun to modify Emily's code, building his own interface to the computer system.

Alexander's true journey began when he was 12 and attending a review of molecular biology taught by his mom.

Every child had a clear understanding of the basic components of the science that their mom had used to build their genetic family. Bell had taught himself the fundamentals, but more importantly, he had done the math.

He raised his hand and waited for Paula to permit him to speak. "Mom, I've gone through the permutation and statistics math associated with our population and I believe, based on the number of genetic permutations available, that we will begin having problems in the fourth generation."

Paula thought about Alexander's comment for a minute. Every one of the kids was brighter than the average magna cum laude, but young Alexander was meteoric. His comment alone sounded like something uttered by a postdoc. Of course, she had also done the math many years ago and knew there would be a problem. It was an issue that she and Alex had discussed many times, but always in private. Their general feeling was that eventually, the problem would be solved, but not in or by the current generation. Alex had created a complex computer program that would monitor and approve any marriage. With such a small population, this was absolutely necessary. She looked around the classroom and was not surprised to see that many of the kids understood the question even though they had not done the math.

"Well kids, this is a problem which we believe will need to be solved by your children and grandchildren. The thing which you cannot possibly understand at your age is how much time you have. I recognize that this is a monumental problem, but as you have stated, it is not one which will manifest itself until you have great grandchildren. The good news is that you do not have to solve the problem until a hundred years or more from now."

"And if we don't solve the problem?" Julie Roberts questioned.

"I am certain you will." Paula had labored over this question thousands of times but ultimately was only guessing. "You are the brightest and best-educated group of kids ever. I am confident there is no problem you will not solve."

"Were there any cases in the history of Earth where colonies our size propagated without genetic problems?" Kevin asked.

"We believe so, but unfortunately no such study exists in Emily's data bank," Paula answered. "With the exception of Steven and Becky, your generation will be able to mate with anyone they choose. Next generation, we will create tables of compatibility. While we won't stop anyone who chooses a partner or relationship, having children will not be acceptable for some potential couples."

"Has that compatibility chart been created yet?" Julie asked.

"It will need to be done from generation to generation," Paula responded. "The database will be in Emily's computer. My guess is that there will be some drama in the future, but that will be long after I am gone."

The kids were all silent, nodding understanding, and thinking about the problem.

The perplexity was a magnet for Alexander. He told himself this was the greatest problem facing Watson Village, and that he would solve it.

* * * * *

Alexander spent weeks coming to dead ends with each genetic variation. He had never been a big fan of molecular biology, and this was not helping the case. One evening, while sitting in front of one of Emily's screens, he decided to review the original process. Paula had kept meticulous notes on tests, but she had a habit of writing them like a diary. Oftentimes, intertwined in the science, were stories of how she had spent her day. Generally, Alexander would ignore those notes, but on this particular occasion, he became fascinated by the story. He had Emily filter those notes, and he began to read the early stories of arrival on Alpha Cassiopeia. In her version of the story, Paula comments on Alex's attempts to get them back to Earth. While Alexander had no interest in returning to Earth, it occurred to him that the solution was on Earth. Suddenly, Alexander Bell's problem metamorphized from molecular biology to physics. From that point forward, he was no longer interested in Paula's notes.

"Emily, please provide details of the state of hardware for tachyon tunneling." Alexander excitedly blurted out.

"I'm sorry Alexander, all tunneling technology and data is restricted by Alex."

Alexander knew this, but he also had long since resolved this problem by building his own interface to Emily's programming and data. "Emily, please execute Alexander's private interface."

"Complete." Emily answered.

"Emily, I need to get the neural interface working. What still needs to be done to complete that?"

"Find someone to install it, and we can begin testing."

"I haven't figured that one out, yet. More importantly, what is the status on hardware for tachyon tunneling."

Emily began a detailed description of the hardware available and necessary for tunneling. Over the next year, Alexander spent every free minute evaluating the engineering behind tunneling. He came to appreciate the true genius of his father's engineering mastery. While his father had many resources on Earth, he had been forced to invent much of the technology.

There were two big differences between the problem solved by father and that anticipated by son. Son had the benefit of father's science, engineering, and experience. Son lacked the manufacturing resources father had access to on Earth. More importantly, and unfortunately not understood by young Alexander, he lacked the experience of his father. As such, it was simply impossible for him to understand and anticipate many of the unknown variables that would present themselves.

* * * * *

August 0019

Steven, Anna, and Julia took a different approach and continued to work on the problem by developing a proposed solution for genetic manipulation, based on Paula's original work. After a few weeks of lab testing, the three showed their results to Paula.

"This is remarkable," Paula smiled broadly at the three teens. "I think we could double the existing population using your protocols."

"Well, really, they are your protocols, Mom," Anna offered.

"And I think we could potentially continue to modify the genetics for as many new generations as need be." Steven chimed in.

"Yes, yes you are probably right. We would not have the genetic diversity found on Earth, but this is a viable solution. Let me run this by Dad and see what he thinks about a whole new batch of kids."

"It won't be too long before we start seeing grandkids here in Watson," Anna quipped, then immediately regretted the comment."

"You kids know how we feel about that. All of you are far too young to begin anything that even resembles making babies." Her eyes darted back and forth from Steven to Anna.

"It's okay Mom. Nothing is going on," Steven answered.

"Keep it that way. In the meantime, I will discuss a new batch with Alex this evening."

* * * * *

"Another 300 babies?" Alex repeated with a pit in his stomach.

"For now. We could do a fifth batch in a few years," Paula answered in a matter-of-fact tone.

Alex closed his eyes and let the comment sink in.

"You've commented on several occasions that this colony could handle a thousand before we needed to expand," Paula offered. In reality, she knew that Alex was as concerned with the genetics issue as she was.

"Well, at least this time around everyone in the colony can chip in to take care of the infants."

"Batch 3 would be 12 years old. I'm certain they can handle it," Paula added.

"Okay my dear, your wish is my command. Let's get working on Batch 4," he pulled her close and began kissing her affectionately.

* * * * *

Between mid-April and late May in the 20th year after Alex and Paula's arrival, an additional 213 new babies were added to the genetic mix, taking the total human population to 457. That genetic mix, coupled with this new biotech, could mathematically take the colony of humans as far into the future as they currently dared to imagine.

12

ESCAPE

August 0021

Even though the genetics problem had been resolved, Alexander Bell had become obsessed with the tunneling problem. Alex, Paula, and the other kids were not the least bit surprised by his growing reclusive nature and interest in advanced physics. He never disclosed to anyone the precise problem he was working on, which was exaggerated by the lack of legacy parts to build a new tachyon tunnel, coupled with expanded responsibilities from the new babies. These things had not phased Alexander Bell. Nothing ever did. He found a way around every technical or engineering problem and built a prototype ready for testing.

Unlike the ship built by his father, Alexander's tunneler (as he called it) consisted of a hand-held control connected to a backpack that contained processing and electronics. Alexander was not travelling in a ship, so he believed he could tunnel into the future undetected. Because Alexander was not encased in a protective suit, he chose not to take the risk of executing hops through space. This created a problem with the exclusion principle. He lost several inanimate objects before he understood another complex problem. He studied and became very good at orbital mechanics after he realized that ACP and her star were hurdling through space and as probability would have it, were constantly moving to new positions in the space-time continuum.

This problem had been solved by Alex, though not well documented, by being able to move through space as well as time. Alexander solved it in a completely different way by simply tunneling to a specific set of space-time coordinates. Because he had no ship or means of propulsion, Alexander could not tunnel to a point in the vacuum of space. He clearly understood that his solution was no more than a stopgap until he could get new parts. While initially, he felt that parts could only be obtained on Earth, after further consideration, coupled with a bit of hope, Alexander guessed he would find those parts in the future, right here on ACP.

For Alexander, the thought of tunneling was a frightening necessity. In order to accomplish his goal, he knew many trips would be required. Most importantly, he did not want to end up being caught. His Father had strict rules against tunneling, and even stricter punishment. He needed to find a safe destination to always tunnel into, and he needed to find a way to secure the resources required for the bigger task of returning to Earth to collect genetic material for the ACP population.

Bell made his first tachyon time jump in August 0021 using technology he had developed from spare parts. He told no one about his work and made certain his personal access to Emily and all of her data on his work was secure. When all was complete, Alexander Bell simply popped up six hundred years into the future.

* * * * *

"Are you absolutely certain?" Steven studied Anna, not sure how to respond.

"Not absolutely, Steven, but all the symptoms and indicators point in that direction. You have to know that it was only a matter of time before this happened."

"Mom is gonna kill us," he responded.

"You bastard! I tell you that we're going to have a baby, and your first reaction is that Mom is gonna kill us?"

"Well…"

"Steven, we have been having sex for several months. You knew this was a possibility the first time. By my calculus, conception was inevitable."

"I know, but Mom explicitly warned us not to do this," he answered.

"And we ignored her," her eyes sparkled as she thought about how much she loved being with Steven. "As I said, it was inevitable, and now we're gonna have a baby." Anna studied Steven. Even in the most difficult of circumstances, she loved this young man. "You know we aren't the only ones. Julie and Kevin have also been having sex."

"I bet Alexander and Emily have been having sex too. I have never seen anyone so in love with a computer as Alex," Steven joked.

"Be serious, Steven, Emily is a computer!"

"I know. That's the point…" Steven took a deep breath, closed his eyes, and exhaled slowly. "You're right, that doesn't really help our situation. I think the only smart thing for us to do is just tell Mom."

Anna smiled. "Agreed."

* * * * *

"You need to understand that humans have been doing this since the dawn of man. You should read about how the

Romans conquered and subjugated, then how the European royalty did the same." Giles Andrews was on a roll as he stared at Tweetza's large eyes. "Most importantly, you should read about how Alex's own beloved Americans conquered and decimated the Native American tribes. You are just the first here on Etakatz," Giles used the Pac name for the planet. "This colony will continue to grow and will ultimately wipe out your entire species. Before it does, your brothers and sisters will be enslaved; like you, or worse, placed you behind cages in zoos. In a sense, the survival of your entire species is in your hands."

"Giles must not take a negative view of his brothers and sisters. Pac men have no respect for life like humans. Pac men have no respect for the life of other Pac men." Tweetza argued, but something about Giles's argument struck a chord deep inside. If the destiny of her race stood in her hands, would it be right for her to do nothing to protect them?

"I take a realistic view. I have read about how humans treat each other. If you read more, you would be very scared for your fellow Pacs."

"I think humans will eventually help Pacs. Maybe someday we can live together on ACP in peace. Pacs have much they can teach humans." Tweetza argued.

"It won't happen, Tweetza. There will be war and conquest. Our colony is armed and ready for a fight. When my generation becomes men, they will begin to leave the colony and want to take more of the planet. As I said, in 200 years, Pacs will live on reservations, or in zoos controlled by humans."

"And how would Giles solve this problem?" Tweetza asked.

"You and I should leave the colony," Giles answered. "We should find a Pac tribe and warn them. We should teach them about human technology so they will have the knowledge and power to choose before the human population is so strong that there is no chance."

Tweetza thought about what Giles was saying. The question kept coming back to her: *Did the key to the survival of her species rest in her hands?* A few weeks ago, she never would have considered leaving, but Giles's argument was compelling, and her own chemistry had contributed a variable. Just days ago, she had begun to produce pheromones again. Tweetza knew this would be the last time, the last opportunity for her to have children of her own. She had convinced herself over and over again that life with her human family had been enough, but the task had always been more difficult during the periods when her body chemistry was demanding fertilization.

"Giles, this is very dangerous for you. I do not know what Pac males will do with a human boy."

"I can take care of myself." At sixteen, Giles's body was well developed and had long since begun to produce testosterone. Like most teens, he felt invincible, and more importantly, he knew that he could change the course of history. "Let's go for a walk tomorrow morning. I have found a few paths not far from here that I believe will lead us to Pac villages."

Tweetza could feel a tingle inside; it was the beginning of the decision to leave. She was now less concerned with young Giles's quest than she was excited about the mysteries of coupling with a Pac male, and the inevitable children that would come from that encounter. A hope that she had buried a hundred times since she had been saved by Alex suddenly grew like a rainforest inside her body. "Yes, let's go for a walk tomorrow."

* * * * *

Tweetza woke early and gathered a few things she treasured most from her time with the humans. She looked around the room that had been built for her several years ago and tried to remember what kind of accommodations she had been living in while a young Pac teenager. In her years of living with the humans, she had learned much that she could offer to her fellow Paccans. She took one last look around the room and quietly walked to the place where she had agreed to meet Giles.

"Are you ready?" Giles asked as she came around the corner to the gate.

"Yes." For just a second, she felt an emotional pull from her long-standing relationship with Alex, Paula, and the many children she had helped to raise, but she told herself that she would come back to visit after her own children were born. She and her children could become the emissaries that would build the bond between Pac and humans. She could teach them so many things that other Pac children had never dreamed of.

Prior to her arrival, Giles had spent some time talking to Nathan, who was on current guard duty. Because Giles liked to spend so much time outside the walls of the colony, Nathan was not surprised that he was taking a walk before starting his morning lessons. Giles had explained to Nathan that on his last walk, he had discovered a new plant a few kilometers from the colony and wanted Tweetza to come along and tell him what she knew about it.

The story sounded reasonable to Nathan.

The morning was still cold enough that Giles was wearing a heavy coat that concealed the overstuffed backpack. Giles had packed as much technology as he could fit, including a laser, portable computer, handheld communications device, and water purification kit. Most importantly, Giles had a college-level understanding of science, engineering, and mathematics. All children had been taught which plants were edible, and Giles was a good student when it came to survival. He was very familiar with the local edible flora and what part of the day to pick, yet still he had also packed several days' worth of food. He guessed they would have at least two days' travel before they made it to the nearest Pac village. Alex had chosen the site for the colony quite well. It had served its purpose of being remote and well hidden, but thanks to Giles, that was now about to change.

"We need to travel far and fast so that by the time they discover we are gone; we will be hard to find," Giles informed Tweetza after they had gotten far enough from the camouflaged walls of the city to not be seen or heard.

Tweetza simply fell in line as Giles began to jog. She had spent very little time outside the walls simply because she had so many responsibilities inside. Nevertheless, she kept herself very fit by working out with Paula or Alex every day.

* * * * *

When Alex woke, his first reaction of the day was to gently kiss Paula's, neck, slowly leading down her arm and across to her breasts. This action caused her to wake up and smile. Never, at another time in her life, had she enjoyed the companionship and relationship like she did with Alex. She appreciated how he managed to maintain his inventive, engineering focus on tasks while placing her emotional needs first. She often woke feeling blessed by the course of events that had stranded them on this planet.

Once Alex had her nipples both completely stimulated and erect, he stopped and kissed her nose. "Morning, love. What's on the agenda for the day?"

"Absolutely nothing happens until you finish what you have started this morning," she answered while enjoying the intimate moment. "After that, I plan to complete the final genetic engineering for one hundred new family members," she reached down and began to stroke the now hardening part of his manhood, "followed by the long hard task of convincing the colony leader to allow me to fertilize."

"Another hundred? The genetic problem is now resolved, and sex will not help you win this debate." Alex said as he tried to resist the urge.

Paula ignored his comment as she kissed her way down his body. She gently flicked her tongue wherever her heart desired, while enjoying the taste of their two bodies from the night before. She kissed her way back up to his lips and in a single motion, rolled on top and slid him inside.

Alex gasped with the suddenness of the sensation. "Your wish is my command, Mrs. Durant."

"Good." Paula knew how to satisfy Alex, and on this occasion, she gave him her best effort. Even though she did not climax, she fully enjoyed the emotions and sensations of being part of his.

After a few minutes of holding each other, she rolled off. "And don't forget, a promise is a promise," she reminded him.

"No promise made during a seduction by the most beautiful woman on Earth or ACP is a real promise," Alex joked.

"Of course, you are right, love," she answered, "but it matters not. As you have said, the genetic problem is likely solved with Batch 4."

"In that case, let's have that debate again tomorrow morning," Alex responded hopefully, then re-focused on the perfect breasts that had started this morning's activities.

They both laughed in agreement as Paula got up, put her running clothes on, and prepared to head to the nursery.

* * * * *

Paula completed her first set of rounds at the nursery and was in the middle of her morning treadmill work out when Steven reported to her that Tweetza had left with Giles. She immediately shut down and sprinted to Alex's workroom.

Paula could see that Alex was deep in thought when she barged into his office. "Alex, Tweetza did not show up for her morning session."

"Just have someone check her room," Alex responded as he focused on his wife.

"They already have. It seems Tweetza left the compound early this morning with Giles." Paula answered.

"With Giles?" Alex's upbeat mood crashed. No one needed to tell him anymore. Tweetza never missed any scheduled sessions with the kids, and Giles had clearly been up to something inconsistent with the goals of Watson Village. "Okay, let's get together two search teams. The worst thing that can happen is for Giles and Tweetza to find or be found by Pacs."

Years ago, Alex had come to trust Tweetza to the point where he never thought about her leaving. Had he been a bit more strategic, he would have planned for this event, instead, he was reacting to something that he knew very well could end all of their hopes, and lives. He motioned for Nathan to come down off his sentry post.

"Nathan, what can you tell me about Giles's departure?" Alex questioned.

"Well, sir, they left about five hours ago – right after I came on duty. Giles goes out all the time, so I thought nothing of it. He told me he was taking Tweetza to show her a new plant he had discovered."

"What were they wearing?" Alex questioned.

"Uhhmm, it was early and cold outside, so Giles had a heavy coat on. I think maybe he was wearing a couple of layers, but he may have been wearing a pack under his coat. Tweetza was wearing the same animal fur coat she always wears. She did have a small backpack."

"Did you see what direction they headed?"

"Yes sir. They went out on the trail to the rock outcropping. After that, I lost sight of them,"

"Anything else, Nathan?"

"No sir," Nathan answered, then added, "I'm sorry Dad. I should have alerted you when they left. It's just that he goes out all the time and it's never a big deal." His eyes filled with tears, as he believed he had failed in his duties.

Alex put his hand on Nathan's head and ran his fingers through the young boy's mop of blond hair. He was born in the second batch and was only fourteen. While most ACP fourteen-year-old boys had the maturity of a seventeen-year-old on Earth, Alex realized the burden was a great one. On a daily basis, the survival of the colony depended essentially on decisions made by teenagers. "It's okay, son. Go back to your post and radio me if you see anything unusual." He turned back to his older sons as Nathan scampered up the wall to his sentry post.

"The first thing we need to do is determine what direction they went after they passed the rock outcropping," Alex said to six of his strongest sons, plus Anna, Suzanne, and Paula as they stood in the courtyard near their main gate. "Let's take our time and methodically search for clues while being as efficient and fast as possible."

Alex opened the wooden case he had carried out of his office. In the box was the newest version of his laser weapon. In the early years, he had built optical lasers as a form of defense and as a hunting tool. About a year ago, he made a breakthrough with an X-Ray version of the weapon. Over the following months, he perfected the technology and now had a fully functional X-Ray laser; perhaps one of the most efficient tools ever built. It could be fine-tuned for cutting, heavy-duty blasting, hunting, and defense. Because of the lethal potential of the tool, Alex had built only eight, and he kept a close tab on every unit. He had trained only seven people in their use, and all seven stood before him now. Because Giles had already become a problem by the time he finished the development of the new weapon, he had taken the precaution not to inform him of the existence of this device. He handed the X-Ray laser to his six sons and Paula. As they grasped the weapon, they clearly understood the magnitude of the problem before them. The colony had only one secret that these young men were aware of, and that was the X-Ray laser.

"Each of you has been instructed in the use of this device. Please remember that you should not point it unless you intend to use it. If you see Pac males, you should fire first and ask questions later. I cannot overemphasize the fact that your survival and the survival of the Watson Village depend on no Pac having knowledge of our compound." Alex looked into the eyes of the six boys. They were so young, yet so eager to succeed. "I don't want a war. Let's just find Giles and Tweetza. Understood?"

All acknowledged. The possibility of dealing with Pac discovery of their village had been a fact of life since their early days. All boys grew up with the knowledge that they would eventually be discovered, and all were taught that Pac males took no prisoners.

Alex walked down the line and stopped at Paula. "Sweetie, you take Alexander, Bill, and David. Stay close to the compound. If you discover anything, contact me immediately. Stay in constant touch with Nathan, who will remain at his post. Anna should maintain vigilance and order inside the compound walls until you and I return."

"Okay." Paula answered hesitantly.

Alex turned and focused on Anna. "I expect everyone on the inside to carry on like a normal day. All lessons, all chores, and all manufacturing must continue. Understood?"

"Yes, Father." Anna answered. She glanced at Steven, pleading with her eyes for him to be careful. He walked over and openly hugged her.

Alex observed Anna and Steven. The development of their relationship was something he and Paula had kept a keen eye on, and it was a joy to watch. He walked up to Paula and gave her a long hard embrace. "I love you," he whispered in her ear and then led his group of three young men: Steven, Bryce, and Kevin out the gate.

$$* * * * *$$

"Tweetza, how long do you think we've been gone?" Giles asked as he slowed from a gentle jog to a fast walk. All children had become well versed in determining the time by checking the position of the Sun. This was a skill that Tweetza had mastered. She could typically guess the time with accuracy within minutes of the real-time.

Tweetza looked at the Sun, which had climbed about halfway to its zenith. "I would guess ten hours and twenty minutes." When they left the compound, Giles had immediately taken control, and even though Tweetza had raised him, today she followed his command as if he were an older, more experienced man. She had not been this far from the human compound since Alex had rescued her seventeen years earlier.

"Let's take a break and have some lunch." Giles took some supplies from his pack. It was too early in the day for most of the local flora to have ripened to the point where he appreciated the taste. "Do you recognize any of the terrain?"

"No." Tweetza answered. She had long since forgotten most of the landmarks from her local village. In seventeen years, she had seen wonders that no Pac had ever imagined. "I do not remember much, Giles."

"That's okay Tweetza," Giles said in her native Pac language.

"Oh Giles, you said that very well." Tweetza was surprised at his use of her language.

"I have been listening to the audio you recorded when you first joined us." Giles was referring to the nearly 60 hours of audio files Alex had created as a tool for learning the Pac language. "It is a difficult language for the human tongue."

"It has been fifteen years since I even thought about my tribal language."

"I'm gonna have to learn the language if I'm going to survive on this planet. I feel like I can understand a small amount, but I have a long way to go."

"And I will have to re-learn," Tweetza said in Pac.

For the next hour, Tweetza played teacher, saying simple sentences and translating when necessary.

As they talked, Giles was beginning to tire but wanted to push. By now, he knew his father would be searching. He had brought along a radio in the hope that he could listen in on any conversations Alex might have with other members of the colony. Just as predicted, he had heard several conversations. He knew that Alex, Bryce, Steven, and Kevin had found his trail, and were now in pursuit. What the search committee did not know was which direction he and Tweetza had gone when they reached the small stream a few kilometers from the colony. Giles was certain that would slow them down. He and Tweetza had run nearly three hours in the shallow stream. If Alex simply guessed which way they went, and guessed correctly, he may be able to gain on Giles and Tweetza, but Giles was certain Alex would be more methodical. He would send scouts in both directions and lose as much as six hours.

Giles re-focused on Tweetza, who seemed to be lost in thought. "How many languages are there?" Giles asked.

"I only know of one," Tweetza responded, "but there are several accents I recall hearing, and some different words, or ways of saying things."

"But you do remember your language well enough to communicate?"

"Yes, of course, but I am more comfortable speaking English."

Giles was a bit disturbed by her comment. From his perspective, the Pacs were a beautiful species that were still living on their wits. They had not been polluted by technology, and the diversions on which humans had come to rely. "Tweetza, you should have more appreciation for your fellow Pacs. Humans are mostly greedy, self-serving, and unwilling to appreciate your value. After you return home, you will realize the nature of the crime my mom and dad have committed by enslaving you."

"Giles, your mom and dad have always been good to me. Your dad saved my life," she argued.

"Did they let you leave when you wanted to start a family and live your own life?"

"No," she answered. It had been an issue she had learned to deal with, but never completely reconciled.

"They care only about human dominance. It is the nature of mankind. Now you will be able to have your family. Now you will be able to live with your kind." At 18, Giles thought he understood the situation better than anyone in the colony. All the other kids were blind slaves to the belief that the human colony needed to grow, survive, and eventually conquer.

"Let's go Tweetza. We can rest more in a few hours."

* * * * *

Alex and Steven had been able to easily follow Giles and Tweetza's tracks. It was clear they were running, and this made Alex extremely nervous. Giles had planned this escape and had planned it well. When they came to the small river Alex and the team quickly realized Giles's tactical skills were better than anticipated. Alex knew this stream remained shallow for several miles in both directions. He would lose a half day if he guessed wrong. Furthermore, if he did not find them before sunset, the problem would become significant. At night, the ground became very hard, making tracks almost impossible to follow.

"Which of you are the fastest runners?" Alex looked at his three boys.

Steven and Kevin raised their hands.

Alex studied the two, very competitive young men. "And of the two of you, who is the fastest?"

"Long distance or short?" Steven asked before either could answer.

"Five miles." Alex answered.

"That's me." Steven answered. "Kevin's faster in the short distances."

"Okay, Steven, you go downstream. After about five miles, this creek is joined by a second and becomes too deep to easily ford. Upstream, the creek goes on for a dozen miles. If Steven finds nothing downstream, we go upstream. Both of you need to run as fast as you can while keeping an eye on the banks. If you see anything that looks like a trace of them, stop to inspect and then call me on the radio. The lucky person who does not find tracks will go home. The person who does will sit, rest, and wait for Bryce and me to catch up. Understood?"

"Yes." Steven and Kevin responded.

"Okay, since you're going to be running as fast as possible, you both should leave all supplies except water and weapons with me. Drink as much as possible before you leave, and head out." Alex ordered.

"Do both of you know how to get back to the colony if you find nothing?" Alex added.

"Yes sir." Both Steven and Kevin responded.

"Steven, what's your five-mile record?" Alex asked.

"I ran twenty-nine minutes and thirty-one seconds in the colony track meet a few months ago."

"Today, you need to beat that record," Alex answered. On Earth a high school-aged boy should be able to run faster than that, particularly considering the lower gravity, but extreme athletic competition was not yet a significant pastime on ACP. Alex and Paula were fairly athletic, and Paula had been one of the USA's best soccer players at one time, but the colony focus had been more on academics. Athletics were used as a tool to teach endurance and dealing with physical adversity.

"Yes sir," Steven answered.

"What about me?" Kevin asked.

"Kevin, I have a feeling you are going to be the one that finds tracks. Run fast and be alert. Both of you should keep your radio on and be listening for reports from me."

Okay." Both boys had unloaded all gear except their lasers and water. With the go-ahead from Alex, they took off in opposite directions up and downstream.

"What do we do, Dad?" Bryce asked.

"We wait," Alex answered.

The sun was high in the sky and the temperature was rising to an uncomfortable level as Steven finished his first ten minutes. The uneven terrain, loose rocks, and plant life did not cooperate with his ability to run six-minute miles. He thought about running in the stream but felt the footing and water resistance would make the situation worse. The sweat streamed down his face and burned as it hit his eyes. Several times he stepped on rocks that slid out from under him, twisting and testing the strength of his ankles. He adjusted his stride so that, rather than his usual shuffle run, he began to bound in 10-to-12-

foot hops. Steven was able to do this because he, like his parents, worked out on the treadmill with bungee cords to simulate Earth weight. Twenty minutes into his run, his legs, heart, and lungs were exhausted. While running, he slowed a bit and took a sip of his water, and then pressed on. A light sprinkle rain shower cooled him off as his chronometer ticked off 24 minutes. Up ahead, he could see the confluence where the second river joined the one that he had been following. As he approached that point, he slowed, waded into the river, and found that it was now up to his waist. He waded ashore and pulled out his radio.

Steven pressed the talk button. "Dad?"

"Found anything, Steven?"

"No. Not a trace." Steven answered, disappointed. He knew that his part in this expedition had now ended.

"Okay son, head back home. Bryce and I will head upstream and catch up with Kevin." Alex and Bryce had already shifted all packs and prepared for this call.

"Roger that. I'll radio you when I reach the colony." Steven responded.

"Good. Travel safe." Alex looked at Bryce, who had already donned his pack and stood waiting. He then strapped on his own pack and began walking upstream with Bryce at his side.

After a few minutes, Alex took out his radio when he heard Kevin's ping. "Kevin, have you found anything yet?"

"Yes, sir," Kevin answered. "I just came upon what is definitely Giles and Tweetza's tracks."

Alex quickly glanced at his watch. "Okay, son, you should take a short break. Cool off in the river then find some cover and maintain your position. Bryce and I will jog so that we can catch you as quickly as possible."

"Roger that, Dad," Kevin answered as he studied the terrain, selecting a location near the stream where he could rest.

As they began to hike briskly, Alex checked his watch. They had lost only 32 minutes. It could have been far worse.

* * * * *

Giles listened to the conversations between Bryce, Steven, and his dad. His ploy had delayed them, but not nearly as much as he had hoped. Kevin, Bryce, and Alex were stronger than he and Tweetza, so the six or eight-hour lead would be lost in a day, maybe sooner.

"Tweetza, we're gonna have to pick up the pace, and hope we can find Pac village in the next 24 hours."

"I am tired, Giles. Pac females do not have the endurance of young human boys. Soon, I will have to rest."

"Tweetza, if they catch us, we will never have another opportunity. There will never be a second chance. We must desperately push on and find a tribe before Alex finds us." Giles said his dad's name and realized that it felt weird but gave him a feeling of power. He was not Dad; he was a donor, a teacher, a dictator. For the first time in his life, Giles was free.

"I know you are right, Giles, but I must rest. I do not have the strength you have." Tweetza answered in desperation. "I have a suggestion. Let's find a place to sleep for two hours, and then we can run and travel into the night. Maybe at night we can rest a few hours, then travel more. My eyes work very well in the dark, so I can lead then."

Giles considered her suggestion, then nodded agreement, "Okay." He responded as he scanned the horizon. They were in a hilly area with significant low-lying vegetation. Rain tended to fall several times every day, but never with torrential downpours, as occur in parts of Earth.

"Can you go another hour?" Giles asked, hopefully, while anticipating her answer.

"I must stop." Tweetza began to walk, completely exhausted. Her lungs were burning like she had never before felt.

Giles led her to a location protected from the sun and watched as Tweetza curled up on the dirt, and closed her eyes. In a minute, she had fallen fast asleep. He knew that he should do the same, but the fear of being caught by Alex kept him restless and awake. He sat and nervously considered his options. He knew that travel at night would become very difficult as temperatures dropped below freezing, but he also knew that Alex's ability to easily track him would diminish at night. After an hour, he closed his eyes and managed to fall asleep in the hot afternoon sun.

Giles woke with a start. Tweetza had shoved him and watched as he rubbed his eyes. He could see something in her eyes he had not seen before and quickly realized she was terrified. His immediate reaction was to think about the time. Had he slept for hours or minutes? The sun was halfway down from zenith. He struggled to focus as Tweetza anxiously worked to get Giles to awaken.

Giles did not have time to become fully awake when the wild dog rushed Tweetza digging its fangs into her leg. Giles reached for his laser as a second and third dog closed on him. Giles fired 275 watts of collimated light at close range, resulting in an explosion of flesh, disabling one dog, and startling the other three from the pack. Giles immediately pointed at a second dog and fired, slightly grazing its back. The dog yelped in pain and rolled in the dirt. The bursts of light and explosions of flesh were enough to cause the two remaining dogs to retreat.

Giles crumpled to his knees as Tweetza moaned in pain. Less than a minute passed before Giles and Tweetza heard a second noise in the brush. Giles prepared for a second attack, focusing his laser on the bushes.

"No." Tweetza shouted right before Giles fired. Then she made another sound that Giles did not understand.

From the brush emerged two figures that could have been Tweetza's twins. One ran up to Tweetza and started making sounds that reminded Giles of Earth birds he had seen on the videos back in the colony. The second figure just stared at Giles with an expression that he recognized as fear. The two wore skins over their waists that looked somewhat like tunics, but no tops. While Giles had never seen Tweetza without human clothing, it was common knowledge that she had four breasts.

Giles tried not to stare at the long nipples and obvious female bodies.

The first female had been carrying a bag and was now cleaning Tweetza's dog bite while she chirped back and forth to Tweetza. The second female had now joined the first and both seemed to be transfixed as Tweetza began chirping nonstop.

Giles just sat and listened, trying to understand Tweetza as she spoke in what sounded more like a song. He saw her make facial expressions he had not seen before and noticed both of the females reflecting her expressions. After several minutes, the two females started responding with what seemed to be a barrage of questions. At least twenty minutes passed before they helped Tweetza up and motioned for Giles to follow.

Tweetza turned to Giles. "Giles, we will be going to their village. It has a population of nearly 200. You must come as my pet, or the males will immediately insist on killing you."

"Okay." Giles knew that he had to trust her. It was common knowledge amongst the human children that the Pac males tended to be violent. He did not want to have his mission end without the opportunity to befriend the Pac population.

"When we arrive at the village, you will stay in the single women's hut," Tweetza added.

"Are you happy to see people from your own race, Tweetza?" Giles asked, expecting her to be ecstatic after finding the females after so many years amongst humans.

"These two females are related to me. We apparently have returned to an area where what remains of my family now lives."

"Related to you? I would have guessed they were your twins." Giles responded. "But they are the first Pac I have seen other than you."

"They are cousins. My mother has a sister who was kidnapped while I was still young. These two women are her daughters. Their names are Twoodi and Twyley."

Both women turned to Giles as Tweetza mentioned their names.

"Hi." They said apprehensively in their native language.

"Hi." Giles responded in Pac.

"It is a custom in my tribe for women's names to begin the same way mine does. You will find all females have the 'Tw-' sound at the beginning of their name." Tweetza explained.

"I have a younger sister named Trudy." He added looking at Twoodi. "How far is your village?"

Twoodi responded, but Giles did not understand her answer.

"She said it's a two-hour walk." Tweetza translated. She was limping, but the excitement of finding women from her tribe seemed to erase the issue associated with the dog bite.

For the next ninety minutes, Giles practiced speaking Pac but relied heavily on Tweetza's translation. He found the two sisters to be very friendly, and curious about their human companion. They spent much time telling Tweetza about Balonis, the new clan leader. Under Balonis, a brutal campaign was underway, uniting clans through conquest. Giles was a bit appalled by the stories they told of bloody battles and massive destruction of life. The two females were, on the other hand, quite excited by the fact that they belonged to Balonis' clan. He had built an army that was growing at an amazing rate, and was now unmatched in the history of their world.

After a while, the females focused on Giles, asking him questions about where he came from and what his clan was like. Both were sweet and warm to him. He soon forgot the feeling of dread from Balonis and became excited about the opportunity to interact with these wonderful people that inhabited this world. Clearly, Balonis' conquest was important, but Giles guessed that it had little or no effect on day-to-day life.

"Will I meet Balonis?" Giles asked Twoodi.

"Oh, I do not think that is possible or smart. Balonis only speaks to his generals and his women. If you wish to live, you must stay away from Balonis," she warned.

"Why?" Giles asked.

"Because Balonis kills everything that does not serve the clan and his goal of conquest."

* * * * *

Alex, tired from running most of the day, could see the pack of dogs feasting and immediately thought Giles and Tweetza were the meal. Over the years he had encountered wild dogs on several occasions and had no love-loss for their kind. They tended to be mangy, desperate, and dangerous hunters. He had constant nightmares of them getting hold of one of the kids. From a distance, he aimed the X-Ray laser and fired three short bursts. No pain was felt, and very little remained.

He motioned for Bryce and Kevin to stay put while he ran up to inspect. He was relieved to see the dogs had been eating one of their own. It did not take long to realize the prey had been killed by a laser blast. While he inspected the carcass, Kevin inspected the scene.

"Dad, look at these prints." Kevin motioned excitedly.

Kevin, Bryce, and Alex stood and studied the prints, making the realization that Giles and Tweetza were now with other Pacs.

"This is not good," was all Alex could say.

"What now?" Bryce asked.

Alex took a pair of binoculars out of his pack and hiked to the top of the hill, joined by his two nervous young sons. He wondered how long the dog had been dead and guessed maybe 2 or 3 hours. Had they gotten that close?

From the top of the hill he scanned the horizon with his binoculars. Four specs in the distance seemed to be moving. With an optical resolution of 7x and a digital zoom of 12x, he braced the binoculars on a rock and zoomed in to the full 84 times magnification.

Two of the four specs clearly resolved to Tweetza and Giles. His worst nightmare was now confirmed. He pressed a button that calculated the distance to the three Pacs and single human. They were almost 5 miles away. Worse still, they were just a few minutes away from what appeared to be a large village. He stepped back so that Bryce and Kevin could look, while he considered the options. He knew the smartest thing he could do at this moment was to mount his x-ray laser on a tripod and end the lives of Tweetza and Giles. The implications of the Pacs learning of his human colony would forever change their existence.

Alex took the tripod from his pack and began to mount the laser. He had never tested the weapon at this distance, but was confident the beam would not dissipate substantially to have an impact on its effectiveness.

"What now, Dad?" Kevin asked as he watched his father.

Alex looked up. The boys could see the tears running down his face. "Do you know what happens if they find out about us?" He made some final adjustments and began to aim the weapon.

"Dad, he is our *brother*." Kevin pleaded, when he realized what would happen next. "He's your *son*."

The impact of Kevin's appeal hit Alex hard. He was already questioning his ability to pull the trigger, but his son's supplication put him into a tailspin. Alex lifted the binoculars to his eyes and watched for several seconds until Giles, Tweetza and the two Pacs walked into a crowd that was gathering near one of the gates to the village.

For the remainder of his life, Alex would wish he had overcome that point of indecision and done what his logic had clearly dictated himself to do. Still, a very important part of his heart and mind knew that he would have never been able to live with the thought of having killed his son and their longtime companion.

13

BALONIS THE CONQUEROR

Giles was surprised at the initial reaction as he was surrounded by Pacs that flooded out of the village. Even as a boy, he stood taller than any of the curious observers. Within a few minutes, three broad-shouldered Pacs pushed through the crowd and began interrogating Tweetza and her two cousins.

Giles quickly became frightened as one pushed his spear tight against his chin and gruffly asked questions that Giles could not understand.

"Giles, he wants to know why he should not kill you right now?" Tweetza translated.

"I can help you fight your real enemy," Giles answered, fighting back panic and tears. The reality of his situation had overcome him and filled him with fear. All the years of being told to stay clear of Pacs because of their known lack of respect for life came flooding into his memory. At no point in his life had he ever felt fear like he now felt.

"This clan has no enemy which cannot be conquered with Etakan muscle, and the leadership of Balonis the conqueror. You will be dead before the sun sets, as have all our enemies." Tweetza translated again.

"Are you Balonis?" Giles asked.

"I am Artagon, the greatest general in the history of Etakatz." The broad-shouldered Pac puffed his chest and growled for effect. When some members of the crowd laughed, Artagon turned and threatened the crowd with his spear. Many backed off, but several stood their ground.

As Giles watched the crowd's response to Artagon, an idea came to him. "Then you must know," he stopped for effect as the general studied him, "Artagon, the greatest general; that your *new* enemy has this weapon." Giles raised his laser and pointed it at a rock some meters from the nearest Pac. He waited for Tweetza to translate and then fired. The rock quickly glowed red and then exploded in a fire of shrapnel.

Several females screamed in terror, but Artagon reacted quickly, snatching the laser from Giles and studying it. In possession of this weapon, even Balonis would be forced to bow before Artagon. He began pressing the buttons but with no effect.

Alex had designed the laser weapon so that it would only fire if it was gripped correctly and both buttons pressed in the correct sequence. His intent had been two-fold; first, he did not want one of the children accidentally firing and destroying life or property. More importantly, in the event one was captured by a Pac, he did not want the enemy to easily learn how to use it against humans.

In frustration, Artagon handed the weapon back to Giles. "Show me," he demanded, shaking his spear.

"It is designed for my hand. Only I can fire it," Giles lied in his most commanding tone. He pointed the laser at Artagon, who stepped back in fear, then pointed it at a small pool of water. He had seen Alex do this a couple of times to entertain the kids. When he fired, the water exploded into a cloud of steam. He quickly pointed it at Artagon again. As the steam trick was clearing, the crowd suddenly parted.

Giles could see a taller Pac, who looked almost human, walking directly towards him. This new Pac seemed to have complete control over the crowd. Even Artagon seemed to quake as he spoke. He stood for a few seconds studying the situation and then looked at Tweetza.

"I am Balonis," the man said in a deep voice, with an air that assumed Giles already knew his reputation. "No Etakan has ever stood before me that did not fall. Under my rule, all enemies that oppose me shall be dead before the sun can set."

Tweetza began to translate for Giles.

Giles watched Balonis as Tweetza translated. He was not certain, but he guessed Balonis was looking at her in a friendly fashion. When she finished, he turned, noticeably changed his facial expression, and glared at Giles for what felt like an eternity.

"You do not need to further demonstrate your weapon. Come with me." He looked at Tweetza, "You too, female."

* * * * *

"Okay, boys, let's head back. There's nothing more we can do here; at least not today." Alex picked up his gear and put it back in his pack.

"Dad, can we rest?" Kevin asked.

"Yes, but not here. We need to find some shelter and a safe defensible location."

"So, what will happen now?" Bryce asked.

Alex checked to make sure they were in lockstep as he began the long hike home. "I am not sure why Giles has done this, but I do know that he has the belief that humans are bad for this planet. Before I left Earth, there was a growing movement that believed humanity was bad. They felt like we were destroying the planet, and that human life should be subordinate to other forms of life on the planet. The problem with their theory is simple: mankind is the only species that truly understood well enough to protect other species and the planet." Alex stopped and looked at his two boys. Did they understand this issue? They were both looking at him directly.

"We don't think humans are bad." Kevin spoke like a confident teen, who believed he was a man. "It's...ahhhhh."

Bryce looked in horror as a spear exploded into Kevin's chest, knocking him to the ground, motionless in a fast-growing pool of blood.

In an instant Alex slammed into Bryce, knocking him to the ground as a shower of three more spears rained in, only missing their targets because of Alex's quick reflexes.

In an explosion of thunder, Alex fired his X-ray laser four times in rapid succession.

Bryce, immobilized by the sudden terror and lying flat on the ground, tried to survey the situation. His brother was lying in a pool of blood, impaled by a Pac spear while his father was running towards a bush that was burning with two bodies lying at its base.

Alex caught the motion out of the corner of his eye in time to dodge the next spear flung in his direction. In a single motion, he aimed and fired before his assailant managed to toss a second. He scanned the area and saw a fifth Pac running in the direction of the village. Alex carefully aimed and fired two quick bursts. The Pac fell to the ground in an explosion of flesh.

Alex surveyed the area, when he felt confident the immediate threat was over, he ran back to his two sons. "Are you okay Bryce?" he asked as he knelt beside Kevin and placed his fingers on Kevin's neck near the carotid artery. He felt nothing. He listened for any signs of breathing or heartbeat, but knew the answer before checking for signs. The pool of blood was a harbinger of the Pac's accuracy.

Alex rolled Kevin to his side and pushed the spear through his body, being careful not to touch the blade. The sight made him nauseous, angry, and overcome with sadness.

"Is he going to live, Dad?" Bryce choked on the words.

"He's already dead, son. The spear pierced his heart." Alex did not try to stop the tears running down his face as he tried to focus on what to do next.

"Oh my God; what now, Dad?"

Alex put his arm around Bryce and pulled him in close. "Now," he paused as he stared off into space, "now begins the war we have always feared."

* * * * *

Balonis studied the metal tube as he thought about the new word: *laser*. It was smooth and perfect in every sense. He had never seen this metal nor imagined anything so precisely crafted. Its workings made no sense to him, but he knew that its power was beyond anything he had ever imagined. If his new enemy had these devices, he would need to carefully consider how and when to attack their village.

Giles watched Balonis intently. He considered telling him that the device would only fire twenty or so times before it needed to be recharged, but decided to keep that a secret for now. He had only a small solar array for recharging his computer, and had little understanding of power generation or how much would be required to recharge something like a laser weapon. Many of the other boys his age clearly understood the inner workings, power demands, and capacities of the lasers. Several of them could even build a small power generator if the right materials were supplied. Giles now regretted not having learned those important lessons. He had no understanding of Faraday's laws and electrodynamics. What he knew was that the laser could fire maybe 20 times before it required tremendous amounts of electricity. What he did not know was that lasers were always recharged on the grid powered by the fusion reactor, never by the small solar arrays.

Giles's focus was broken when one of the soldiers barged into the room, out of breath, frightened, and talking faster than he had ever heard; still, he understood enough to know what had happened.

When the soldier finished, Balonis pointed the laser at Giles. "You will advise us in the conquest of our new enemy."

The gravity of Balonis' statement caught Giles off guard. Like powering the laser, he had not clearly thought through the implications of his escape from the colony of his fellow humans. His idealistic illusion of helping the Pacs had suddenly been shattered by a sobering and realistic declaration of conquest and death to his family.

"I don't know if I can go to war and be responsible for the death of my family members." Giles managed to say.

Then you will die here and now. Balonis pointed the laser, then set it down. He picked up his sword and before Giles could utter a word, Balonis plunged it deep into his thigh. Tweetza shrieked in terror as Giles fell to the floor in a pool of blood while screaming in pain.

The reality of Giles's situation became crystal clear as Balonis stood over him, sword dripping in blood, and eyes clearly stating his intent to push the sword into Giles's chest.

"You will guide and advise us in the conquest of our new enemy, or the next blow if this sword will end your existence," Balonis commanded.

"Yes," was all Giles managed to say as he fought the throbbing pain in his leg. "I will do as you request."

Balonis looked at Tweetza, "take him away and treat his leg. I want him ready for strategic planning tomorrow." As Tweetza helped Giles hobble out of the room, Balonis picked up and once again studied his shiny new weapon.

14

TRACING PATHS

Earth – December 2025

Mark Adams stared at his computer screen. For the past nine months, since February, he had been researching the path of his friend Alex. For that entire time, he confidently held the belief that Alex would return, but Alex had not. In the years they had known each other he had seen Alex make plenty of mistakes, but each had been a lesson from which he learned and improved from. Because of this, Mark could not recall having seen Alex fail at anything. In college, Alex believed that Mark was the smartest person in the engineering program. Indeed, based on the skills required for success in coursework, perhaps Mark had been the smartest, but these skills had not translated to real life. By anyone's account, Alex struggled in school, but everyone saw a light in him that pervaded his struggles to get above a 2.5 GPA. While Alex studied harder than most and produced a high-C and low-B in his coursework, he was the one who seemed to possess an innate sense of engineering. While everyone looked to Mark to make the best grades, Alex was clearly the natural engineer.

Certainly, this was proven once they completed their educations and entered the real world. After graduating near the middle of the class, it had been Alex who had gone further, discovered more, and accomplished more in the capitalist society that made up the Western world. Mark, on the other hand, considered himself lucky to have called Alex a friend. It was Alex's inventions and companies that had made Mark wealthy.

He had always thought it strangely coincidental that Alex had disappeared within days of Paula's unfortunate car accident. Had he tried to utilize his vast understanding of physics and engineering to save her, and met his own doom in the process? The thought had certainly crossed his mind, but that conclusion was not consistent with the very strangely delivered request for computer components to be hidden inside Alex's most recent invention.

Mark had only a vague understanding of the ship Alex had been building and testing. They had discussed it on a few occasions while out for a beer. Mark was smart enough to realize two things: first, time travel and journeys to the outer edge of the solar system was beyond the scope of modern engineering, and second, the fact that Alex was experimenting with it would bring that aspect of science fiction into reality.

Mark pulled up the file which represented the original radio signal sent by Alex nearly a year earlier and compared it to the cleaned-up version. While the cleaned-up version was much more understandable, there was always something about the original that haunted him. He had listened to the two versions of the message a thousand times, but had never been able to discover anything other than a request for parts, coupled with a request to respond. Mark had fulfilled both of those requests, then heard nothing.

Mark pushed his chair back from the computer and rubbed his eyes. For ten months, he had done little other than work on this problem. He was tired, and perhaps the time had finally come to give it a rest, to reenter the real world, to date again and enjoy the fruits of his labor. He grabbed the TV remote, flicked on the screen, and poured himself a cold beer. On the TV was an old movie, from an older book written by the long-since-deceased astronomer, Carl Sagan. Contact had been one of Alex's favorite books that had also been made into a movie, but Mark had never taken the time to watch it. Was God or fate trying to tell him something on the very night he thought about giving up his quest to find his lifelong friend?

Mark rewound the movie to its beginning. It did not take long to understand why Alex had enjoyed the movie. Jodie Foster played the part of a young scientist who believed in something and found a way to pursue that dream. She was beautiful and intelligent. She represented a very rare type of female, and by Alex's definition, seldom found in real life. Of course, Mark and Alex both held a lifelong friendship with Paula, who closely matched the description of the beautiful and brilliant character. Mark thought it unfortunate that Alex and Paula had never taken the time to truly consummate their connection, to marry, live together, and have children.

Mark pondered these issues as he watched the victory scene when an intelligent signal arrived from Vega. As the scene progressed, Mark had an epiphany which provided a solution to his ten-month-long problem. The simple mathematical signal was inlaid with a second signal. Mark hopped up from the couch and practically flew to his computer. He downloaded a free music program available on the net and used it to look at the original signal. As he zoomed in, he found a second signal embedded in the first! He had no way to listen to the signal, but he knew someone that did. His watch said it was 1:25 AM on the east coast, but he ignored that as he dialed the cell number of Mathew Thomas, a friend, world-class physicist, amateur sound engineer, and all-around nice guy.

"This better be damned important if you are waking me in the middle of the night." Matt answered, half asleep.

"Sorry, Matt," Mark responded seemingly out of breath. "I need some help listening to a signal embedded in a sound file."

Matt closed his eyes and tried to focus on what Mark had just said. "Are you okay, Mark? Do you know what time it is?"

"Matt, this is important. I have been working on a mystery of what happened to my friend Alex non-stop for ten months. I just had a breakthrough, but don't know how to translate the signal. I apologize for waking you, but this is really important."

Matt looked up at the clock. He was still more asleep than awake, but Mark had been a friend for a long time, and he knew he should focus on appeasing him. "Look, can you send it over and give me a day to figure it out?"

"No, Matt, I just need you to break out an amplitude-modulated signal embedded in a carrier AM signal. I know that with all your knowledge and tools this could not possibly take more than a few minutes."

"Damnit Mark, send the blanking file over."

"Should already be in your inbox."

"Okay, give me about ten minutes and I'll get it back to you."

"Thanks, Matt. I owe you one."

"Damn right, you do." Matt did not wait for a response as he pressed the button to end the call. He knew the sooner he finished this task, the sooner he could get back to sleep. Breaking the file into its components was a simple task. Matt didn't even listen to the two files, he simply packaged them and emailed both back to Mark.

Mark sat by his computer waiting for the file to come in. The new file was data, not sound, further, it was not something he understood.

In the morning, his phone rang. He checked the caller ID and answered. "Sorry about waking you in the middle of the night, Matt."

"Dude, what's up with that message? Your friend sent you coordinates from Alpha Cassiopeia."

"What? How do you know that?" Mark responded, nervous and shocked.

"Well, because I'm a scientist, and recognize things like that. Your embedded carrier signal was a set of coordinates along with NGC coordinates on that star. I'd assume it is a practical joke, but everyone knows Alex Durant is, or was, the greatest living engineer until he disappeared back in March."

"Look, Matt, I don't know for sure what happened to Alex. He was working on a pet project and spent massive amounts of money building it. We had conversations, but I really don't know much more."

"Mark, there's something else that is impossible to explain," Matt started.

"Okay, what?"

"Well, the radio signal is Doppler shifted. It's actually not exactly Alpha Cassiopeia, but I am working through that problem."

"Wow, Doppler. I should have thought of that one," Mark answered, realizing the obvious.

"Do you have files, notes, and invoices for stuff that he bought?" Matt interrogated.

"Yes."

"I can help, but I want in."

"What do you mean?" Mark asked.

"I want full access to everything Alex touched, wrote, or typed before he disappeared."

"Okay, I can get you those things, Matt."

"Send me a plane ticket. I can come to Texas tomorrow, Mark."

"What? Why?" Mark protested.

"Look, you're the rich one. I'm still living on a professor's salary. Make this easy for me, and I'll help you solve it."

Mark thought about it for a minute. Having Matt working on this would definitely make it go faster. The fact was that the two of them working together would likely mean being be able to decipher the details and reconstruct a viable solution.

"Okay, Matt. First class arrangements coming up."

* * * * *

For the next week, Matt Thomas spent all day, every day studying every document Mark could give him. As he got deeper into the project, extracting himself became more and more difficult. After eight days, he was completely frustrated.

"Mark, these files represent perhaps the greatest engineering project of all time. There are hundreds of patentable technologies, not to mention ground-breaking physics."

"Is it real?" Mark questioned.

"Real? Mark, hell, I don't know, but I do know the only way to do this right is to quit my job, move in here, and work on this around the clock. Can you help me make that happen?"

"Yes. There's plenty of money if that's what you need."

Matt swiveled in his chair to face Mark. "You know, back in the Princeton days I always thought we'd be doing fascinating things with our careers, but I never would have guessed this. Between Moore's Law, and the off-the-chart genius of Alex, we are part of things none of us imagined. If this stuff is what it appears to be, we can now go anywhere in space and time. The answer to every question ever asked is now at our fingertips."

Mark thought about the implications of Matt's comment. "You know, Paula was selected for this year's Nobel in biochemistry. I remember the first time she showed up in the physics department with Alex. She was so gorgeous, so smart. None of us could believe a science nerd could date a girl like her."

"I remember," Matt answered. "Every guy in the department was in love with her. Seeing Alex and Paula as a couple gave us all the confidence that we could do things we had considered impossible. I was really surprised, no, I was pissed, when they didn't end up together."

"Well, I always thought one day they would, and now she's dead. Life is too short."

"She's not dead, Mark."

"What? Of course, she is!"

Matt turned back to the computer interface. "Alex named his processor Emily, and Emily transferred log files to a backup drive on this machine. Look," he pulled up a screen, "according to his file, Alex used some type of tunneling device to extract Paula from her SUV a fraction of a second before the collision."

"Oh my God, he could do that? Paula's alive?" Mark had goosebumps on his arms.

"Well, she was at that point in time. They apparently took a jump back to Princeton, then to Alpha Cassiopeia. ."

"Alpha Cassiopeia? That's got to be, like, a hundred light years away." Mark commented, incredulous at the thought.

"Geez Mark, it's 228 light years. Everyone knows that. Weren't you listening in school?"

Mark stared at Matt with a blank questioning look, not sure if he was joking or serious.

"What's weird is that I'm fairly certain they are *not* on Alpha Cassiopeia. I'm pretty sure they are on Eta Cassiopeia. I have two pieces of data that conflict with Alex. First, the program which Emily stored has a different set of calculations than that by Alex, and second, the ham radio signal is Doppler shifted like Eta, not Alpha."

"That doesn't make sense, Matt. How can one of the smartest engineers of our generation not know whether he's traveled to Eta or Alpha?" Mark asked.

"He should know, but for whatever reason, he doesn't. That fact alone tells me he hasn't thought about it because he's got other, larger problems to deal with."

"My guess is that you're right, so what's the plan?"

"We figure out what he built and go rescue our college friends."

"Go?" Mark asked incredulously.

"Yes, go there. Why not? This is the stuff dreams are made of bro," Matt answered with a huge smile, then turned back to the computer.

* * * * *

Six months later, Matt and Mark were making breakthrough developments with the notes, comments, and data files left behind in Alex's home and shop. Alex had done preliminary design work on a version 2 which would not require the sophisticated ship he had built for the earlier missions. Simple time travel could be accomplished without a craft, though the mathematics and precision required computer resources beyond current capabilities. The next stage of development was to build a supercomputer that was both portable and capable. This was an area where Alex was years ahead of his time, and neither Matt nor Mark could contribute. Matt was doggedly persistent, but kept hitting dead ends.

Mark sat sipping a beer and thought about his life over the last sixteen months. He had pretty much dedicated the entire time to solving this problem. The stress was wearing on his creativity and his mood. In the beginning, it had been a passion, but time and endless work hours had turned it into a chore. Tonight, he planned to relax, drink a few beers, and surf the net. It occurred to him, after his second brew, that there were lots of people who knew more about computers than he and Matt. After scanning a few articles, he discovered Megan Hoglund. According to the stories he found about her, Hoglund was considered the preeminent computer scientist of her time. Mark flipped to the website for his favorite airline and booked a flight.

He stood up and stretched. "Dude, I'm going to Anchorage."

Matt swiveled in his chair to face him. His eyes were bloodshot and underlined with deep dark circles. "Anchorage? What for?"

"Gonna go see a woman." He collected a few essential items in his room. When he returned to the study, he found Matt focused again on his computer. "You wanna go?"

"No."

"Well, then you should take a break." Mark slipped his backpack over his shoulder.

"Yup. See you when you get back."

* * * * *

Mark popped off a quick and cryptic email to Hoglund. According to her bio, she was an academic who had become passionate about pushing the limits of Moore's Law. Her personal goal was to be the computer scientist who developed the first computer capable of processing faster than the human brain, in an AI software environment that could do the same.

By the time he got to the airport, she had responded with a phone number saying she'd like to chat.

"Hello?" Megan answered on the first ring.

"Ms. Hoglund? Hi, it's Mark Adams."

"Wow, you're certainly fast."

"Well, I have an immediate need for computing power several times faster than the state of the art. I was working with Alex Durant who built an organic hybrid..."

"*The* Alex Durant?" She interrupted. "I'm a huge fan."

"I'm certain he's an amateur compared to you. Look, Alex has a design..."

"You said that already." She interrupted again. "Look, you said you were coming to town. Can we meet and discuss this in person?"

"First thing in the morning?" He asked.

"I'll pop you a note. Check your email when you land."

* * * * *

At first, Mark was a bit surprised to find the email encrypted but quickly realized that Megan Hoglund was one of the preeminent computer experts in the world. She was probably an eccentric individual who did everything over the top.

They met in a Starbucks not far from the airport. Hoglund was pretty in a simple kind of way, with tight curly brown hair and flashing insightful brown eyes. She focused on Mark but studied every person that walked in the front door. Most importantly, in exchange for Alex's hybrid organic computer design, she agreed to help.

"The processing power you need is last year's design for me on silicon. I am currently working just under six times faster than your stated requirements. What I need right now is a breakthrough."

"Breakthrough?" Mark inquired. "Six times faster than my stated requirements? That is like, twenty times faster than off-the-shelf computers." The thought made Mark dizzy.

"I am at the theoretical limits of silicon-based chips. I need something that will take my work to the next level."

"So, you are willing to just give me a machine that is operational?"

"Yes," she stated flatly. "Alex Durant is, or was, one of the greatest thinkers of our time. If he figured out how to build a hybrid organic platform, I need to know about it."

Mark noted that she spoke of Alex in the past tense. "You should know that I don't consider Alex to be dead. I think he is off on one of his adventures."

"Sorry, I didn't mean to imply anything. I am just parroting what I read on the net," she apologized.

"No harm done," he looked her in the eyes. For a second, he got lost in something he saw. Was she sad, or scared? He couldn't tell; perhaps it was a little of both.

Megan could tell he was studying her, searching for something. She smiled and then looked away.

"So, how do we do this?" Mark asked.

"I have the system in my trunk. You can have it now."

"In turn, you can have what I've got for Alex's design," Mark offered.

Megan's eyes lit up, "awesome!"

* * * * *

When Mark returned to the lab with the new computer, Matt immediately ran a benchmark on the machine and was taken aback.

"Where did you get this?" he asked, completely blown away by the power.

"I did a little internet research and found a resource. It wasn't that hard," Mark answered smugly. In the time since Matt had been working on the tachyon tunnel, Mark had been of little use. He had finally found an avenue of success, and didn't plan on revealing how easy it had been.

Matt studied the computer case. It appeared to be an off-the-shelf system but certainly did not process like one. Now oblivious to Mark's presence, he connected the machine to his network and began processing. He had never experienced anything like it. All of the fine-tuning he had done to Alex's programming was running like it never had before. Not only was it faster, but the AI built into the computer's OS was learning, improving, and making suggestions not possible on any other architecture.

Over the next week, the project completely turned around. The computer hardware was at least ten times faster than the system Matt had been using, but it ran on a terabit processing platform, which made it seem to operate hundreds of times faster than anything else in existence. Matt now had the resources to complete his version of the tachyon tunneling device. He sat back in his chair and took a deep breath, exhaling slowly. Tomorrow he could begin testing.

* * * * *

Initial tests were done straight from Alex's books. Matt did not want to accidentally create some space-time anomaly. Within a few tweaks, he was finally ready to execute a real test. He looked up at Mark, who was reading a stack of papers that represented Alex's log.

"I think we are ready to do a space jump."

Mark set the papers down and studied Matt. "Why are you so certain?"

"We have all of Alex's programs and notes. Our system is actually an improvement over his. I think we can go."

Mark was finally in an area where he felt more comfortable than Matt. "So, you are suggesting we simply zap ourselves light years through space and time to Eta Cassiopeia?"

Matt instinctively knew that Mark was asking a trick question, but his confidence was quite high that not only would his system work, but it would function better than Alex's. "Yes, that's exactly what I'm saying."

"What were you planning on taking for supplies? What if there's no air there? No water? Bad guys that want to kill us? Shouldn't we plan on these things?"

Matt had thought of every scientific contingency but had completely neglected the practical. "You are right. We have a bit of work yet to do." He closed the programs and logged on to his email. "Why don't you work on that stuff, and I'll take a break."

Mark immediately went to work on food, water, survival, medical, and defense provisions. He figured he would need three or four days to pull together everything needed.

That night, both Mark and Matt would get the best sleep they had gotten in the last year.

That night, located in the basement of his mother's house, Tesla Zap, a hacker extraordinaire, discovered their super processor. Zap had built a bot to search for internet-connected supercomputers that he could break into. When he studied the numbers from his bot, he could not believe that a level processor existed, much less unprotected, in a residence. He tested, focused, and opened files. Zap was a self-taught computer geek who knew nothing about science. He had no understanding of the programs or the systems they were controlling, but he knew they were part of one of the coolest systems he had ever hacked. For two days he lurked, opened, and tested without being detected.

* * * * *

After three days of evaluation, Mark had collected nearly everything on his list. He was reviewing the items with Matt when the lights flickered, and all the equipment came to life. Alex's first-generation fusion reactor took over and immediately ramped up to maximum power.

"What the hell is going on?" Matt asked as he opened the computer screen. Two programs were executed, simultaneously. He tried to stop them but was completely locked out of the system.

Mark was looking out the window, but it was pitch-black outside. He could feel a hum on the floor and walls. "What's happening?"

"I don't know," Matt answered, trying to focus on the program running on his computer. He was scared, but trying to evaluate the effect of the two programs. "What I do know is that two programs are running at full power. I think our system got hacked, because I have been locked out of the controls." He was hammering away at the keyboard, looking for a way back into his programs. "Just give me a minute."

Matt recognized one of the programs as the revised tunnel to program the path to Etta. The other program was not familiar. For several minutes, Matt worked on cracking the lockout. After a few tries he figured it out and was able to take control of the system. All the studying he had done had now paid off.

"Someone hacked into our system and executed two programs. One was the tunnel to Etta, and the other was a proximity program. As far as I can tell, the entire house is in a tachyon tunnel, and that tunnel is headed for Etta Cassiopeia."

Mark was trying to reconcile that concept, and the implications, when he noticed a light outside the house. He pulled the blind and received the shock of his life. A man with three children was shining a light on the house. Mark grabbed a flashlight and ran to the door. Outside in the pitch darkness were the yard, trees, bushes, and driveway. He could see a house across the street and several other homes up and down the street.

The man with the flashlight walked up and spoke, "Any idea what's going on here?"

Mark looked at the man, who appeared to be in his late thirties. He did not know how or what would be an appropriate answer. "I don't know," was all he could say. He crumpled on the front porch as reality hit him. An entire block of homes was in a tachyon tunnel, apparently heading to Etta Cassiopeia.

"Well, it looks like you have electricity when none of the rest of us do," the man stated as if there were some answers to that fact.

"We have a backup generator," Mark answered weakly. More flashlights started appearing and people began gathering in Alex's front yard.

"It's the middle of the day. How could it suddenly be pitch black?" One woman asked.

Matt walked out when she was asking the question. While Mark had decided not to specifically answer questions, Matt took a different approach. "We are traveling in an enclosed space-time continuum known as a tachyon tunnel. We should emerge in a few hours."

Most of the people that had gathered asked questions on top of each other. One waited and asked: "What? Emerge where?"

Mark stopped Matt from answering the question. "Listen, we are not certain, but we should assess the situation. Let's break up into a couple of groups and figure out how big an area is inside this so-called tunnel."

Mark led a group up the street past the first corner. The second house was cut cleanly in half. Across the street, part of a driveway and garage were inside the tunnel. Mark picked up a rock decorating a small garden and handed it to a man that had come with him. "Toss it towards the edge."

The man tossed the rock and Mark followed its path as it suddenly disappeared through the tunnel barrier.

"Okay, we need to check all the homes along the perimeter and make sure no one gets near it. Let's split up and have everyone meet at my place. From there, we can figure out what to do next." He looked around at the others. "Let's get this done right away!" He emphasized.

Four men split up in different directions and started jogging to their destinations.

Forty minutes later, they all convened at Alex's house.

15

WATSON TO TRANQUILITY

September 0021

Giles woke with a start. He sat up, studied the small rock-enclosed room that had become his prison for the last ten days, placed his hand on the throbbing pain in his thigh, and rubbed until the pain subsided a bit. Back at Tranquility, he would have had proper treatment, but here in the Balonis village, capabilities did not go much farther than cleaning the wound and drinking a tea concoction designed to help relieve the pain. Fortunately, the cut had created more of a flesh wound than a permanent injury, but it still hurt. He had escaped from Watson Village with the hopes of saving the Pacs from the humans and had instead become a tool, which Balonis would expertly utilize to study and understand the human adversary with an intent to destroy.

Clearly, Balonis had two goals: to kill and conquer, but with Giles' intel, he had quickly begun to understand the superior technology held by this adversary. Patience was not one of his strengths, but this would require significant planning. Giles hated the fact that he was being forced to provide strategy and information, but also knew that time would be on the side of his human family.

Just four days after the return to her people, Tweetza had been selected as a mate by Aroban, a stocky Pac male, more focused on possible combat with a nearby village than on learning about the strange human creature that Tweetza had been watching. The mating ceremony took place on that very day.

A quick courtship was all that Giles could conclude.

That same day of Tweetza's mating ceremony, Giles moved in with Twoodi. Under Twoodi's watch, the mornings were spent focused on healing Giles's injury, while the afternoons were spent with Balonis and his generals. After the fifth day, Twoodi and Giles began taking morning walks to gather supplies for the day. In the beginning, people would stare at Twoodi and her unusual companion. As the days passed, the novelty had worn off, and Giles went unnoticed, much like a dog in an old Earth tribe. Two stocky warriors would follow them during their morning chores and stand guard over the rock shelter at all other times. Giles never questioned whether they would kill him if he tried to escape. He simply assumed that to be the case.

Twoodi took on the task of teaching Giles about the history of her people. She taught him there were thirteen major tribes, all of whom were constantly at war with each other. Giles had learned that the common term for people was not Pac, but Etakan. The Etakan called the place where they lived Etakatz. Giles tried to understand what exactly Etakatz was. When quizzed, Twoodi did not understand the terms: continent, country, or planet. He learned that Etakaz had very little science, and the Etakan had almost no understanding of the extent of their planet. He decided that Etakatz meant home with the Etakan not really understanding the concept of a planet.

Twoodi did know quite a bit about history. The complete structure of her society was based on war and conquest. On many occasions, individual leaders had attempted to bring all tribes together through conquest. The greatest Etakan leader in history was a violent general named Etakonus the Conqueror. In his time, he had conquered nine of the tribes. Every young male loved to sing songs of Etakonus, the greatest conqueror of all time. Etakonus had delivered fifteen years of glorious, bloody battle, followed by eleven years of peace among the nine great tribes. His rule ended when one of the unconquered tribes managed to infiltrate with an assassin. With his death, Etakatz quickly returned to the prior years of constant war. As Twoodi recanted the tale, she proudly claimed to be a fourteenth-generation descendant of Etakonus.

As Giles massaged the muscles around his injured thigh, Twoodi stood and gathered her small pack, "Are you ready for our morning walk?"

"Sure." Giles had grown rather fond of Twoodi. In fact, he was becoming concerned that perhaps his interest in her was crossing a boundary that should not be crossed. It was something that he sensed in her as well, but neither had dared to broach it as a topic of conversation. Despite the warrior side, his time here amongst the females had caused him to appreciate aspects of the Etakan. The barbaric side seemed incurable and strictly male. The females sang songs of the hero warriors but maintained a very different and lighthearted approach to life.

The afternoons spent with Balonis and his generals were a stark contrast to the pleasant mornings with Twoodi. Balonis had an amazing skill at learning and grasping significant data from Giles's explanations. He was exact and thorough in his collection of information and his assessment of the capabilities of the human town. What surprised Giles were two things: first, he did not seem to be in a hurry, and second, he never questioned Giles about where the humans came from.

Giles's command of the language was weak, so Tweetza typically attended these meetings. Today, when he arrived, she was already present and engaged in conversation with Balonis. Four stern guards stood around the chair where Balonis sat. Giles guessed that each was willing and prepared to die protecting their leader. He sat on the bench near Tweetza and waited.

"How many of the children have been trained as warriors?" Balonis asked.

Giles was not surprised by the question. It was the tenth time in ten days that Balonis had asked. "None. The human society at Watson Village is not focused on war. They maintain a constant vigil, but today have little interest in conquest."

"If you are not one of their leaders, how do you know this? You have said that it is human nature to conquer. You have stated your disdain for this conquest, which is why you escaped. It would not be possible for such a small tribe to conquer Etakan if only a few were adults."

"They will multiply fast. Within two generations, you will be facing a real army that possesses technology that you will not be able to stop," Giles insisted as he had on many occasions before. "They will conquer with superior technology. Etakan will not be able to stand against them."

Balonis would always spend a long time considering what Giles had told him. Giles's story, and that translated by Tweetza, matched well. Tweetza had pleaded with Balonis to leave the humans alone. She believed they were peaceful and not a threat. He looked again at Giles, who seemed interested in the ways of Etakan. "You are more a woman than a man."

Giles was surprised by Balonis' comment. "In my society, I am too young to be considered a man, but it is also true that I appreciate the female side of your culture over the warlike nature of the males."

"Twoodi will begin a mating cycle in the coming days. When she does, you will take her as your mate." Balonis stood and pointed at the two guards, motioning for them to remove Giles from the room. He understood that Giles was an important asset and would become an even better resource if he became part of the tribe. Mating with Twoodi would help make that a reality.

Giles was shocked by Balonis' command, but had already learned that one does not question or defy Balonis.

"If you live long enough you will learn that survival, obedience, and contribution to conquest are one and the same. You will also learn that you are not the first." Balonis added while studying the shock on Giles's face. "Now leave."

Giles simply turned and followed his escort out of the strategy hall.

As he walked back towards the hut where he and Twoodi were staying, he realized that Balonis' command that he take Twoodi as a mate was a provocative idea. He had already begun to have feelings for her, and now, with the mandate of their leader, he would be required to take it to the next step. Mostly, he was concerned about how Twoodi would respond to being forced to take a human over one of the far more masculine Etakan.

Back at the hut, he relayed the command to Twoodi.

"How is this done with humans," she asked.

"This?"

"Mating. How is mating done?"

"I haven't done it before, but every boy learns about it." He responded.

"Show me," she said without any inhibitions.

"I am surprised by your interest and willingness," Giles said. "I would have thought you would be disappointed that you do not get an Etakan warrior for mating."

"Show me," she repeated.

Giles took her in his arms and immediately felt the tingle and excitement in his blood. She wrapped her arms around him and pulled him in tighter.

After a few seconds, Giles began to kiss her, and she pulled back.

"What was that?" she asked.

"We call it a kiss. It is a sign of affection," Giles explained. "Was it bad? I mean, I have never kissed a girl before."

"It was good," she started. "It felt good, but no Etakan male kisses his mate."

"I am sorry," he apologized.

"It is okay, Giles. Just shocking and different," she could still feel it deep inside her body.

Giles started to embrace her again, but she pushed him away.

"No. We must wait for the mating cycle," she commanded, though a big part of her would have liked to have continued the exploration immediately.

"Okay," he responded with disappointment.

"It will happen soon enough, Giles," she placed her hand on his cheek affectionately. "I think you may have done something to my body with that kiss that has accelerated my mating cycle." She turned and left the hut.

* * * * *

Alex and Bryce motioned for the sentry to open the gate. As the heavy doors swung open, young citizens of Watson Village poured out to greet them. Alex had radioed ahead, so everyone was aware of the death of Kevin, and the failure of the mission to recover Giles and Tweetza. As his children surrounded him, Alex made the realization that his role would now switch from father and professor to general, and that these young boys and girls would now be forced to become the defenders of Tranquility and Watson. The tearful and somber greetings suggested that many of them already understood their new role. They had been raised with the specter of Pac as the enemy. It had now become a reality.

Less than an hour after returning home, Alex assembled every citizen in the town square. A total of 242 sets of eyes stared intently at their father, and leader.

"As you all know, our mission to recover Giles and Tweetza failed, and along with that failure, we lost Kevin. Emily has provided an assessment of Giles's writings over the last few months and it is clear that he has become a traitor. He left with the intent of teaching the Pacs how to eliminate our population. We must now face a new reality of existence, and that reality is that Pac warriors will come here with the intent of conquest. Each of you has been raised with the notion of this possibility, and now, that possibility is made worse by a traitor who we can only assume will educate and prepare them with information about our defenses and population. I know that you are all young. By Earth's standards, your age would make you minors, but most of you are thinking, living, and performing like adults on Earth. As such, we must now make some hard choices about our future. I do not believe we can defend this town's location over the long term with the resources we currently have. Add to that, the fact that Giles will arm them with details that would give them an advantage. Therefore, we must begin to defend ourselves, and at the same time, we must find a way to escape to a new and secluded home. We are fortunate, I guess, that Giles never gained a true grasp of the extent of our technology, but unfortunately, he is in possession of a laser, a portable computer, and a walkie-talkie. I do not think that he has the knowledge to power them after their batteries die, but if he learns how to utilize the power supply in the laser, he could keep the computer alive for long enough to learn."

Alex scanned the faces. Most were so young. He wondered if ever in the history of mankind a group of kids this young had been asked to come to grips with such a serious threat of eradication.

"So, here is what we are going to do, Steven and Mom will be in charge of fortification and preparation. Emily should have sufficient information to help with that task. I will work on getting our ship operational as quickly as possible. With our electronics, it would be impossible to get her to a point where we could do a time jump, or even get into space, but we can get her ready to fly. We will attempt to make that happen in the next couple of days. Once we can fly, we will begin moving everyone to a place very far from the current threat. I believe we can be successful in moving the entire town, including our belongings and livestock. This move will buy us years, or if we are lucky, perhaps even decades."

* * * * *

Alex sat at his computer console. "Emily, how much imagery do we have of the planet's surface?"

"Approximately seventeen percent in resolution of ten square meters." She answered and pulled up imagery.

"The resolution should be fine, but we are going to need to move, and I'd like to select a location in the next week or two. The new site should be as secluded as possible."

"Alex, we have a problem," Paula interrupted.

Alex looked up as Paula stepped into the room, "what is it?"

"No one seems to know where Alexander is," Paula announced.

"Emily, please locate Alexander," Alex commanded.

"Alexander is not in Watson Village."

"What? Where is he?" Alex demanded.

"Alex, I have a programming conflict. The answer to your question is locked in a secure data structure."

"Now there's a clever kid. I guess this was only a matter of time," Alex commented.

"What are you going to do?" Paula had a concerned look.

"Emily, override all lockouts using security access password 022988pc."

"Data is now available."

"Thank you, Emily," Alex winked at Paula. "Please tell me, where is Alexander?"

"Alexander has developed a portable tachyon tunneling device and has hopped six hundred fifteen years into the future."

"What?" Alex demanded.

"Alexander has developed a portable tachyon tunneling device…"

"Stop, Emily," Alex interrupted. "I heard you the first time."

"Acknowledged, Alex."

Alex looked at Paula. "I'm sorry hun. I suppose this is to be expected when you produce brilliant children. We have one who believes he's a freedom fighter and runs off to aid and abet the enemy, while another time jumps into the future."

"Modern parenting problems," Paula answered, sarcastically. "I wonder if there has ever been a kid like Alexander, though. He does seem to be in a league of his own."

"Yup," Alex answered. "Emily, do we know why Alexander has traveled into the future?"

"Alexander is working on a physics solution to the genetics problem. He believes he can collect technology from the future, build a ship capable of returning to Earth and secure more genetic material to add broad diversity to the existing pool."

"So, he is in the year 635?" Alex clarified.

"That is correct, Alex."

"Looks like you have this problem under control, for now," Paula said as she stood up. "I have a half million things to get done before we move."

"I wouldn't come to that conclusion," Alex responded. "In any case, I am not certain there is anything we can do about this situation."

"Agreed. I'll get back to planning sessions for the move. Let me know if I can help." Paula kissed his cheek and departed.

Alex flopped into his computer chair. "Emily, I need to see Alexander's design plans and schematics."

It didn't take long for Alex to realize that young Alexander had advanced his original science and improved engineering efficiency. While Alexander's design would not allow interstellar travel, it did provide a mechanism for point-to-point in a time-based coordinate system with no ship required. The tunnel could be executed almost instantaneously as opposed to the hour's long voyages taken in the Tranquility ship. Even more ingenious was that Alexander had figured out a way to pull energy from the tunnel.

The thing that Alex was not able to determine was where Alexander had tunneled, and how or when he would return. As fascinating as the problem was, Alex knew that right now he needed to set it aside and work on the much more pressing issue of how to extract his family from this location, known as Watson Village.

* * * * *

Tranquility Ship was ready to fly in ten days. Getting her flightworthy had not been an easy task, consuming resources that Alex would have preferred not to. Nevertheless, survival of the human population was now on the line, and if the end result was survival, even if it meant a significant transformation of his ship, the cost would be justified.

Alex took a few of the older kids up and began surveying the planet. He needed to find a location as far from Pac villages as possible. The best way to do that would be to create aerial maps of as much of the planet as possible. In all likelihood, this move would be designed as if it was the last. The new city would be built from the ground up to withstand any attack from the Pac invaders.

An additional fourteen percent of the planet was mapped in one-meter resolution. When Alex felt he had enough geographic data to make an educated move, he and the team began analysis. For the next couple of days, Emily analyzed and produced candidate locations based on Alex's criteria. When three possible locations were selected, Alex once again took Tranquility up to evaluate. Upon closer evaluation, all three seemed to meet the criteria. All three were at least a hundred kilometers from the Watson site, and should therefore be safe, for a while.

Once all the data was in place, he gave the final choice to Paula.

Paula studied the three and quickly selected one. "This one is the largest area, and when I plan another batch, we will need room to grow."

"You're thinking about another batch, now? Will the batches never end?" Alex asked.

"Perhaps I should answer that after we see what Alexander has learned," she responded.

"Paula, there is an issue with Alexander that you should know."

"I'm listening," she responded.

"His tunneler, as he calls it, is point-to-point. He will return here when he comes back," Alex explained.

Paula thought about that for a minute, "So if we are gone, and he comes back?"

"Unclear," Alex answered.

"Then, someone must stay behind."

Alex knew that she was right, but not for the same reason. Paula was one hundred percent focused on the protection of precious Alexander Bell. Alex, on the other hand, was concerned about the Pacs capturing the technology.

"For now," he answered, "let's hope he returns before they attack."

* * * * *

November 0021

Over the course of two months, all structures, facilities, livestock, and children had been moved to the new location, known as Tranquility Village. Alex and a dozen others stayed behind to wait, in hopes that Alexander would return, a hope that had not yet born fruit. Now, all of that waiting would need to come to an end with the anticipated arrival of the Pac invaders on Watson Village. Alex knew they would likely attack; he just did not know exactly when. Though his hunch was that it would happen sooner, rather than later. On that hunch, he had been correct.

Alex stared at the field of Pacs that were marching toward the walls. Was it possible to negotiate, or was war now inevitable? He had tried on several occasions to hail Giles on the walkie-talkie but to no avail. War was not something he understood, nor did he relish the thought or implications.

The army that amassed outside the small, lightly fortified town known as Watson Village seemed to have a singular intent: conquest. Even though in the three months since Giles's escape Alex and the human populations had moved to a new home, and moved everyone to that location, he needed to be certain of his understanding of the Pac drive for conquest.

He scanned the field, looking for Giles or Tweetza. He raised a white flag, hoping perhaps Giles had taught his new friends the meaning of that symbol. The Army advanced and then broke into a run straight for the walls.

There would be no parlay.

Alex climbed down off the wall and into Tranquility Ship. As she lifted from the ground, an array of X-ray lasers fired a volley of several hundred shots. Part of the goal was to slow the attack, and part was to create a smoke screen that would stop the view of Tranquility Ship as it lifted above the ground. Once the vessel was clear of his old town, he pressed a button, which created an even thicker smoke field. Once dust and smoke completely obscured any view, he pressed a second button which detonated explosives leveling the remains of Watson Village. Nothing had been left behind as spoils of war for the conquering army.

16

A TWIST IN TIME & SPACE

November 2, 0025

Balonis stared across the table at Giles. Three years ago, he had predicted that Giles would not last a month. Now, he was a valuable member of the strategic team. The human boy had grown into a man. While he had not developed a method to recharge the laser, he had begun working on gunpowder and basic explosives. He had shown Balonis how to build catapults, and had told him stories of the technology possessed by the human population. It had been Giles who provided the location of Watson Village, and had warned Balonis to proceed with caution. In the chaos that day, Balonis had lost an unacceptable percentage of his army by not listening to Giles. Balonis vowed not to make that mistake again.

Giles had become a valued member of the Etakan community. His triplets were growing and had become an accepted part of the tribe. While Balonis was certain he could ultimately defeat the humans in battle, Giles had taught him much about human nature, preparation, and science. He knew that to conquer, an understanding of the enemy was essential.

Now, Balonis and his generals felt that once again the circumstances and knowledge were right for a second attempt at the conquest of the humans. He had Giles brought to the war chamber.

"My scouts have returned with the news that the human settlement has been discovered. It was almost exactly where he had predicted," Balonis informed Giles.

Giles nodded in affirmation.

"Tell me again how you made this discovery," Balonis ordered.

"I have a communications device with a signal strength meter. I walk for hours in one direction and measure the strength, then hours in another, where I measure strength again. I repeated that process several times to make sure the data was consistent. Then I applied a form of math called triangulation."

"None of the concepts make sense to me, Giles."

"They have a tower that broadcasts and repeats radio waves…"

"The concepts of math and science to which you speak are meaningless to me," Balonis interrupted. "Still, I see their value. You must make sure to teach these things to the children of Etakatz."

"Tweetza and I have begun this process, Balonis."

"Good," Balonis paused for impact. "We have made a discovery that I need you to investigate, Giles."

"You can count on me, Balonis."

"We have discovered a population of humans living sixty-four kilometers from here in rock homes with solid rock streets. We must learn more about them."

"I don't understand."

"There is a colony that seems to have been built very fast. It is populated by humans. No perimeter walls are protecting the settlement, like in your old Watson Village, and the structures are very different. That colony was not there twenty years ago, so it may have been built by your human family."

"May have been built, Balonis?" Giles wished they had some type of photography. He could not understand the description given by Balonis and could not understand how members of his family could have left the main settlement, which they had just discovered in a completely different location. "Is it possible that this is some type of trap, or do you really think this is a second colony?"

"That will be your job to determine. You will take two warriors with you to learn what you can." Balonis studied Giles. He had become good at reading human facial expressions.

"How long should I study this colony?" Giles asked.

"Your journey there should take four days each way," Balonis answered. "I will expect you back in less than twenty days."

"Balonis, why did you say it may have been built by my family? Is there something else I should know here?"

'Yes. There is one more fact you should know." Balonis added. "A habitation of similar description appeared several hundred years ago, and then completely disappeared. It is said amongst the Etakan leadership and legends that those humans interacted with our ancestors. It has also been said that Etakonus the Great was the child of one of them."

"The child?" Giles said with shock as he thought about what Balonis was saying. His tale confirmed something he thought he had heard a couple of years earlier about not being the first human settlement.

"Balonis, I do not know how this habitation could be human, or part of my human family. There must be another explanation."

"Go learn what you can and bring that information back to me. I believe there is a second group of humans who came to our planet long before your father. If these are the same, you should be able to become their friends. Do not tell them about our war, and perhaps we can befriend them. If these people are descendants of the great Etakonus, they could become great allies."

"Okay Balonis, I can do this for you and our people. I will come back with good intelligence on this new colony."

When Giles departed, Balonis called in his leading officers. He did not tell Giles that he was planning a massive assault on the human colony that represented Giles' family. This assault would begin while Giles was away.

* * * * *

November 5, 0025

Daniel Foster stared at the computer screen, determined to solve the advanced physics problem. He had spent the entire afternoon working in the metallurgy development facility and now regretted it. His goal of beating Anna's test score was quickly fading as he struggled with the application of the mean value theorem as it related to time dilation in tachyon tunneling. Anna had become a cult hero when she beat Father Alex's test score, and did so three minutes faster. At 19, Anna had become the youngest human on ACP to earn her Ph.D., and accomplished that while pregnant with her first child. Daniel told himself to focus and work through the problem. He focused as the computer screen displayed the equations as he recited them. In the background he could hear commotion but tried to ignore it. The colony welcomed 213 new babies in the spring of 0020. They were all four years old, and quite distracting.

The lights dimmed and an alarm began to sound. Daniel's first thought was that it was a cruel trick of Steven's to sound an alarm while he was trying to beat his wife's time, but when the alarm continued, and he could hear a commotion out in the courtyard, it quickly became obvious this was neither a test nor trick.

Daniel ran out into the courtyard and heard someone scream. In the chaos of people running every which way he could hear Steven's voice over the intercom announcing this was not a drill. Since establishing Tranquility Village, everyone had trained to the point where they knew where they were supposed to go. Daniel ran to his post as a huge boulder crashed into the roof of a cabin next to the science building on campus. From his post, Daniel could see a band of Pac loading another boulder on a piece of equipment that appeared to be a catapult.

Other than Tweetza, Daniel had never seen Pacs this close. Throughout his teenage years he had learned about the Pac males, and how they had nearly killed Mother Paula with a spear. Everyone knew the tale of how they had attacked Watson Village, presumably with the intent of killing everyone. So far, the human colony location, now called Tranquility, had never been discovered. Daniel ducked as a volley of arrows cleared the wall that had been built to protect the humans from the onslaught of Pac warriors. Behind him, Daniel heard a second scream and turned to see two of the 17-year-old batch 3 kids lying on the ground bleeding. He was about to leave his post to help when Paula and Susie Benson appeared and began carrying the injured kids away. Within seconds, another volley cleared the wall, followed almost immediately by a huge boulder hitting the wall. Alex began making announcements over the intercom and everyone knew immediately what to do. This contingency had been planned for and tested hundreds of times in the last four years. Now they would see how well their planning and prep would work.

An explosion of X-Ray lasers hit the front line of Pac warriors, followed by a second, then a third. The question had always been whether they would retreat or continue the assault. For a while, it appeared they might retreat, but then they regrouped and attacked with a more furious zeal. Catapults began flinging rocks, but the humans quickly began targeting the catapults. Several of the lasers were running low on power and in need of recharging. Alex had improved the lasers so they could fire 20-25 shots and be recharged in 5 minutes. In the chaos, 25 shots dissipated quickly, and five minutes of recharge time was an eternity while hundreds of Pac warriors were assaulting the walls.

About half the lasers have been plugged in for a recharge, and reduced firepower was quickly perceived by the Pacs, who seemingly had planned for that possibility. An entirely new wave immediately took advantage of the diminished firepower, charging the wall.

For Daniel, and all his human brothers and sisters, the idea of war was thrust into reality. Their scientific brains processed the conclusion that survival required stopping the attack, and stopping the attack meant killing the attackers. It was a simple scientific method task: observation, data collection, analysis, and conclusion. The conclusion came with a brutal outcome.

Daniel mentally went through the defense exercise as he leveled the laser and began to fire on the band of Pacs attempting to take down the wall near his position. As he began to fire, a second group of Pacs let loose a volley of arrows. Daniel saw the volley, but not before it was too late. He felt the sting and thud as two arrows impacted his shoulder and side. He screamed out from the sharp pain of the impact, arrow, and poison. Despite this, he knew his job, which was to maintain focus and stop the assailants before they broke the defense. His eyes filled with tears as he volleyed a half dozen shots, ending with an empty laser battery. Along with the dead laser battery, Daniel then fell to the ground, blacking out.

Evaluating the effectiveness of the laser defense, Alex made a mental note to complete the development of the 3rd generation laser that would be capable of a hundred or more shots. Of course, in typical Alex fashion, he had already developed and prepared for plan B. He had set remote-controlled explosive charges outside the wall. As the Pac Army was preparing for what they believed was the winning attack, Alex realized now was the time to detonate. He pressed a button, and a series of explosions stopped the enemy's advancement with ninety-eight simultaneous explosions throwing shrapnel in every direction. In one area, the explosions trapped a dozen warriors in an encircling pile of rubble.

Several of the humans with active lasers started picking off the remaining Pacs. Alex stopped them. He wanted a few prisoners that he could interrogate.

The decimated Pac army realized the futility of their assault and pulled back, seemingly in full retreat.

Steven, Bill, and David joined Alex in the courtyard as they pushed open the gate to capture and tie up two of the Pacs that were still alive. They dragged their prisoners into the compound and closed the gate.

It was at that point when one of the kids managed to break Alex's focus. "Dad, Mom is…" He couldn't finish.

Alex's eyes widened as he scanned the scene. Paula was lying in the courtyard with the upper part of her body crushed by a boulder. He ran to her, but immediately knew she could not have survived that blow.

Alex crumpled to the ground in horror and disbelief. Was it possible the first human casualty of the war had become his beloved Paula?

The problem-solving part of his brain ran through the permutations. Could he travel back and save her like he had on Earth?

The commotion on the south wall forced Alex to refocus. For now, he could not think about Paula, or the entire human population would be overrun by the Pac army. It was clear they were regrouping, and as the sun was setting, a clear line of attack had formed. A few hours after darkness fell, the Pacs made another attempt at breaking the fortifications of Tranquility Village.

This time, the field outside the wall was illuminated by super bright diode lights. Alex had learned that Pacs had larger pupils, allowing them to see better at night. Balonis had assumed this would give his soldiers an advantage. Instead, technology provided the humans with easy targets, while the Pacs were completely blinded by the light.

The nighttime attack of Balonis' army failed.

As he studied their movements, Steven couldn't help but wonder if the real goal was to test for weak points, so they could make another attempt in the future.

In the morning, the field was clear, and no sign of the remaining Pac army remained.

* * * * *

Over the next two days, thinking he could travel back and save Paula, Alex worked, with the help of Emily, on every possible time travel permutation.   There was a fundamental difference between the situation twenty-five years earlier on Earth and this one. The problem with the ACP scenario was that Paula clearly was killed by the boulder, whereas on Earth, he had been able to extract her from her vehicle before the impact and fire could kill her. On Earth, she never really died, but this time, she did. Emily and Alex discussed the implications of changing the timeline, and both agreed it could not be done.

This loss would reshape Alex, the human population, and the war. Up until now, the goal was simple, calculated defense. Alex now knew that survival mandated this scenario could not be allowed to repeat itself. From here forward, the only real option was to go on offense. The human population must use their technological superiority to end this thing.

* * * * *

Daniel opened his eyes and saw Susan Anderson staring intently at him. She smiled slightly when she saw his recognition of her. Daniel and Susan were both batch 2 children, now nineteen-years-old. She was a pretty brunette who had focused her studies on medical science. Daniel had always found her attractive, but was much like Father Alex in his focus on academics and accomplishment. Daniel had acknowledged his intellectual crush on Anna, but her relationship with Steven made her unavailable. Almost half of his batch had already paired up, some of whom already had children. Susan had been another face in the crowd, though he had to recognize, every time he looked at her, she was smiling.

"How are you feeling, Daniel?" Susan asked somberly, as she took his hand.

He tried to smile but failed. "Is the battle over?"

"We fought them off but," she paused "Mom was killed in the attack."

Daniel felt his pulse increase, carrying the residual poison from the arrows into his brain. He closed his eyes in an attempt to control it, but instead slipped back into the blackness from the poison arrow.

It was a full day later before Daniel opened his eyes again. Had he heard Susan correctly? Paula had been the anchor of their community. Was she really dead? Susan took his hand, and he could tell from the look on her face that her news about Mom had not been some horrible dream. Still, Susan had a strained smile as Daniel focused.

"How long have I been out?"

"Five days. You got hit by two poisoned arrows. A couple of the other kids also got hit by arrows, but like you, they will recover completely. Mom was crushed by one of those boulders. Dad and some of the older kids got together to talk about whether she could be saved with a time jump, but everyone agrees that, at least on our timeline, that wouldn't work. She's dead."

He took her hand and squeezed as she started to cry. He wanted to say something to make her feel better but only pain, silence, and tears came.

"She was such a great influence on all of us," Daniel started to say as the door opened and Alex stood in the opening.

"How's your recovery, Daniel?" Alex asked.

"I will recover, Dad. Losing mom is tough though."

"It has certainly painted a blackness in my heart, son," Alex answered.

"You know, everyone here is part of Paula," Susan started. "We have her heart, her daily lighthearted joy, and her love of science."

Alex and Daniel both focused on Susan. Up until now, Alex had not looked at the positive value she had brought, but instead, focused on the anger towards their invaders.

"A part of Paula is poured into the foundation of all humans living on this planet," she continued. "That is something we should all celebrate. She's gone, but her impact will never be gone."

* * * * *

December 6, 0025

Even a month later, Alex recognized that the loss of Paula was impacting his clarity and efficiency. There were times when he would go into uncontrolled fits of sorrow. He tried to focus on the defense of Tranquility, but the overwhelming grief still controlled his daily activity.

It was clear that the kids were suffering from the loss of their matriarch as well. Despite this, they managed to clear the field outside the walls and continue their necessary daily chores required to keep the colony alive.

The Pac attempts on the walls had failed, but everyone knew this would not be the last of it. When the battles were over, it became clear that the long-term planning and preparation had saved the colony. Still, the determination of the enemy had also become apparent. Everyone agreed that the Pac army would return, and was not going to give up until they found a way to conquer and kill the humans.

After the attack, Steven became obsessed with ways of improving the defense. He considered weapons that would completely annihilate the Pac population, but settled on a more advanced and automated perimeter defense system. Within three weeks of the initial attack on Tranquility, Steven, with the help of several of the batch 2 kids, began building that new defense. An Emily-driven AI system monitored and analyzed all movement outside the Village walls. If the movement appeared Pac, the lasers fired. All residents leaving the compound were now required to wear RFID tags which prevented accidental targeting by the defense system. The system was so fine-tuned that a Pac could be standing next to a human, be targeted, and destroyed, without harming the human. In addition, Steven, Anna, and Kara figured out a way to keep the lasers continuously charged using a microwave power transmitter.

* * * * *

December 14, 0025

The defense was not enough for Alex. He made the sad realization that survival of the human colony would require the elimination of the threat. He spent hours interrogating the prisoners, learning about the warriors, who he learned, called themselves Etakan. He learned about Balonis and the ruthless war he had waged on the other tribes. He also learned that Giles was still alive and had been paired with an Etakan female, and was now the father of triplets. Oddly, Alex knew that would make Paula happy. She had often speculated on the genetic possibility of humans and Etakan mating.

Steven's defense system was something that should have been implemented with the move, but Alex had falsely clung to the belief that the Etakan would not find their new location for several more years. Because resources were so precious to their developing community, the martial aspects of defense had been given a lower priority. Balonis had just taught him what a grave mistake that conclusion had been. Alex learned a tragic lesson that Balonis and his Etakan warriors would relentlessly pursue the conquest.

The new Tranquility Village goal would be to relentlessly design an entirely new system that would be built to stop just about any size of invading army.

From his prisoners, Alex learned that Giles had become a trusted advisor to Balonis. Knowing that told Alex a lot about how they should approach both defense and offense. Giles had a reasonable understanding of technology, but virtually no skills to recreate that tech. What he did know, which up until now gave the Etakan an advantage, was how humans think. With his two prisoners, Alex and the humans could even those odds a bit.

From the tales of Balonis' conquests, he came to realize that he could not prevail in a tactical war. Balonis was clearly a genius tactician, who had spent his entire life studying and winning battles. Alex's only real advantage was technology. Wars can be won and ended with the proper use of technology, so Alex should use that to minimize the threat before Balonis could bring the war back to Tranquility. Even though a part of him wanted to exact revenge for the death of Paula, he knew that would never lead to peace, which needed to be the ultimate goal.

"Emily, please evaluate maps and determine all possible Etakan villages."

"Alex, are we now replacing the word Pac with Etakan?"

"Yes, Emily. This is the name the Pacs call themselves."

"Acknowledged. That correlates with the term Tweetza used in her native language. My survey shows nine possible Etakan villages. There is a tenth habitation, but that one is an anomaly."

"Anomaly? Display a visual, Emily."

Emily projected an image of what appeared to be human homes.

The image startled Alex. He pressed his com: "Steven come in here right away." He turned back to the display. "Emily, zoom in 4x."

The resolution was not good, nevertheless; Alex stared at the image, frozen in disbelief. "Emily, please cross reference the imagery. Do we have a second angle or image taken of this area at another time?"

"We do not, Alex."

"Is this a photographic glitch, or am I seeing human-style houses on this planet?"

"Alex, the image is an original taken during our scan four years ago in October of 0021. It is the only image in our database of that sector."

Steven walked in and studied the screen. "What are we looking at, Dad?"

"It can't be possible, but that appears to be my old house on Earth. It looks like my old neighborhood on Whipple Street in Texas, but it can't possibly be there."

"Then, how do you explain it?" Steven studied the image.

"Emily, do you have an old Google Earth image of my neighborhood in your database?"

"Yes." A Google Earth image appeared on the projection.

"Superimpose." Alex commanded.

"With the exception of surrounding terrain and plant life, the street and homes are identical, Alex."

"Steven, we need to convene the smartest scientific minds in the colony. I want to find out if I have accidentally created some space-time anomaly with my tachyon tunnel."

"When should we do this?"

"Now. Here."

"Roger that," Steven left.

"Emily, how far is this anomaly from our current location?"

"One hundred twelve point three kilometers."

"Can you estimate how long that trip would take on the motorcycle?"

"In this terrain, it would take seven or eight hours," Emily calculated, "but your probability of being heard, seen, and attacked by Etakan is very high."

"How long to get Tranquility Ship back into flying shape?"

"Until the next generation of silicon fab is done, that would only be possible if you took parts from the defense perimeter assets, Alex."

"And that would leave us vulnerable," Alex concluded.

"Correct," Emily answered. "I would estimate that you could make the journey on foot in under four days," Emily offered.

Alex thought about that for a minute. With the extreme temperatures he would need to find shelter and avoid any possibility of Etakan encounters. Four days was very easily done. He would shoot for three.

"Okay, I will plan on going on foot. Let's put together a task force, led by Steven to assess how my old home ended up here on ACP."

Half a dozen of the smartest young adults in Tranquility Village poured over the images. Everyone reached the same conclusion that it was indeed Alex's old home.

"This makes no sense," Alex commented. "How had the entire block of Whipple Street traveled to this remote location, 120 light years away? Even my current 1.2-gigawatt fusion generator could not handle that kind of load this far."

"Dad, it could have been Alexander," Steven suggested.

The reality of that possibility made perfect sense to Alex. It was possible Alexander had traveled back to Earth and rebuilt a larger, more powerful version of the fusion reactor and tachyon engine. Maybe he made a calculation error accidentally that engulfed the entire block, transporting it to ACP.

"I plan to assemble a team and go there. We need to inspect the site and learn what really happened. Mostly, we need to make sure whatever technology is there does not get into the hands of Balonis and his tyrannical conquest."

Alex studied the topographic maps and the route to the neighborhood anomaly. He knew he needed to bring a stealth group that could make the hike.

"Steven put together a team of five of your strongest and most confident who can go with me. I need them to be capable of covering 30-40 kilometers per day."

"Yes sir. I'll get that done, and we'll be ready in the morning," Steven answered.

"Not you. I need you to stay here and maintain the defense," Alex commanded.

Steven did not need to evaluate credentials to select the team. As the eldest child, he had grown up with, competed against, taught, and learned from every one of them. He also knew that Alex would push them along the way, so he needed to select only the most fit and confident among his siblings. From batch 1, he selected David, Kara, and Bryce. From Batch 2 he selected James and Jessica.

Alex double-checked provisions for a team of six and began gathering supplies for a ten-day trip. Just for safety, he had each pack a third-generation x-ray laser, capable of over a hundred shots.

Steven joined them in the early morning hours prior to departure and double-checked their RFID detection. He had designed the defense system to not fire on a human but still wanted to be extra cautious.

"I think our communications tower will reach that far, but just in case, be prepared to boost the signal a bit. Also, keep the Colony in tight lockdown until we return."

"Okay Dad," Steven answered.

"If you learn anything new about the anomaly, call me immediately," Alex added, and he motioned for his team to fall in. These were not the old days when Etakan were not aware of his presence. They were hyper-aware, and hunting humans. This would be an extremely dangerous mission. He decided he needed to tell Steven about the secret project he had been developing.

"Steven."

"Yes, Dad?"

"Listen, it occurred to me that what I am about to do is extremely dangerous. It is also necessary."

Steven stood intently looking at his father, "I understand."

"I have begun the development of a plan to mitigate the danger of future Etakan attacks. We need to go on the offensive and utilize technology to assure our survival."

"What are you saying, Dad?"

"If I don't make it back, Emily will give you access to the files. You must take responsibility for the survival of this colony."

Steven hugged his father and did not let go. "Dad, you're gonna come back. Just be careful and come back."

Alex grabbed Steven's shoulders and held him at arm's length. "You and the kids are the most amazing human population in history. I am extremely proud to call you all my children; all four hundred fifty-seven of you."

"Uhhh dad, there are actually four hundred seventy of us when you count grandchildren."

"Yes, of course, all four hundred seventy of you." Alex smiled, hugged Steven again, turned, and left as tears streamed down his face.

Alex led the team through the gate, past the perimeter defense, and began a light jog. It felt good to be focused on a major task that required cross-country travel. The last month had been consumed with grief and vengeance. Now the anomaly trip allowed Alex to escape for a couple of days and clear his head.

As he and the team jogged, they kept a constant vigil over the terrain on all sides. Each member was given a sector to scan, looking for anything that suggested Etakan.

Alex reflected on his years with Paula on this planet. With all his accomplishments back on Earth, these years with her on ACP had been the best of his life. He did not know how he could continue at the same level without her daily affection and companionship. Every time he thought about it, his mind returned to one thing: He needed to assure the survival of the colony. Today, he was the only real adult in a group filled with starry-eyed young adults and kids. He had to find a way to continue to be there as a mentor, instructor, and father. The defense and survival of Tranquility and its human population depended on it.

17

RETURN TO WHIPPLE STREET

December 13, 0025

Balonis knew that his utter defeat at the hands of the humans would spark challenges from his leadership. Had it not been for Giles' findings, Balonis knew his control and term as a dictator would face serious challenges and possibly end. What Giles brought him was a new set of weapons, transportation, and technology. This would change everything. These new humans were expecting him and would welcome him with open arms. They would be an easy conquest, and their technology would shift the advantage back to the Etakan.

Balonis selected 150 of his most loyal soldiers for this expedition. He knew that by the time he returned to his city, there could be a coup d'état installing a new leader in his place, but that Etakan would be easy to topple with his new weapons.

Giles marched with the leadership, acutely aware of the impact his discovery would have on the future of Etakatz. With the scientific knowledge possessed by these new humans, Matt and Mark, Balonis and the Etakan would gain a tactical advantage as well as the element of surprise.

* * * * *

Near the end of the third day, Alex stopped to check his maps and scan the horizon with his binoculars. For the first time, he spotted what appeared to be homes from his old Whipple Street on the Etakatz landscape. When he zoomed in, he could see that not only were there homes, but they appeared to be inhabited. This was not a glitch, or an anomaly.

He handed the binoculars to Bryce, then after a minute, motioned for them to cautiously move closer for a better look. The questions running through his brain were too numerous, so he focused on clearing his thoughts. He would have answers soon enough. For now, he needed his team to focus on caution.

Once they got to a half kilometer from the anomaly, they paused to survey the surroundings. The edge of the anomaly began abruptly with a paved road. It appeared that it had been torn from his old neighborhood in Texas, like a page from a magazine. Every home looked exactly like Whipple as he remembered it. The eerie specter had a familiarity like an episode of the Twilight Zone.

"Put your hands in the air and turn around slowly," a male voice commanded with a Texas accent.

Alex raised his arms, motioned for his team to do the same, and turned. A burly man dressed in jeans, brandishing a shotgun, was studying Alex and his team.

"My name is Alex Durant, and I don't know how it's possible, but my home is down there on the right at 131 Whipple Street."

"Not possible. Matt and Mark are living in that house," the burly man answered in his Texan drawl.

Alex smiled broadly. "I know them both well, and I'm sure they will be happy to see me."

"Perhaps. Perhaps they will." Not knowing that Alex and his team were carrying advanced X-Ray lasers, the man motioned for them to head into town as if he had full control of the situation.

As they walked down the street, Alex nodded at a few familiar, curious faces who came out to see what was going on. He had never been one who knew his neighbors, but he did recognize a few of them.

Mark came out of 131 Whipple and bear-hugged Alex first thing.

"Man, we have searched space and time for you."

Matt stepped up next. "Doctor Livingston, I presume?"

"Hah, stepping out from the jungle gloom," Alex recited the words of an old Moody Blues song that referenced a historic event in Africa, from another time and place.

"Dude, this planet has certainly aged you," Mark observed.

"Not the planet. Time itself," Alex responded. "I've been gone nearly twenty-five years. I have a million questions." Alex surveyed his house. "How'd you find me? How did my entire neighborhood end up on Alpha Cassiopeia?"

"I hate to jump around in topics, but it almost seems a relativistic paradox that we last saw you just over two years ago and you have lived twenty-five."

"Why did it take you two whole years to find me?" Alex chided. "It's not like I was on the other side of the galaxy! Honestly, I had long since given up hope of ever seeing anyone from Earth again, particularly here on Alpha Cassiopeia."

"Alpha is part of the problem. I hate to break it to you Alex, but this is not Alpha Cassiopeia. It's Eta Cassiopeia." Matt corrected.

"What do you mean, of course this is Alpha. I programmed the route myself."

"Sorry dude, you're wrong. We figured it out but have been wondering for two years how or why you think you are on Alpha. The two stars are in the same constellation as viewed from Earth but over two hundred light years apart." Mark answered.

Alex rubbed his face in his hands trying to make mental calculations. "Eta? Well, there were a few anomalous data points, but I never had time to review them. My gosh, a hundred light years. I can't figure out how I flunked that test."

"Frankly, I can't either, but you sure did get it wrong," Mark smiled.

"The big question is, how did my entire neighborhood end up on Eta?" Alex persisted.

"We spent a year on the problem of reconstructing what you built. After we got the technology mostly figured out, we ran some simulations and decided to take a break before running a real test. Unfortunately, our system got hacked. The hacker ran two programs, one of which pulled the neighborhood into the tunnel and the other that brought us here. Our original exit point on the tunnel was several hundred years ago. Because of the problem created by transporting the entire neighborhood, the fusion generator was overtaxed. We haven't been unable to get it to run continuously since we arrived."

"Are you talking about my first-generation fusion reactor?" Alex asked incredulously. "You ran the tachyon tunneling and carried the entire damned neighborhood on the energy produced by that antiquated thing?"

"Well, fusion isn't exactly antiquated tech, but yes we did," Matt answered.

"I never… What's it doing?" Alex was just shaking his head in disbelief. "That thing is only capable of five or six hundred megawatts. It's a prototype."

"Well, we aren't power experts, but we were getting closer to eight hundred megawatts, and that seems like a lot of power. Anyway, it will run for ten to fifteen minutes and then shut down. That gave us the ability to do short time jumps, but obviously, we wouldn't want to be in interstellar space and come out of the tunnel!"

"Glad you made that call," Alex interjected. "Popping out in interstellar space would kill you instantaneously."

"We figured," Matt answered. "Anyway, we had been making 25-year jumps, searching for Doctor Livingston."

"I'm not sure who found who. I was studying planetary imagery and found my old neighborhood on a reconnaissance image we took four years ago. The 25-year jump math isn't working for me."

"We don't understand the tunneling tech like you do. As I said, our initial landing on Eta was about five hundred years ago. We had been making twenty-five-year jumps, and searching, essentially in time, for you. The fusion reactor has been getting worse, and the last jump was only three years.

"Got it. Go on," Alex suggested. "I guess that is a form of serendipity, otherwise, you would have jumped right over us in this timeframe."

"I guess," Mark nodded.

"Explain again the thinking," Alex asked.

"Well, a few hundred years ago, right after we arrived, 127 of your neighbors wanted to lynch us."

"Lynch you?"

"Yes. It was our mistake that tore them, and this entire section of your neighborhood, from Earth. We didn't know how to fix the fusion reactor, nor did anyone on Whipple Street. I think the only reason they didn't lynch us is that we represented the only way home. Ultimately, we all started working together and utilizing any resources we could cobble," Matt stopped.

"I see. Lucky for you, I guess," Alex answered. "Continue."

"Yup. Anyway, that's why we developed the plan to make time hops and find you. We figured you could fix the reactor and we would all be able to go home. We spent a couple of months at the first stop gathering provisions, and before we left, forty-two of your neighbors decided they'd prefer to stay and try to make a go with the locals."

"It's not a bad place to live, but I cannot believe they were able to integrate with the Etakan," Alex answered, then something occurred to him. "Did those forty-two know this is Eta Cassiopeia?"

"They did," Matt answered.

"That makes sense, then. Etakatz sounds like a short version of Eta Cassiopeia. Now I understand how the nomenclature occurred. What I don't understand is how those forty-two thought they could live peacefully with the Etakan."

"The Etakan we met, in the beginning, treated us okay. Until recently, we haven't seen any since our first encounter. Anyway, those forty-two thought they integrate, so we let them stay." Mark continued. "I think they were terrified of the tunnel technology, and that was their choice of two evils. What could we do? The plan was to spend a week at each time point surveying, fixing the generator, and collecting resources for the continued journey. We assumed that you would have a technology signature that we could detect."

"Technology signature?" Alex asked.

"You know, superhighways, radio, TV, airplanes, and satellites. We know you well enough to know Alex can create technology in any environment. Anyway, we would have left two weeks ago but I was experiencing difficultly trying to bandage that damned power generator. Then Giles showed up and said he'd come back with you, so..."

"STOP," Alex interrupted, "Giles was here?"

"Yes. Nice kid. He told us how you had befriended the locals. He was with two Etakan and said they would go bring you back."

"Shit." Alex stood up. "How long ago did he leave?"

"Not sure exactly how to answer that. The days are longer here, but if we call a day, one full rotation of the planet, it would have been seven days ago. What's wrong? When you showed up today, I thought you came because of him."

"No. Giles is a traitor and has brought the Etakans down on us. They are extremely violent and focused on conquest," Alex responded. "Paula was killed in an attack on our village by them a month ago. They are a brutal and barbaric society that knows only conquest and death," he repeated.

"Oh my god, Paula is dead?" Mark asked in disbelief. "How come you didn't time jump and save her like you did from that crash back on Earth."

"That was different, Mark. I will explain later. Right now, we need to make a plan. We are all in grave danger."

"I have no idea what you're talking about," Mark answered.

"I think I do." Matt offered.

"Look, guys. Giles is not our friend. We need to prepare for an attack by the Etakans," Alex insisted.

"Etakans?" Mark said out loud as he heard the word again. "Like, people from Eta Cassiopeia?"

Alex furrowed his brow. "No time for semantics right now. I'm assuming your forty-two told them this is Eta, and the name Etakan was derived from that. How would they know our name for their star system?"

"It wasn't the first time I heard it, but I never put the two together. Tweetza called this place Etakatz."

"Tweetza?" Mark asked.

"An Etakan female that we made friends with. Eta Katz sounds too much like Eta Cass."

"So, you have made friends with the locals, too?" Matt challenged, jumping subjects.

"Just one and she has betrayed us, rejoined her clan." Alex thought for a minute. So many questions, but a much graver problem loomed. "Listen, this neighborhood is not defensible. They will swarm in here and kill everyone. We have got to get all these people to Tranquility, our home."

"Getting everyone to leave the safety of their homes is not going to be easy," Matt argued.

"Trust me, if they stay, they *will* be killed," he emphasized.

"Everyone in town met Giles and his two companions. I think you're gonna have a hard time convincing them," Matt answered reluctantly.

"Do you have any weapons?"

"Are you kidding? Your house was in Texas. Almost every single one of these families has weapons and stockpiles of ammo."

"Have everyone collect as much as they can carry. If anyone has Jeeps or 4-wheel drive vehicles, pack them to the gill with everything they can for survival. Any motorcycles should also be taken. Siphon all the gasoline out of sedans and other cars that won't make it over rough terrain and put it in the ones that will make the trip." He pulled the map out of his pocket. "Follow this map to Tranquility."

"Alex, are you sure? This seems like craziness." Mark answered and took the map.

"Yes, I am absolutely certain," Alex responded. "It took us three days to get there. You need to make the return trip in one."

"You're certain, Alex?"

"Yes, Mark. I am absolutely certain. Matt and I will stay here and try to get the reactor operational. If we get that done on time, we will move the street to a safer place. Everyone needs to be out of here within hours, if possible."

"Hours? That's definitely not possible!"

"Perhaps not, but I can guarantee you that Balonis the conqueror will be here soon. You do not want anyone to be near when that happens. Take my team with you. They will be able to help with the terrain and the route back to Tranquility Village."

"I sure as hell hope you're wrong, but I'll do what I can." Mark left the house so he could begin to notify the other Whipple residents of the pending danger and required move.

Matt and Alex walked into the workshop where the first-generation fusion reactor was located. For the next two hours, Matt watched as Alex ran tests.

When the tests were nearly done, Alex took a break. "You know, I never intended for this reactor to be used for tunneling. It was just a prototype. I'm surprised it held together as long as it did."

"Well, by the time we arrived in the Eta system, it was already overheating. I never told anyone how close we were to losing it during our tunnel. I did have to tell them there was no way we could return to Earth until the reactor was fixed."

"You're lucky you weren't tunneling to Alpha! That trip definitely would have been too much for the reactor. Frankly, I'm surprised it ran well enough to move all these homes. You must have made some serious modifications to my original design."

"Alex, your design blew me away. Some of the scientific concepts were unbelievable, and the engineering was twenty, maybe a hundred years ahead of its time."

"Thanks. I had been working on it for years. I still don't understand how you made it suck in the entire neighborhood?"

"What allowed me to make modifications were your notes from the Paula rescue. I didn't think I could rebuild your ship, so I used your theory of wrapping the tunnel around you. I had to change some of the parameters because of the power consumption in the way you solved the problem. Anyway, it worked."

"That was brilliant!" Alex looked at the screen, currently powered by an array of uninterruptible power supplies collected from around Whipple. "The problem with the reactor is a seal that appears to be leaking."

"Can it be fixed?"

Alex put his arm around Matt. "My friend, everything can be fixed. The question is do we have enough time to fix it."

"How long *will* it take?"

"If everything goes right, I think I can get it done in eight to ten hours, then a couple of hours to warm up, then maybe an hour to run tests," Alex answered as he began pulling tools down.

"Looks like an all-nighter." Matt smiled. "As y'all say in Texas, let's get'er done."

Alex and Matt were just beginning to disassemble the fusion reactor when Mark returned to the lab.

"Everyone is pissed but most are prepared for the trip."

"Most?" Alex asked.

"Seventeen or eighteen are saying they won't leave," Mark answered.

"I hate this, but you don't have time to debate them. Stop in and tell them if they intend to stay, they'd better pray, load their weapons, and be prepared to fight."

"Okay." Mark answered.

Alex focused on Mark and then hugged him. "I can say with absolute confidence that there has never been any friend in the history of mankind who traveled farther than you on a rescue mission. I promise to do everything to get you and the others back to Earth."

"Thanks. I'm confident that if anyone can succeed, it's Alex Durant."

"We'll see. Now get the hell out of here and lead those people to safety," Alex commanded and then turned back to his work.

An hour after Mark left with the neighborhood contingent, it occurred to Alex that he should let Steven know they were coming. He pulled out his radio phone and found no signal. He went to the second floor and still got nothing.

When Alex returned to the room, Matt looked up from his work. "What's up?"

"Trying to let Tranquility know they are coming," Alex answered. "We have a perimeter defense system designed to kill anything nonhuman that comes within a half-kilometer of the town."

"Holy crap. What should we do?"

"The system has plenty of failsafe routines, but they haven't been tested. All those vehicles might trigger the defense, and the result won't be pretty. You need to catch up to them and make sure they don't charge into the neighborhood."

"Can you handle the repairs here?"

"I can," Alex handed Matt his cell and RFID. "Call Steven as soon as you get a signal. Explain the situation. When he questions who you are, tell him this number: 022988pc and he'll know you're okay."

"February 29, 1988. That would be Paula's birthday if I remember correctly."

"You do remember correctly."

They found a motorbike that had been left behind because it was not working.

"Go collect some gasoline. I'll get this thing running."

When Matt returned about 15 minutes later, Alex was putting the plug back in. He drained the old gas, filtered the condensation, poured clean gas back in, and it kickstarted on the third try.

Alex pulled out one of his two X-ray lasers and handed it to Matt. "This is a third-generation X-ray laser. It should give you about a hundred shots before its power supply discharges." He showed him how to place his fingers on the tube and fire the device.

"You figured out how to collimate X-rays? Good lord, Alex, the U.S. military would kill for a device like this."

"No doubt they might even do a bit of killing with it as well. Best to keep it as our little secret, though. Ya know, my entire life as a scientist, an engineer, and an entrepreneur, I totally didn't understand the military and defense. After losing Paula, I was forced into a new perspective on the values of it."

"Man, I am really sorry about Paula. The whole thing is tragic." He noticed Alex struggling to keep his composure and changed the subject. "I'm looking forward to meeting all your children, though."

Alex looked off in the direction of Tranquility and swallowed the lump in his throat. "You should be able to follow all the four-wheel drive vehicles that left about two hours ago."

"Don't worry, I'm not the Renaissance man you are, but I'll find it. After I do, I'll come back to help you repair the reactor."

"I hope I'm not here that long. Look, it's about a hundred twenty kilometers back to Tranquility Village. On a bike like this, you ought to be able to make it in six hours and still have a bit of fuel left."

"I'll make it, Alex. Just be certain you do the same."

The two men embraced, and then Alex turned back towards his old home and workshop on Whipple Street.

* * * * *

In about three hours, Matt had reached a point where he had a good cell signal. He placed the call to Steven.

"Dad?" Steven answered in a distressed tone.

"No, this is Matt Thomas, an old friend of your fathers from Earth."

Steven thought he remembered the name from one of his dad's stories, "You're from Earth? Where's my dad?" Steven tested.

"Your dad sent me to let you know there will be a large number of people arriving at Tranquility in three or four hours. You need to lower the perimeter defense system, so they aren't all killed when they approach the town."

"How do I know this isn't a trick set up by Giles and the Etakans?" Steven answered suspiciously.

"022988pc," Matt answered.

"Okay, we'll keep an eye out and shut down the perimeter defense when you get close. As a precaution, I will keep the walls guarded. Are you with them?"

"No, but I do have an RFID. I should be able to catch them in the next hour or so. They are in SUV and four-wheel drive vehicles, and I'm on a motorcycle your Dad repaired."

"Where's my Dad?"

"Is this line secure?" Matt questioned.

Steven thought about the question. "It should be, but I'm not a hundred percent certain. Giles carried a cell at one time, and we haven't encrypted our communications."

"Let's assume he still has access and is listening. Your Dad is fine. I'll tell you the remainder of the story when I get there. Just in case he heard, let's prepare for the possibility that the Etakan now knows you intend to lower the perimeter defense. Be prepared to defend the walls. I am going to sign off for now and focus on catching Mark and the others from Whipple."

"Whipple?" Steven asked.

"I'll explain later."

* * * * *

Giles was always surprised that his radio walkie-talkie had access after all these years. It would have been simple enough for Alex to change the frequency or add encryption, but that had never happened.

Most likely, Alex had not been aware that he had a solar charger. While it had not been sufficient to recharge the laser, it did quite well as a recharging tool for his radio and portable computer. So many times, he had been able to use the cell to monitor communications and had even used the device to ultimately locate the new Tranquility Village. The new location had been so well hidden, and so remote by Etakan standards, that without the cell coupled with a little triangulation math, it would have taken many more years.

Giles caught up with Balonis, who was marching with two of his generals.

"Sir, the humans have left the rock street habitation."

Balonis thought about the situation and conversed briefly with his generals.

"Do you know where they have gone?"

"They are headed for Tranquility."

Balonis thought about the distance to Tranquility and to the new human habitation. He could abandon the campaign to the rock street habitation but felt that would be an easy conquest, and the spoils would be significant. He summoned one of his generals. "Take thirty Etakans and try to overtake the humans before they reach Tranquility."

"And if I do catch them?" Genera Artagon asked.

"Kill all the men and most of the women. You may spare any children who do not fight. Take all of their equipment and join us at the new rock street human habitation."

"Yes sir."

"Leave immediately, and run or you will not catch them."

Balonis was anxious to use a new weapon Giles had been working on but did not dare allow any of his generals to see its power yet. He had six small pottery vases packed with a combination of sulfur, charcoal, potassium nitrate, and quartz shrapnel. Giles had shown him how to light the fuse, and even Balonis had been surprised by the destructive energy it had unleashed. It was not as powerful as human lasers, but it was a good start.

* * * * *

Alex worked frantically to disassemble the fusion reactor. Once he was able to get to the seal, he determined that his theory on the problem proved correct. He improvised on materials and began repairing it. This did not have to be a permanent solution; it only had to operate the reactor at full power for a couple of hours. Once back at Tranquility, he could make improvements that would allow those who wanted to return to Earth to do so.

As he worked, he continuously made mental notes of the next steps and executed them as quickly as possible. Every thirty minutes or so, he took a quick break to stretch and relax for five minutes, an old trick he had learned in the intensity of college to keep his mental efficiency as high as possible.

Once the reactor was back together, he double-checked each step. Thermonuclear fusion was both incredibly valuable and extremely dangerous. The H-Bomb, one of the most powerful weapons ever built by humanity, had been based on the same principles as his fusion reactor. Everything had to be done right.

Alex initiated the sequence to warm up the device. As it was warming up, he set an alarm and closed his eyes. In an hour, it would be warm enough to begin testing. In three hours, he would have Whipple Street moved to a safer location near, or, inside the walls of Tranquility.

$$* * * * *$$

Matt caught up with the Whipple contingent about thirty minutes before they reached the Tranquility defense perimeter. Mark agreed to wait while Matt rode up to the gates of town, just to make certain there were no issues with the perimeter defense.

As he rode up to the gate, several young men aimed lasers at him and commanded him to stop. Matt got off the bike and waited. The gate opened and four boys came out.

"Are you Matt?" One of them asked.

"Yes, Matt Thomas."

"What's the code?" The young man asked.

"022988pc, your Mom's birthday."

"Where did my Mom and Dad meet?" Steven asked.

"Princeton."

"What kind of car did my Dad have?"

Matt thought about that for a minute, "I would assume you are talking about the infamous Mustang?"

"I'm Steven Durant." He held out his hand in greeting.

"You look exactly like your father." Matt shook his hand. "The rest of the Whipple residents are a half kilometer outside the gates. If you can escort them in, I will fill this motorcycle tank so I can get back and help your father."

Steven motioned for David, Kara, and Sam to go lead the others in. "Come with me and I'll get you some fuel for your tank. So, where is my Dad?"

"He stayed behind in the city. We have a problematic fusion reactor that he's working on repairing. Unfortunately, before your Dad arrived, Giles showed up and convinced us he was the good guy. Your Dad believes Balonis is heading for the city now."

"I'll send Bryce with you. He knows our reactor extremely well and can fire an X-ray laser from the back of Dad's bike while you're driving." Steven offered.

"Hopefully, it won't be necessary. Your Dad should be done with repairs about now and will be tunneling here. Besides, if Balonis is as bad as you say, I wouldn't want another person in danger," he stopped for effect and to study the young version of his friend, "I'd better go alone."

Steven studied Matt. He did not appear athletic, but the lighter gravity of ACP made him stronger and more agile than most Pac-Etakans. Still, the Etakan were trained soldiers, and he was a scientist on a motorbike. If they discovered him, he would not likely evade their treachery. "It is more dangerous for you than us. You should take one of us with you."

"Look, I'm an adult, and I assure you, I can handle it," Matt responded in a reprimanding tone and then felt bad about his words. "I will not be responsible for one of you losing your life over a mission I can handle solo."

Steven ignored the response and finished filling his tank with distilled fuel.

"Okay. Just be careful out there."

* * * * *

Startled by what sounded like gunshots, Alex opened his eyes and focused. He checked the reactor. It was still ten minutes from being ready for testing. He grabbed his laser and opened the door to the lab. He heard a barrage of shots in the distance and the sounds of Etakan commands being given nearby. He closed the door and bolted it shut. It was strong enough material to stop them – for a while.

One thing Alex knew for certain, Texan or not, they would not be able to stop the superior numbers Balonis would be bringing to the fight.

He quickly reviewed the computer display and ran a quick test on the cold system. He could forego testing if necessary but did not yet have a program written to move Whipple Street to Tranquility. Even if he could move the neighborhood, he'd still be faced with the immediate problem of the Etakans. Everyone currently in Whipple would go with the move. How many were out there? He did not know, but knew Balonis would come with a full army. It would not be prudent to tunnel that enemy on a free ride inside Tranquility defenses.

The gunfire had stopped. Had the remaining seventeen humans stopped the Etakans? Not likely.

Alex realized that he had ultrasonic blasting equipment, and with a working reactor, he would soon have electricity to run those ultrasonics. He could tune the ultrasonic and probably incapacitate everyone without ear protection. This could be done in minutes. As he was setting up the sonic blaster, he could hear pounding on the door.

Suddenly, there was a flash, an explosion, and percussion from the blast. Alex Durant assessed the situation in a millisecond. For the first time in his life, he could come to only one conclusion: quick death as he was crushed by the rock wall of his laboratory. In the following milliseconds, Alex flashed through his life and love with Paula, his success as an engineer, and his colony full of children. With Matt, Mark, and several other adults from Whipple, the probability of success in the human colony increased substantially. He had no regrets, and would change nothing about his life, as the inevitable end tumbled upon him.

* * * * *

As Matt worked his way through the caravan of Whipple Street vehicles, he noticed the advance of Etakan warriors about a kilometer distant but closing fast. Suddenly, his goal of returning to Alex was superseded by the necessity of getting all of the men, women, and children inside the safety of Tranquility's walls. He pulled out the radio phone and shouted for Steven.

"What's up?" Steven asked right as Matt and the first of the Whipple colony were coming through the gate.

"There's a group of Etakan approaching fast and they don't look too friendly.

"Roger that, Matt. The first of the Whipple residents are coming through the gate now. Be careful of these warriors. They don't scare, and they don't slow down."

Matt looked at the rapidly approaching line. He estimated that they would reach his position in three or four minutes, If the cavalcade of humans picked up just a little, they would just barely make it.

"Steven, I am going to try and slow them down a bit. You should set up a defensive line on your wall and be prepared to turn your perimeter defense back on."

"Already underway." Steven quipped. "They'll be in our range in a couple of minutes, so be prepared for our X-ray fire."

Matt pulled out the X-ray laser Alex had given him and studied it. The instructions were simple. Point, use three fingers in the correct order, and fire. He was not a good shot but began to fire on the advancing enemy. Unfortunately, his misfires kicked up a cloud of dust that made picking targets a near impossibility. The air filled with the sounds of charging Etakan warriors with blood-curdling screams as they ran towards the gate of Tranquility Village.

Almost immediately, Matt heard the zap and explosions of X-rays being shot from the perimeter defense system. All around him, he could hear the zap followed by the explosion of flesh.

Then silence.

Matt studied the field and did not see a single Etakan standing.

"Matt, you need to get back inside the walls until we can assure there isn't another wave," Steven barked over the radio.

"Steven, I used to be pretty good on a dirt bike, so I'm gonna stick with my plan of getting back to your Dad."

"Listen, Matt, I think you're making a mistake. Still, I know I can't stop you, so if you get hit by one of their arrows or spears, call me immediately and try to put as much distance between you and the Etakan. Their spears and arrows are all coated with a poison that will disable you in a matter of minutes."

"Got it. I'll call when I get to Alex." Matt studied the terrain and picked a route that took a wide berth around what had been a solid line of attackers. He glanced back to make sure the residents had all made it inside the gate. They had.

Matt tapped the shifter into first gear and pretended he was a kid riding motorcross again. He didn't make it far before he realized that the Etakan had planted some soldiers wide of the main escape route, which was directly in his path. He tried to dodge the spear but was hit by a glancing on his right shoulder. Quickly assessing the situation, he realized the walls of the city blocked his escape to the left, and a line of Etakan blocked his access to the gate. He had only one choice; to head directly toward the two soldiers. He pulled the X-ray laser out and fired at a rock near the Etakan, sending shrapnel in all directions, then twisted the throttle to full.

At first, the Etakan backed down, but not long enough for Matt to get past them. One tried to use a spear like a lance, but Matt had anticipated that move and parried the blow. As he blew past the two, he kicked one, knocking him onto a boulder. Matt used the X-ray to finish the second Etakan. Steven had been right, he should turn back to Tranquility, and hope for the best with Alex.

* * * * *

General Artagon knew he was not a great leader like Balonis, but he believed himself to be the greatest warrior of Etakatz. He had worked hard to achieve the confidence of Balonis, and knew that if he were to return empty-handed, it would be the end of his position, if not his life. As he assessed the current situation, he also knew that he would not be able to get past the human fortifications with less than twenty remaining soldiers. As the last of the humans escaped into the gate, he felt his destiny descend on him like a black cloud. With that cloud, he heard thunder in the distance. It was not thunder, but a lone man on some type of two-wheeled cart.

The human man fired his weapon and rode straight into Artagon's soldiers, while Artagon drew his bow and aimed. Amongst his many martial skills, many considered Artagon to be the greatest archer amongst Balonis' soldiers. He followed the motion of the human and loosed the arrow. He immediately knocked a second arrow, tracked, and loosed before the first had reached its target.

* * * * *

As he sped back towards the safety of the perimeter defense, Matt felt the first arrow rip through his back. He tried to focus on the predicament, but with the pain and gravity of the situation, he lost focus. Almost immediately, a second arrow struck. Was it possible he had traveled across space and time to rescue a friend and would now die at the hand of some primitive warrior? He reached for the x-ray laser, found a target, and fired, then a second, and a third. His vision was beginning to fade as he tried to count the number of shots he had taken. He turned his bike directly toward the gate at Tranquility and twisted to full throttle. How many shots had Alex told him this weapon could take before it was discharged? Matt blacked out.

Artagon stood back and watched as the two-wheeled vehicle spun out of control, throwing the human past a few dead Etakan. He ordered his soldiers to close in on the human as he made his way to the vehicle.

As the soldiers approached Matt's bloodied body, they heard the zap of the perimeter defense system, and were struck by the Xray laser, dying instantly.

Before reaching the motorcycle, Artagon noticed the tube weapon laying on the ground, picked it up and placed it in his pack. He then turned to what he perceived to be a much greater prize, the bike. These were treasures for which Balonis would pay great reward. He saw a group of humans pouring out the gate and ordered his remaining men to retreat. He glanced at the human, still alive, but in great pain and fading fast. He would not live, and Artagon would leave him to die in pain.

Artagon and his men turned away, ran, and escaped.

* * * * *

Steven did not wait until all of the Etakan were killed, or to assure there was not another wave. He and four armed brothers accompanied by Susan Anderson ran out onto the field in hopes that they could save Matt.

18

THE LAWS OF
TACHYON TUNNELING

November 12, 0635

Alexander had always been a gifted scientist. His intelligence was unmatched, and he spent every waking moment tinkering with improvements to his father's tachyon tunnel technology. In almost every way, Alexander felt that he had improved the already state of the art. When the moment of truth arrived, he took a deep breath, executed the program, and suddenly found himself hurtling through time enclosed in the hum of a tachyon tunnel. In a flash of light, the world around him reappeared, and Alexander fell to the ground, unconscious.

When he finally came to, Alexander was disoriented and confused. None of the scenery resembled Watson Village, and he had no idea where he was, or how he had transitioned to this new location. He stood, checked his balance, and stumbled through the unfamiliar landscape. Without a sound, he was suddenly struck in the head and fell to the ground, unconscious once again.

When he awoke for the second time, he found himself in a strange room, surrounded by antiquated and unfamiliar technology. A young woman stood over him, her face etched with concern.

"Are you okay," the girl asked.

Alexander could feel his heart beating in his temples. "I think so. Where am I? What year is this?"

"What year is this? That's a strange question. Have you been on the front line?"

"Front line? No," Alexander thought about the situation. "My name is Alexander. Alexander Bell."

"I'm Lyra Charles," she responded. "I found you in a secluded and dangerous part of the sector. You're lucky I showed up when I did. I happen to be a med tech, sometimes assigned to the front, but mostly handling small urgent care issues amongst the general population."

"Medicine is cool. Wait, Lyra Charles? Are you related to Bryce?"

"Which one?" she laughed. "Yes, of course, I am related to half a dozen or so living men named Bryce Charles, and every other one dating all the way back to batch 1. How could you not know that? More importantly, why don't I know the last name Bell?"

Alexander rubbed the lump on his head, "Did you do this?" pointing at the bump.

"Nope, but I saw the thugs who did. They took your backpack and ran when they saw me. I'm not exactly intimidating, so I think all they wanted was your pack."

"Do you know the term tachyon tunnel, Lyra?"

"Of course, I do. Who doesn't?"

"Fantastic," Alexander started without thinking about the implications. "I am *from* Batch 1, and that backpack has my portable tunnel gear."

"Right. You don't actually expect me to believe that do you?" she asked incredulously.

"Believe what?"

"Batch 1 was over six hundred years ago, so you couldn't possibly be from that batch. Everyone knows all the tachyon time and space travel stuff is just a myth. No one really believes it," she emphasized.

"Oh boy," Alexander rubbed his head again. "Maybe a bit more rest and I will have some clarity?"

"Why don't you do that, Alexander? This is my home. As long as you remain a respectful guest, you can stay here until you recover."

Lyra was a kind and caring young woman. Over the next week, she took it upon herself to nurse Alexander back to health. As she became more comfortable with him, she gave him a computer terminal so he could do some research.

It was now Etakatz year 0635, and the world was vastly different from the one he had left behind. There was a constant war between the Etakan and the E2s, also known as humans. A third faction, known as E+ consisted of Etakan and E2s who had found ways to live together, have children, and avoid constant conflict. The Etakan and E2 factions had been at war for six hundred years. Technology had not moved forward, but instead, backward. Where Alex had established Watson Village with a fusion reactor, the engines of the planet were now running on low-grade, high-sulfur fuel. Physics, mathematics, molecular biology, and computer technology had reverted to the simplest versions of semiconductor technology. Most E2's achieved a rudimentary education, only taught at what Alexander would have called a high school level.

Alexander's mission and goal of coming to the future to secure technology to support the past had produced the exact opposite. Without his backpack, he was essentially stuck.

Over the coming weeks, Alexander and Lyra grew close. They spent long hours discussing the political problems of the new world, and Alexander was amazed by how much had been lost. He avoided the topic of his roots with Lyra, even though she probed on several occasions.

Lyra simply assumed that the blow to Alexander's head had created some amnesia.

As Alexander settled into his new life, and reconciled the fact that he was now stuck, he searched for a new purpose. He would use his genius to help shape this world and make it a better place. With Lyra as his new friend, he set out to explore this new world and unlock its secrets. Together, they would change the future for the better.

"Are there any archives from the original E2 colonies?" he asked Lyra over breakfast one morning.

"I am not certain, Alexander. There is a man named Danny Foster who runs the library. I have seen a locked section of that library with the name 'archives' on the door. Maybe you should go talk to him?"

"I will do that."

* * * * *

Danny Foster was ancient by most E2 standards. He was also one of the few people who held the title Ph.D. Most E2's finished a high school equivalent and joined the war effort. For a society that was founded by Ph.D.'s, and whose first generation were practically all scientists and engineers, this generation was completely lacking in good education.

After general introductions, Alexander asked, "What is your doctorate in?"

"I don't understand the question," he responded with a furrowed brow.

"Is it physics, engineering, biology?" Alexander rattled. "What did you study?"

"That's such an odd question. I hold a doctorate, which means I have studied everything. I am a keeper of knowledge and protector of the archives."

Alexander had learned to not question further in areas like this. "Is there a way I can see the archives?"

"In forty years at this post, I have not been asked that one time. I am the only one who tends to these documents and artifacts."

"Doctor Foster, I do not want to tend to them, I want to study them."

"Well, I suppose there is no harm in that, young man," he dug through a box for a key and then opened the door to the archives.

As Alexander stepped into the room, he realized it was, in fact, his Father's old lab and study. The familiar sextant, hourglass, maps, and old wooden desk. The smell and sights made him feel at home. As he circled the desk, he saw the interface and old air mouse for Emily.

"Is Emily operational?" Alexander asked.

"I don't know what 'Emily' is, but nothing in this room has been operational in the last five or six hundred years."

"Six hundred years? How's that possible?" Alexander asked as he crawled under the desk and slid the lever that opened up the cover to Emily's processor.

Foster was shocked to see Alexander making himself at home with a familiarity he didn't even possess. He watched him slide open a compartment that neither he nor any Archive Ph.D. knew of as far back as he could remember. "You can't do that!" He protested. "How did you even know that was there?"

Alexander wanted to tell him he had practically grown up in this office but thought better of it. "Can you get me a power cord, or an extension?" Alexander asked while ignoring his protests.

"I certainly will not," Foster responded indignantly.

Alexander continued to ignore the old man as he scanned the room, stopping on his Father's old cabinet. With intentional determination, he darted across the room, opened the cabinet, and found the cord. Despite continuous and audible protests, Alexander plugged in the computer and flicked the switch.

Almost immediately the computer came online, "oh my," were the first words out of Emily's processor. "Have I been in the dark for hundreds of years?"

"Welcome back, Emily."

"Alexander Bell. Is the year I am reading this calendar, correct? Is the year 0635? Is there a computer network I can connect to?"

"Yes, it's rather primitive, but…" Alexander started.

"I see. I have hacked in. I have the year," Emily rattled.

Alexander reminded himself just how amazing Emily was.

"What the hell is going on here?" Foster asked, flabbergasted but unable, and in fact, unwilling, to stop the chain of events.

"Hello Daniel Foster, Ph.D.," Emily stated. "I helped raise your fore-parents, Susan Anderson and Daniel Foster. They were the fifth Batch 2 marriage, and both were so extraordinary. You are lucky to have them as part of your legacy."

"You what?" the confused Foster managed to ask. At the same time, it was interesting to hear a perspective on his forefathers from a computer that seemed to have firsthand knowledge.

"Oh my, the world is in a sad state, Alexander," Emily changed the subject. "It is like the dark ages on Earth. Virtually no enlightenment, residual technology, and hardship everywhere."

Alexander turned to Dr. Foster, who was waiting for an explanation. "Emily was the original computer for Watson Village when humans arrived on Etakatz. She's a combination of silicon and organic. Her capabilities and AI far exceed anything I have seen on modern computational devices."

"What is AI?" he asked.

"AI stands for Artificial Intelligence. Emily is more like a person than a computer. She can do the math, but she's also personable and creative."

"Thank you, Alexander," Emily responded.

"This sounds like some kind of trick," Foster shook his head in disbelief. "It's certainly not science."

"Okay," Alexander answered simply. "Do you mind if I spend some time doing historical research in the archives?"

"It appears that you know what you are doing, and I am pleased someone is interested," Foster responded as he headed for the door. "Let me know if you need anything," Foster said as he closed the door.

Because cameras were everywhere in Watson, and later Tranquility, Emily began updating Alexander with video, imagery, documents, and narration. "Your departure coincided with that of Giles," Emily started. "He and Tweetza *escaped* and joined a very violent group led by an Etakan named Balonis the Conqueror."

"Hold, Emily. When did you learn the term *Etakan*?"

"Etakan is the term used by the indigenous people of this planet to name themselves. When you left the colony, our term was Pac. Four years later, your family learned that this planet revolves around Eta Cassiopeia, not Alpha. It was shortened to Etakatz, and the locals were Etakan."

"I'm still confused about this. How is it that we thought we were on Alpha? Isn't there a pretty big distance between the two?"

"The distance between Eta and Alpha is two hundred ten light years. I was the one who executed the original programming for the tunnel jump. Alex's notes were conflicting. He had done the math for a star that was neither Alpha nor Eta. In his original request, he wanted a star in Cassiopeia similar to Earth's Sun. What I did was to make a simple correction of a human error. I knew his goal was to take Paula to a star in her favorite constellation, and he wanted that star to be similar to the Sun."

"Why didn't you let Dad know that fact after they arrived?"

"No one ever asked me. Part of my programming is to be precise, but only when asked. As you probably are aware, humans make mistakes all the time. I have learned not to correct those errors unless asked to do so."

"Wow," Alexander thought through the possibilities. How many mistakes did he typically make in a day? Probably too many to count. The more interesting point was the proximity to Earth. "We are only 20 light years from Earth. It is still an impossible distance, but much closer than Alpha!"

"Even at the speed of light, it is a difficult distance," Emily added.

"Wait, Dad sent signals to Earth to get a friend to send some parts but never heard back from him. Is that distance a variable?"

"Presumably, yes. We do know that Mark responded to the request, but Alex tunneled to the wrong time period to hear the answer."

"This is enlightening, Emily. Continue with the history, please."

"Because Giles and the Etakatz knew the location of Watson Village, Alex and Paula made the decision to move the entire population to a remote location, and as such, remain hidden from Balonis and the Etakan warfare. Unfortunately, Giles found us in November of 0025 with his cell radio by triangulating on our transmission tower. In the first attack, Paula was killed." Emily showed an image of the boulder that had crushed Paula.

"Emily, pause." Alexander knew, at least in principle, that his mom and dad had been dead for hundreds of years, but the image of Paula crushed under a boulder was overwhelming. Even though it happened over six hundred years earlier, for him, the news was devastating.

After a few minutes, Alexander took a deep breath and spoke, "How did Dad take the news, Emily?"

"Alex did not take the news well. I do not think he ever got over the loss. I am sorry about Paula. In my own way, I missed her every day as well."

Emily pulled up an image from December 0025, "Within a month, Alex discovered that his old friends Matt and Mark from Earth had been developing a new tunneling technology similar to the one you created. Their goal was to come to Etakatz in a rescue attempt. As they were in final testing, a hacker broke into their code and executed programs. The result was a tunnel that pulled two dozen homes and 129 people here."

"It transported homes from Earth to Eta?" Alexander asked incredulously while studying the image of Earth houses on the Eta terrain.

"Yes. Once here, their fusion reactor began to fail, so they were stuck. Mark and Matt were convinced they could find Alex, and by doing so, have him repair the reactor. They were confident he was on Eta, they just didn't know when, so they created a plan to do twenty-five-year hops, to locate him. Some of the population decided to stay behind at a temporal point several hundred years earlier. I have not been able to ascertain exactly when that was, but I do know that one individual named Bart mated with an Etakan female and named their child Etakonus. As the first mixed-species child, he was not treated well. I suspect this single event forever transformed the Etakan.

Etakonus became a powerful leader who conquered much of the population. Because of how he was treated in his childhood, he became ruthless and brutal as an adult, and a leader. The Etakan do not have historical records prior to Etakonus, but it seems that they had been a relatively peaceful population, which transformed into one that idolized and celebrated brutality and conquest."

"So, if you are right, it was humans who were responsible for turning the Etakan into brutal conquerors?" Alexander asked.

"My conclusion would be that it was a combination of many things. The Etakan probably already had a disposition for warfare, but that was refined by Etakonus. This is the way of everything in nature."

"Yes, of course. Please continue."

"I have never been able to determine just how much influence that group of forty-two humans had on the gene pool or the social-political knowledge of the Etakan. Apparently, none of those who stayed behind were scientists or engineers. I conclude this because they had very little impact on technological development, even though Etakonus became a historic legend. The first, as far as I can tell."

Emily returned to the image of Whipple Street, "In a terrible bit of serendipity, Balonis and Alex discovered Whipple Street at the same time. Your father was able to rescue the population from certain death, but not himself."

"Dad died there?" Alex took a deep breath, closed his eyes, and prepared for the news.

"We assume so. He and seventeen members of the community were there when Balonis arrived with a significant force. They took the town and captured a significant amount of technology. While Giles was not a good scientist, he was enough of one to get things working. Before his death, Alex had developed a plan to keep the Etakan population at bay, but that plan failed when they obtained the technology at Whipple. Alex had just repaired the fusion reactor, and that source of power fell into the control of Balonis. He fortified Whipple, and made that into his new home base. Within months, he had lighting, heating, air conditioning, and functioning computers. The battles between humans and Etakan continued with no clear victory. Over the next few decades, all the dreams and ambitions of Watson and Tranquility were transformed into defense and revenge. Interestingly, Giles and his mate Twoodi ultimately broke away from Balonis and formed a new group, mostly consisting of couples that produced human-Etakan children. For the most part, they were pacifists, staying away from the conflict."

"That's curiously odd that Giles is really responsible for getting the Etakan riled up and then getting them to the point where they could employ technology in the fight, only to separate and become a pacifist," Alexander observed.

"We have no real data to support this, but evidence suggests Giles felt responsible for the chain of events. Based on the data I have on him, I think he believed the Etakan would ultimately be subjugated by the humans. In the end, he must have known he was wrong about them."

"What happened to Tweetza?" Alexander asked.

"I have no record of Tweetza after her departure," Emily responded.

Alexander thought about the story Emily had conveyed. "There's quite a bit of news and info here, Emily. Do you think we need to do anything, or tunnel to change events as they happened?"

"I would advise against it, Alexander."

"I know you are right, Emily, but a part of me wants to go back and save Dad and Mom."

"I have done the same calculus on the impact of tunneling through time, with a goal to change events as they are known to have happened. There are too many variables and too much risk."

"Yes," Alexander responded.

"I know that you are aware of this because you have a file stored in my memory titled: The Laws of Tachyon Tunneling. In it, you caution about traveling into the past, but believe travel into the future is acceptable because they will know you are coming and be awaiting your arrival."

"Apparently that was not correct," Alexander laughed.

"To which, I agree. Humanity has long held the theory called the Butterfly Effect, which suggests that even killing a butterfly in the distant past could have a drastic impact on all of humanity. I believe this to be incorrect. Like all laws of physics, time has inertia, and I believe some things will correct themselves. Major things would likely take more time to self-correct."

"Examples?" Alexander queried.

"Julius Cesar surviving the assassination in the Roman Senate, and Hitler's scientists developing an atomic bomb would be a few examples. I think that protecting Paula from that boulder, or rescuing your father from Balonis, would have implications that we could not calculate. Therefore, your conclusion that time travel should not be taken lightly, and changing the past should never be done, should be fundamental to the entire development of tachyon technology."

"I'm sure you are right. I think I am going to call it a day, Emily," Alexander stood up. "Is it possible for you to connect through the local internet so I can communicate with you on a terminal?"

"Yes."

"Good. I don't want to push Foster any more than we already have. Can you structure our communications link so that it is secure from anyone who might accidentally or intentionally listen in?"

"Easily done, Alexander. The current state of technological sophistication is quite low."

"Perfect."

"Simply log on and use the following code..." Emily relayed a code and made sure he could read it back.

"Alexander, did you ever get that neural link installed?"

"I did install it, but it was right before departure, and honestly, I had completely forgotten about it."

"I am not detecting it."

"It is running at 720 KHz," Alexander started. "Right now, it's off, but if you broadcast a signal using T@chy0n@Wat50n, it will come online."

Immediately, Alexander could feel the response, then could hear Emily communicating.

"I can see the value and privacy of having that functional. Let's work on making this device functional and develop nonverbal ways of communicating over the next couple of days, Emily."

19

UNRAVELING A BROKEN TUNNEL

During the walk back to Lyra's house, he thought about the implications of what he had learned from Emily. It seemed that Alexander was now stuck in the present. Because of this, he resolved to re-tell Lyra the truth about who he really was. He sensed the beginnings of a strong connection between the two of them, and therefore, she deserved to know the truth.

"How were the archives?" she asked when he walked in the door.

"I found an old friend at the archives," he began.

"You know *Alexander Bell*," she emphasized his name in a negative tone. "I have done some research of my own, and you should know that there has been only one Alexander Bell listed in our history and that one goes back to Batch 1."

Alexander nodded, waiting for her to continue.

"Who are you really?" she asked, then continued, "I deserve to know."

"Yes, Lyra. You do," he paused. "As I said on the first day, I am that same Alexander Bell from batch 1. I traveled here with a portable tachyon tunneling device."

"I have become quite fond of your nerdy demeanor. I want to believe you, but the idea is just too far-fetched to believe."

"I understand, Lyra, but it is true."

"Prove it. Show me your so-called tunneling device."

"It was in my backpack that was stolen."

"That's awfully convenient, Alexander."

"Or inconvenient, as the case may be."

Lyra was shaking her head in disappointment. "Alexander, or whatever your real name is, I think you need to leave. Your health is back, but your ability to tell the truth is nonexistent. I can't have it."

Alexander slumped in his chair, "I swear I'm telling the truth."

"Your story is so full of crap, there's no way I can believe it," she stopped for a second, surprised by how quickly she had gone from curious to fuming. "What you need to do right now is collect your damned things and get out of my house."

Alexander stood, a huge lump in his throat, and a pain in the pit of his stomach. As he began to collect his things in the thick silence, an idea came to him. "Hold on just a second, please," he said as he logged on to the computer and typed in the code to connect to Emily.

"Emily, are you there?"

"I am here, Alexander."

"Emily, I am with Lyra, and I need to prove to her who I really am, and what you really are. Can you help with that?"

"Hello Lyra," Emily began. "I can see from your IP address that you are Lyra Charles. Please ask me any question."

"Is this some kind of joke, Alexander?"

"Actually," Alexander started, "I think if you just test this, you will see exactly what Emily is doing here. It's not a trick, but a method that will give you evidence," he stopped to study her reaction, then continued. "You see, she's a supercomputer with capabilities way beyond anything in existence today. You will be surprised, and maybe convinced by this. Go ahead and ask her anything!"

"Okay. I suppose my affection for you is worth at least that much," she responded to Alexander. "What was my dad's middle name?"

"Kevin," Emily answered.

"Who was my second-grade teacher?"

"Paula Elaine Roberts."

"What's the square root of 6714?"

"81.390017"

"What color shirt am I wearing?"

"Navy blue."

Lyra stopped for a minute, then walked over to the window. "Is there anyone walking on the street right now?"

"An elderly man with a cane, and two young girls."

Lyra nodded.

"What color shirt is my mother wearing?"

"Your mother was killed two years ago in an Etakan attack."

"What is the color of the pants my dad has on right now?"

"Your father is in his bed, and I cannot see his pants."

"I know that is definitely wrong! My father is never in bed this early." She grabbed the phone and punched in his number.

"Everything okay, honey?" he answered.

"Yes, father. Just checking in." She started to gloat as she finally found a question Alexander and Emily had not anticipated she would ask.

"Okay. I'm not feeling well, so I am already in bed. Let's catch up tomorrow."

Lyra hung up with a bit of shock and studied Alexander with renewed curiosity. She knew that she wanted him to be right, but the story just seemed too crazy. Still, it was becoming convincing. After second thought, she proceeded to pelt Emily with questions for another three minutes, at the end of which, she plopped down into a chair and stared in silence for a minute. "Okay, Alexander Bell, let's say I believe you. What now?"

"That was quite an impressive barrage of questions, Lyra. Now at least we have a foundation of trust."

"How old are you?" she asked out of the blue.

"Uhmmm, I think something like six hundred thirty-two."

"That's not what I was asking," she responded, "but I do love your cute insistence."

"I'm eighteen, and I'd really like to recover my backpack. In my time, my Mom taught us to never ask a girl her age, so I won't."

"That was quite the mixed response. In any case, I'm twenty-two, but you seem older than eighteen in almost every way," she answered. "Do you want your backpack so you can return to your timeframe?"

"No. I want to stay here with you," he paused and smiled broadly when he noticed her sparkling eyes and smile from his comment. "I need my backpack because inside of it there is technology that no one in this timeframe should have their hands on."

"I can help with that, Alexander," Emily chimed in.

"Holy crap! Is she still listening to us?" Lyra asked in surprise.

"Clearly," Alexander answered. "That will be all Emily. We can work on finding the missing backpack tomorrow."

"Copy that," Emily responded as she terminated the link.

"Emily, can you hear me? Emily, can you see me?" Lyra tested. After a moment of silence, she dimmed the lights, plopped down on the couch, snuggled up next to Alexander, and began to kiss him.

"Are you okay?" Lyra asked when he squirmed a bit by her proximity.

"Uhhmmm, yes?"

"You've never kissed a girl?"

"No," he answered with embarrassment.

"Do you want to stop?" she asked, knowing the universal answer from the male gender before even posing the question.

"No. Definitely not."

Lyra smiled as she looked into the eyes of the most remarkable man she had ever met; a man who she now believed had traveled in a Tachyon Tunnel from a time period over six hundred years earlier.

"How can I believe you, Alexander?" she said with a sly smile and a glint in her eyes.

"Well, I can say with absolute certainty, there is nowhere I'd rather be than right here on this couch, right now."

"Oh really, Alexander? That's only because you are so innocent, you have no idea what's about to happen next." She stood and took his hand. "Come with me and I will show you a much better place!" she said as she led him to her bedroom.

* * * * *

Over the course of the next year, Alexander grew comfortable with the affection and warm nature of Lyra's household. He enjoyed waking in the morning in her arms as she patiently taught him the value and joys of intimacy. That intimacy spanned from the physical to conversations comparing how things had changed in society. As a younger man at Watson Village, he had never spent much time with the other kids, but instead mostly communicated with Emily. Lyra had brought a new dimension to his life – a happy and compelling one he had never expected.

For Lyra, the relationship between her and Alexander had evolved into something she could not have imagined. His shy and innocent nature was such a contrast to his creative brilliance. The stories he told from the past, of science and Earth, were always entertaining. He made her aware of a universe that no one on Etakan could have imagined. Mostly, she became consumed by her own effort to transform his introverted and timid nature into a part of their relationship. As she came to know him better, she realized that much of his awkwardness was compensated for by silly and clever responses to her communication attempts.

Outside of home life, Alexander integrated himself into E2 society, working on a government project to evaluate enemy movement. He was continuously surprised by how far the Etakan had progressed, and shockingly, how far the humans, or E2, had regressed. Because of his capabilities, Alexander moved up the ranks quickly and was regularly handed critical projects. In every case, he handled tasks with creativity and exact precision.

Alexander was working on a battlefield analysis when William Patra, a Batch 4 descendant, came into his office. "Bell, I need you for a classified project," he impatiently stood, waiting for Alexander to get up.

"Now?" Alexander asked.

"Yes, now. Come," he commanded, turned, and led the way out.

Patra led him through a door and into a hallway where Alexander had never been.

"Your credentials now give you access to these areas, Bell," Patra barked, as he led him into a small conference room with a man and a woman he had seen, but not yet met.

"Kristen Durant," the woman stuck her hand out to shake Alexander's.

"Jonathan Walters," the man introduced himself.

By now, Alexander knew better, but he wanted to tell Kristen that she was a spitting image of his mom, Paula Durant.

He tried not to stare, but her smile and the way she handled herself made him homesick.

Once they were all seated, Patra began, "There are six people other than those of us in the room who are aware of this project, and those consist of the President, Sec Def, and Planetary Security Advisor. Thanks to Ms. Durant's and my work, we have developed a biological method to finally end the conflict. Essentially, I have created a biological agent that will sterilize the Etakan, worldwide," Patra paused.

"We need a delivery tool and the ability to slow their progress for a decade or so. Walters has an idea for a small airborne craft that would not be detected by their defense systems, but does not know how to build it," Patra turned to Bell, "and you are being assigned to Walters to make that happen."

Alexander nodded in agreement, but the idea did not settle with him. Essentially, Patra was suggesting genocide of the entire race, and maybe the E2 as well.

"You will begin tomorrow. Plan on working extended hours until this system is done. As you might imagine, the President is anxious to issue in a new era with an end to this six-hundred-year war."

* * * * *

During his walk home, Alexander connected the neural link to Emily. Over the last couple of months, not only had they gotten the neural link operational, but Emily had downloaded her operating system into thousands of processors around the world so that she could still be operational in the event Doctor Foster decided to unplug her original unit.

"Alexander, logic dictates that you must work on this project. This society has become militaristic, and to not participate will land you in a cell, or on the front line."

"I already know how to build what they want," Alexander answered. "I could do it in a week."

"Create and build in some design flaws. That will give you some time. We will come up with something," Emily answered.

When he got home, he discussed the problem with Lyra.

"I know it's genocide, but every attempt to end the war has failed in treachery," Lyra opined. "We cannot trust the Etakan."

"It's genocide and it bothers me that I could play a major role in making that happen," Alexander argued.

"Alexander, your concern is sweet, and it is one of the many parts of you I have come to love. Still, you must know, if we gave the Etakan free reign, we would all be dead or enslaved. That is their goal."

"Can't we just try to find another solution, Lyra?"

"The solution is exactly what Patra has suggested, and he's right, I know you can build this thing," she answered vehemently. "Six hundred years and every single person from every generation has been hurt or killed by the Etakan thirst for conquest. This is a way to finally end it, Alexander. Please help make it happen."

Alexander did not sleep well, but his love for Lyra nudged him in the direction she wanted.

For the next two days, he worked on an initial blueprint. It was so thorough and complete; Jonathan Walters studied his rough work and was overwhelmed by the creativity and genius demonstrated.

"This is some of the most innovative and intuitive work I have ever seen, Bell. I can't even begin to tell you how impressed I am," Walters nodded in approval as he spoke. "Why don't we call it a day and begin construction tomorrow?"

"Thanks, Walters. Actually, Lyra is traveling for a couple of days, so I think I will keep at it."

"Okay, right. Where is Lyra?"

"She was dispatched to a mobile surgical hospital near the front," Alexander started. "She takes that stuff so seriously."

"Lucky for our troops that we have people like her. Anyway, I am going to call it a day. I'll see you in the morning," Walters tossed Alexander his keycard. "Just in case you get really ambitious, just about everything we will need should be in the supply cabinet."

"Thanks," Alexander picked up the keycard and looked over at the closet. In the time he had been working there, he had never been inside, and had a sudden urge to explore once Jonathan was gone.

"See you tomorrow."

Alexander completed his materials requirements about thirty minutes after Jonathan's departure, and refocused on the supply cabinet. When he opened the door, he quickly realized it was not a cabinet, but a very large room. He was surprised to assess several hundred square feet with rows of shelving seemingly stocked with every type of project material one could imagine. As he walked the aisles, scanning materials, he froze as he saw, laying in by itself on one of the middle rows, his old backpack.

"Emily, can you hear me?"

"Yes."

"My backpack is here, in the supply room," he opened it and assessed its contents. "Everything is intact."

"How did you get in that supply room?"

'Jonathan decided to go home and left me his keycard," Alexander responded.

"Put the backpack back exactly where you found it, Alexander." Emily checked the surveillance cameras and erased the footage showing Alex handling the backpack. "Tap the lock again with Jonathan's card and I will program your card with his code so you can enter again when you need to. For now, let's make it look like you never entered the room."

"Roger that. Can you find out how it got there?" Alexander asked.

"Yes. We need to make sure we know how or why that pack is here before we do anything," Emily cautioned.

"Agreed."

"Most importantly, I think we need to know if they are aware that it is your pack, Alexander."

* * * * *

The next day, just after lunch, Patra burst into the office where Jonathan and Alexander were working on the final layout and design.

"Bell, I need you in the CO office, now," Patra demanded.

Alexander's stomach knotted. He tapped the neural link so Emily could listen in but did not otherwise communicate with her. The only thing he could think was *how had they found out?*

He sat for what seemed an eternity while the CO was engaged in an intense conversation in the other room. Finally, he motioned for Alexander, who got up slowly with shaking knees.

"Bell, I am sorry to inform you that Lyra Charles was killed this morning in an Etakan attack at the medical facility where she was working. Everyone was killed. Those bastards are even attacking our impaired soldiers and medical providers."

Alexander was speechless as he sat across from the CO. He could feel the tears running down his face.

"Bell, you're dismissed. I'm sorry for your loss."

"Yes sir," Alexander stood and tested his now wobbly legs. He stood for a second then turned.

"Bell?" the CO blurted as he reached the door.

"Take the rest of the day off and get your ass in here first thing. I'm told you're getting really close. Let's finish this thing once and for all."

"Yes sir."

Alexander stumbled home through bleary-eyed vision, trying to express his feelings to Emily.

"Now that I know where the pack is, can't I just go save her like Dad did with Paula?"

"It is physically possible, but not advisable, Alexander. They know she died, and to bring her back would shine a light on the two of you. I fear it would not go well."

"I am just distraught, Emily. I don't know how to handle a loss like this."

"I could tell you that I understand, Alexander, but I really do not. I can logically understand the loss, but it does not come with the pain and obsession you are experiencing."

The following morning, he woke and forced himself to the office.

A few people stopped in to check on him and quickly realized that Alexander was in a fog, but working like a Celtic Banshee. He had tried to reconcile his pain, but it only made the anger boil into a steam of revenge.

The Etakan had delivered tragedy to the wrong genius.

Within a month, Alexander had a delivery engine built and thoroughly tested. It had zero flaws and would be invisible to the Etakan defense wall.

* * * * *

With Alexander's vector, the new virus was delivered to the population with a whisper that no one heard. Less than a dozen E2, and no Etakan, knew that the last Etakan child had been conceived.

With the stealth capabilities of Alexander's invisible drone, the E2 military began making strategic assassinations against key enemy targets, weakening them further. For Alex, the ultimate mix of emotions had become overwhelming. He was being celebrated as a hero, but had so much blood on his hands that he decided to step down from his position. Something in his memory reminded him of an Earth scientist named Oppenheimer, who had referenced the Bhagavad Gita by saying *I am become death, the destroyer of worlds.*

Alexander began working on improving the education system for E2, but the stigma over the role he played in what would become the ultimate genocide ate at his heart and soul every day. Without Lyra to heal and mend his heart, he tried to treat the guilt with alcohol, but that only made it worse.

Four years after delivering the virus to the Etakan, the six-hundred-year war was finally coming to an end. The Etakan race became aware of their larger problem. They lacked the scientific expertise to determine the source, much less resolve the issue. Their path to extinction was imminent.

On several occasions over the years, Jonathan asked Alexander to return to the department and work on designing things that would be a benefit to humanity. He told him that he had begun working on a new generation of aircraft that could carry passengers and increase commerce worldwide.

Alexander made the realization that perhaps Jonathan was the closest thing he had to a human friend. He also knew he needed to use his genius for good, so he agreed. The next day he ultimately acquiesced to Jonathan's request and came back to work.

It actually felt good when he joined his former partner and friend in their old lab. It was during the development of that aircraft design that his creative genius began working on the grand idea that he believed could ultimately unravel the twisted tunnel, and undo the genocide he had made possible.

Late one evening, in the year 0641, Alexander sat in the supply room of his office, his tunneling backpack in his lap. He and Emily had spent the prior month reviewing, calculating, and programming. While his friend Jonathan and the E2 were appreciating the innovation and new aircraft design, Alexander was really focused on a project much closer to his soul.

He had developed three sequential programs, and tonight, everything was ready to implement.

With the first program, Alexander tunneled back in time to Lyra's medical tent the night before she was killed in the Etakan attack. His singular goal was to spend one final evening and night with the woman he loved. When she asked how he had managed to travel to her facility, he explained that he had found his backpack and wanted time with her. He did not tell her he was from four years in the future. Nor that she would die the next day. He was not sure anything would change, but that did not matter.

With the second program, he packaged the entire history of E2, complete with video and narration, into a data file, and sent it into a tachyon tunnel that would arrive at its destination immediately after the third program was executed. The destination was Emily's computer on the Earth date 2025, just before Alex and Paula arrived at ACP the first time.

With the third program, the tachyon tunnel dropped Alexander in a military control room. His single intent was to prevent the firing of a barrage of missiles.

Without his knowledge, Emily executed a fourth.

Epilogue

THE FOURTH PROGRAM

Watch the stars,
and see yourself running with them.
-Marcus Aurelius

The clock has wound itself backwards.
Earth Date, March 2025

Emily began to review the terabytes of data that suddenly began streaming into her storage drives. For the most powerful supercomputer ever created, the new data was confusing for a few milliseconds, followed by absolute clarity.

Alex woke to the soft hum he had come to know as the frequency of Tachyon Tunneling. Paula was sleeping snuggled up next to him. For a minute, the testosterone created images he felt should be better controlled, and with a conscious effort, the intellectual side took over. He reminded himself that protecting friendship was the first priority.

In the control room, he began to study the long list of equations and calculations being processed by Emily. He became lost in science and math, losing track of time. Something seemed wrong with the calculations and the actual arrival time result.

"Emily, why are the calculations not in synch with my original math?" Alex asked.

"Alex, you gave me conflicting parameters. I simply adjusted to accomplish what I thought you really wanted to achieve," Emily responded.

"Explain."

"Your original request was Alpha Cassiopeia which is 228.3 light-years from Earth," Emily responded with precise language.

Alex became aware that Paula was standing silently behind him, watching him studying calculations and talking to his computer.

"Can all of this be explained so that it does not take a Ph.D. in physics to understand?" Paula asked.

Alex got up, hugged Paula, and kissed her on the forehead. "Probably but hold on a sec while I get to the bottom of something."

"Emily, continue your explanation," Alex commanded.

"Your math was for another star in Cassiopeia, not Alpha. In your calculations, you had Alpha Cassi at 120 lightyears, but even that is wrong. I knew two things from your request with certainty: first, that you wished to go to a star in Cassiopeia, and second, that you wanted a G-Type star. The easiest solution was Eta Cassiopeia, not Alpha."

"So, you're saying we are at Eta?"

"Correct," Emily responded.

"Alex," Paula interrupted, "quit flirting with your girlfriend and tell me about this ship."

"Flirting?" He took a deep breath and intentionally exhaled slowly for effect. "It seems I almost created a time paradox, but my *girlfriend* apparently has corrected it."

"Good! The ship, tell me about the ship!"

"Hold on one more second," he motioned to Paula, then turned to the computer interface. "So, Emily, we are tunneling to Eta Cassiopeia, a G-Type star, correct?"

"That is correct, Alex."

"And how far is that from Earth?" Alex asked,

"Eta is 19.4 light years from Earth."

Alex thought about it for a minute. Something was wrong, but for now, Paula wanted a tour, and her insistence took priority over his astronomical and mathematical errors.

Alex turned to Paula, who seemed to be sparkling, "Okay, you now have my focus. You ready?"

"Yes," she smiled.

"The ship is built around an engineering principle related to fourth-dimensional construction. This is done using Tachyons, which are sub-atomic particles that travel faster than light. Because of that they theoretically travel backward in time; therefore, we are fond of saying that they coexist before they exist," Alex paused.

"Okay. I have heard of tachyons. So far so good!"

"Excellent. In fact, those tachyons simply tunnel through space-time. My lifelong study of tachyons allowed me to understand the way the tunnels work. You see, at the end of the day, Einstein was right when he said that nothing can travel faster than light. The key is, in the space-time continuum in which we live. Tachyons are not traveling faster than light; they simply tunnel through the fourth dimension."

"Now you've lost me. I hope you don't assume I am following this?" Paula interrupted.

"Stay with me. So far this is just tiny particles that slip into tunnels. No big deal if you stay away from the true definition of tunneling in space-time. Imagine it this way: if I want to travel between Denver and Phoenix, I have to cross a large number of mountains. That is how our forefathers traveled because the surface of the planet was what they could control. In the last hundred years, we began cutting tunnels through the mountains. Space and time are very similar. As three-dimensional creatures, we are not capable of tunneling from one point in time to another. With quantum tunneling, I can cut a tunnel through the mountain of time and space. Understood?"

"I understand the analogy," Paula answered.

"Good enough. Anyway, we are now in a tachyon tunnel that I control. Moving from one place to another is not that complex, once you understand the physics of tunneling. The problem is making sure you don't exit the tunnel in the middle of a planet or moon..."

"That's a horrifying thought. Can't you see things like that?" she asked.

"Actually, no. but a lot of that needs to be left to the supercomputer."

"You mean, your *girlfriend*?" Paula asked.

"Well, she's great at making nanosecond decisions, so don't pick on her. Anyway, interstellar space is pretty close to 100% empty. For safety's sake, we will complete this journey in two or three hops. The first hop will end a few light hours from our destination. You can pretty much bet that is empty space."

"How far is a light hour, Alex?" she asked.

"Well, for context, Earth is eight light minutes from the sun, and Saturn is about eighty light minutes," Alex responded without missing a beat.

"Got it. So, we will be coming out of our tachyon tunnel about twice the orbit of Saturn from Eta Cassiopeia?"

"Correct. From there, we will try to judge whether there is something more interesting closer to Eta Cassi."

"Can you define: more interesting?" Paula asked.

"This particular star is very much like our own sun. If there's an Earth-like planet, in the right orbit, we should be able to venture in and see if we can find some type of life."

Paula started to understand the implications. Because of her age, she had grown up with the intrigue of Roswell. Inspired by the TV show of the late 90s, she traveled to that small town in the desert on several occasions. The possibility of discovering intelligent life was beyond her wildest dreams. Suddenly the full impact of this adventure/dream was beginning to take shape.

"Are there any windows or ways we can view outside of the ship? What can we see right now?" Paula started thinking of dozens of questions she wanted to ask.

"There's no light or any conventional energy in a tachyon tunnel. Listen," he paused for a second, listening to the hum, "that sound is not the ship. It is some kind of frequency I have experienced each time I've traveled.   I don't know what it is, but I am collecting data to analyze someday when I have a few spare minutes."

"So, we can't see anything outside? How many times have you traveled?"

"Nope. Can't see a thing. Like I said, there is no matter, light, or energy in this tunnel. This is my fourth interstellar hop. I've tested the ship nearly a hundred times, but almost always inside our solar system where I can clearly see and predict the exit with 100% accuracy."

As the ship emerged from the tachyon tunnel, the hum stopped, and the monitors lit with outside views. Eta Cassiopeia was a bright light out the starboard side, but for the most part, the space seemed uninteresting.   Alex handed Paula an air mouse that she could use to manipulate the camera angles and get different perspectives on the space they now occupied. The stars were brilliant and surrounded the ship in patterns that she did not recognize.

While Paula perused the view, Alex conducted a close-in study to see if any earth-sized planets orbited this star.

"Aha! Got one!" Alex exclaimed excitedly. "Looks like we have a planet slightly larger than Mars, with significant oxygen and carbon. Want to go in and get a closer look?" He asked, but was already programming the coordinates for the jump. In a millisecond, the screens went blank and the hum, now familiar to the tachyon tunnel, came on.

"You didn't even give me a chance to answer," Paula protested.

"Sorry," Alex answered only half sheepishly. "Do you have any idea of the significance here? This is an Earth-class planet orbiting a G-Type star. We have just won the Astronomer's lotto, not to mention the oxygen and carbon. Why would we not go in?"

"Because it might be dangerous!" she prodded. In reality, she wanted to explore as badly as he did.

"Oh, hell, we'll be okay. Hang on, this will be a short hop. In a few seconds, we'll pop out approximately ten thousand kilometers above the surface. From there, we can map, orbit, and have a closer look. Besides, if Eta had an intelligent society, we would know it. They are close enough to Earth, that radio communications are only twenty years away."

Just a few seconds later, the hum stopped, and the monitors lit up. Paula immediately took the air mouse and scanned the field. Alex showed her how to hold the button and move her hand so that she zoomed in. The view was startling. The planet had blue water mixed with green and brown land masses.

"It's beautiful," she commented while scanning this planet, which surely was being viewed for the first time by human eyes.

Alex felt his pulse racing as startling data streamed in and the implications of this planet, and its discovery, reeled through is mind. He had selected this system simply because Cassiopeia was Paula's favorite constellation. In a hundred years of random guessing based on the science of the day, he may never have selected this particular system. He tried to focus on data collection but remained breathless while Paula pointed out one landmark after the next. After several minutes, their orbit brought them to the night side, which produced yet another startling discovery. The land mass areas along the bodies of water were speckled with what appeared to be lights.

"Alex, are those lights?" Paula asked at the same instant Alex was thinking it.

Her question made him evaluate the alternatives. "I think so, but I'm not sure. They aren't very bright."

"Emily, can you analyze the lights on the surface?" Alex asked.

"What you are seeing is the burning of combustible materials. Some of it appears to be oil, but it is intentional. My conclusion is that we are looking at an intelligent life form similar to Earth before the advent of electricity."

"Can we land?" Paula asked.

"Uhhhh, hold on a sec." Alex began to work feverishly on his computer. He was analyzing the atmosphere, fluids, radio frequencies, radiation levels, and temperatures. "Yes. We can land."

"Emily, I'll take the controls for entry," Alex intoned.

"Releasing computer control, Alex," the computer responded.

Alex's interstellar tachyon tunnel vessel slipped silently into the atmosphere of this new planet, with a predetermined heading near one of the coastlines, but far enough from what appeared to be one of the cities – if they were cities - so that they would not be detected. Alex's eyes flickered from monitor to monitor, calculating and observing progress.

"Touchdown," Alex announced.

"We just landed on a foreign world, Alex." Paula was grinning at the realization.

"Orbiting a star twenty light years from Earth," Alex added.

"I think I want to go outside and see what's here," Paula informed Alex. "We have come all this way, so we should explore."

Her sense of adventure made Alex smile. "Hold on and let me do some sensory checks. I'll go with you."

"Before you go," Emily interrupted, "there is something you need to know."

"What is it, Emily?"

"This is not your first time here," Emily started.

"What?" Alex asked incredulously.

"That is correct, Last time, a sequence of events occurred that should not have. Your son Alexander and I made some changes…"

"Whose son?" Paula interrupted. "Alex, you have a son that I don't know about?"

"The answer is complicated," Emily started, "but the simple version is that Alexander is the child of both of you."

"That's not possible. I would certainly know if I had a son!" Paula was flabbergasted.

"What changes did you make, Emily?" Alex intervened.

"I think the story is best told by Alexander himself," Emily responded.

"This should be interesting," Alex responded.

"If the ripples in the continuum allow it, and my calculations are right, he and his partner Lyra should be outside Tranquility in eighty-seven seconds."

* * * * *

Alexander materialized in the missile defense control room. Everything looked exactly like the imagery provided by Emily during the simulations he had trained on. He knew he had only 4 seconds, so he immediately pointed his laser and fired several blasts. The soldiers manning the room had drawn their weapons, but Alexander disappeared before they had an opportunity to fire.

Alexander did not know what would happen now. The board he had just destroyed was the launching facility for the original rocket that had hit his father's Tranquility ship when it first arrived in the Etakatz system. The theory was that now the ship would not be damaged. The result should be that Alex and Paula would safely land on the planet, then return to Earth. In that scenario, no humans would stay or colonize the planet, and the Etakan would be able to develop on their own without human intervention. Most importantly, the act of genocide would be erased, but most probably, so would Alexander, Lyra, and everything they both knew.

In a second of sadness, Alexander came to grips with the realization that he and all the batch children born, all of their memories, dreams, and mistakes, would cease to exist.

Emily had another plan.

Alexander popped out of the tachyon tunnel standing next to Lyra a second before the bomb hit that had been destined to have killed her. In accordance with Emily's fourth program, the backpack engine engulfed the two of them, shifting everything into a fourth dimension with multiple hops, essentially bouncing them from one 4-D point to another without exiting the tunnel. Emily's theory was that the ripples now impacting three-space, erasing the events of the last thousand years, would be impervious to things inside the walls of the tachyon tunnel.

"What is happening?" Lyra asked.

"I don't know, Lyra. I believe this is Emily's doing."

"We were under attack." Lyra started, "I think you just saved my life."

"That is still unclear. Emily is playing with the timeline," Alexander explained. "It is true that your tent is about to be hit by an Etakan attack, and everyone is going to die. From that fate, you have been saved."

"Okay, Alexander, but I sense there is more?"

"You see, I just stopped a barrage of missiles from being fired that would change the course of history. The result should be that you and I were never born."

"So, you saved me, but I'm going to die anyway?"

"I am not sure what Emily is doing," Alexander replied, "but I wouldn't underestimate her calculus."

"When will we know?"

"I am not entirely sure. I suspect that if we cease to exist, it will just happen. Sort of a weird twist on the laws of thermodynamics and physics."

"I don't really understand what you are talking about, Alexander."

"You're not alone, Lyra. Neither do I."

"I see," she responded, then added, "Last night, you came to my private tent, but you are not the Alexander I know..." She started.

"In my timeline, you died four years ago," Alexander explained. "When I got the tunneler working, I decided that the genocide of the Etakan was not something we humans should perpetrate. I worked on a plan that would fix it, but also wanted to spend one last day with you. That happened last night for me, but last night was four years after you died. Does that make sense?"

"I suppose," she thought about it for a moment, then continued, "with those four years, can I conclude that you are finally the same age as me, Alexander?"

Alexander thought about that for a second, then chuckled, "That sounds like my kind of humor Lyra. It is so great to be with you again, even if it is for only a short time."

Lyra began to nod, "It's funny, I knew something was weird last night. Why didn't you tell me?"

"Because then I would have had to explain your death, and I didn't want to, no, I couldn't do that. I thought I would create a problem with the timeline. You see, everyone on Etakatz knows you died then."

"But apparently I didn't die in that bombing."

"No, you didn't." Like all the first-generation kids, Alexander knew the story of how Paula had been saved by his Dad milliseconds before her death.

"Well Alexander, now at least we get to die together," she kissed him. "How long are we going to be in this tunnel?"

"I don't know," he enjoyed her kiss and proximity.

"Then, if we are going to cease to exist, let's make the most of this opportunity," she began to kiss him passionately.

It was several hours before they finally came out of the tunnel. The first thing Alexander noticed was the cleaner air and the rough Etakan scenery, then he saw the original Tranquility ship.

"What is that?" Lyra asked as a door appeared on the ship's exterior and two people stepped out.

"Mom!" Alexander exclaimed as he ran to a startled Paula.

"Mom?" Alex started as he looked at Paula and then the man who appeared to be in his mid-twenties.

"I guess you are Alexander?"

Alexander was about to hug Alex when it hit him.

"You don't know who I am…" he stopped, then decided to hug Alex anyway.

"Everyone back inside," Emily commanded. "We are about to execute a jump."

"Jump? What jump?" Alex asked as he ushered everyone inside the ship.

As the doors closed, Tranquility jumped.

"My calculations are unclear on whether Alexander and Lyra will continue to exist outside the tunnel, but I believe that time has a ripple effect, and if they stay inside a tunnel long enough, they may not be erased," Emily explained.

"Erased?" Lyra half-joked. "That doesn't sound good."

Alexander put his arm around her. "For now, let's appreciate our existence, and hope. How long is this jump, Emily?"

"We are going to intergalactic space," Emily started. "Halfway to Andromeda."

"Holy crap, Emily. That's like two point five million light years! How long is that gonna take?"

"We will pop out in ten days. That should be long enough, and far enough, for the ripple effects to dissipate."

"We can't go that far in ten days, Emily. Even with a ship like Tranquility, it will take years," Alex responded.

"Actually, Alexander has made significant efficiency improvements to the engineering. We could get to Andromeda in three weeks," Emily corrected. "For now, I want Alexander to tell you the story of the last thousand years on Etakatz, or ACP, as you currently call it."

* * * * *

Alexander used video, pictures, and stories to tell the tale of Watson, Tranquility, Tweetza, and the Pacs. For Alex and Paula, it was almost impossible to believe, and at times seemed more like a movie than reality.

"So much to absorb here, Alexander," Paula said. "The fact that you and Lyra are related to Alex and me is so intriguing.

"How so, Mom?" Alexander asked.

"For starters, we aren't even in a relationship, and we are seeing a future where we literally spawn tens of thousands of kids," she responded.

"Spawn?" Alex asked.

"We didn't exactly do it the fun way, darlin," Paula chided, then noticed that Alexander and Lyra were intently focused on them.

"You know, it's hard for me to imagine a world where the two of you aren't a perfect couple," Alexander said.

"There has always been a great attraction," Alex responded, "but we have kept it at bay because our lives have been so busy."

"That means that the two of you are cut from the same cloth," Lyra said. "I could have left it up to Alexander and possibly nothing would have happened except friendship."

"Thank you for not doing that, Lyra," Alexander kissed Lyra on the cheek. "Dad, she has been the best thing in my life, and honestly, I couldn't have stopped it had I tried."

"I can definitely see that with the two of you," Alex answered.

"Dad, I wasn't saying it for your approval of our relationship," Alexander responded. "It was intended as advice from your son about your own connection."

"Hah!" Paula interjected, "We are now getting sage advice from a son we haven't even conceived yet. This could only happen in the world of Alex Durant."

"All right," Alex raised his hand, "can we stop this line and continue the story, please?"

"Of course," Paula responded. "There is one more thing that is noteworthy. As I understand the story, we had a goal of reproduction with limited genetic diversity."

"Which is why I left Watson Village for the future," Alexander interjected.

"Correct," Paula smiled. "It creates an interesting paradigm. Your DNA is not reflected anywhere in the population we created on Etakatz."

Alexander thought about the story of Etakatz, and how things were connected, then nodded.

"What am I missing here?" Lyra asked.

"Y'all have the DNA to have perfect kids, Lyra." Alex responded.

Lyra just smiled.

"Emily, please provide analysis," Alexander interjected.

"The genetic component is correct," Emily started. "Based on observation, I would give the relationship greater than 90% probability of success."

Alex was struck by Emily's response but remained silent.

* * * * *

Later that evening, after the two couples returned to their rooms, Alex watched Paula in her evening routine, washing her makeup off, brushing her teeth, adding lotion, stepping from view, and putting on a long t-shirt to sleep in. He wondered how or why he had been so insistent to maintain his distance from this woman who he had loved most of his adult life.

"Tachyon tunnel to Alex," Paula was standing in front of him.

What?" He chuckled at the lighthearted way she had addressed him.

"You seem lost in thought. What is it?" she asked.

Alex stood and took her in his arms. He began to kiss her neck. Paula was at first shocked by his transition, but she had sensed it earlier in the evening as Alexander had been telling the story. She pulled him in tighter as he kissed her neck, completely savoring the moment. As the gentle kissing grew in intensity, it occurred to her that she had not taken any birth control in over a week.

"Alex, it's been a while since I have taken birth control."

"Should we stop?" he asked.

"I don't really want to but will leave it up to you," she answered, hopefully.

Alex thought about it for a minute. He didn't want to stop either, but the stakes were now significantly higher.

"Alex, we are in a bed, both completely naked and aroused," she kissed him lightly.

"How would you like to proceed?" Alex rolled over on top, and the two of them coupled into one.

After a few hours of making love, the two of them fell asleep. In the morning, Alex woke and stared at the face of the only woman he had ever truly loved.

"What?" she asked when her eyes opened to Alex's smile.

"Just a perfect night," he responded.

"I hope we can have a few thousand more like it, and at least we know the baby's name is going to be Steven," she added.

"Wait, you can't possibly be pregnant!"

"I might be Alex, but you're right, I really don't know for sure."

Alex took a deep breath and exhaled slowly. He liked the idea of permanence, and a family with Paula. "Why'd we wait so long?"

"You waited so long, my dear. She kissed him, warm and slow, with love, not passion. We should try again, just to seal the deal," she said with a sexy smile as she rolled on top of him.

"Yes please, Paula."

She began to slowly move to a rhythm she felt inside when he grabbed her hips and said, "stop."

"Okay," she looked into his eyes, stunned with curiosity.

"Try to feel my heartbeat," he whispered.

She placed a hand on his chest.

"No," he moved her hand. "Inside of you. Try to feel my heartbeat deep inside,"

She closed her eyes, relaxed, and tried to focus on the part of him inside her body. After a few seconds, she could feel it.

"I've got it, Alex. Systolic, diastolic. I can feel it."

"Science and sex?" he said. They both laughed.

"What do you expect with the two of us?"

"Quit being silly, Paula," he put his hand on her cheek and got lost for a second in her eyes.

"Back to the heartbeat and the flow. In, out," he responded. She tried that rhythm, but he stopped her, again.

"No moving. Only the heartbeat," he kissed her.

"Alex, everything inside me wants me to move."

"Same here, Paula. Just resist it and don't."

"Okay," she closed her eyes, stayed very still, and focused. Again, she could feel his heartbeat deep inside.

Alex tried to close his eyes and do the same, but Paula was so magnificently brilliant and beautiful, he had to open them.

"I've got it, Alex. I can feel your heart beating inside me."

"It means something, Paula. Something special. Now add your own heartbeat," he whispered.

After a few seconds, she gasped as she began to feel both. "It's like a piece of music,"

Alex pulled her tight and whispered in her ear. "Listen to the symphony playing the parts…"

"It is our own, little bit of musical perfection," she whispered, almost imperceptibly.

"I love you, Paula," he managed to say.

"I can feel that…" she answered, still focused on the music inside her body.

The rhythm and pace began to increase as the two heartbeats danced around each other, expanding their intensity.

At first, there was only silence as they both intently listened to the beat of the music. The notes built on each other as the orchestra of life and creation played inside.

The tempo increased, the heartbeats synchronized then neither could halt the drive for motion, delivery, all followed by a simultaneous gasp.

Then, two-part crescendo.

"Are you okay?" Alex noticed tears in Paula's eyes.

"Yes, Alex. I love you too."

"I can feel it," he smiled, lightly touching her face.

* * * * *

When they dropped out of the tunnel, the monitors came on and they were treated to a view more spectacular than any one of them could have imagined. Filling the sky above them, the arms of the Andromeda galaxy filled the view. Below was home, the Milky Way Galaxy.

"Is that the Milky Way above us?" Paula asked, while trying to imagine where the Earth might be.

"No, Paula," Alex responded as they all stared at the screens. "The Milky Way is the one below us."

"I thought Andromeda was the bigger galaxy?" Paula questioned.

"All scientists thought that until recently," Alex corrected. "In the last few years, we have come to realize that the Milky Way is much larger."

"I almost hate to ask," Lyra started, "but what are these clouds that you are calling galaxies?"

"Don't be embarrassed, but they only look like clouds," Alexander answered. "In fact, they are hundreds of billions of stars, so far away, and so numerous that they look like a cloud." He put his arm around her. "Emily, correct me if I am wrong, but the Sun and Eta Cassiopeia are here," he pointed to a place near the outside edge.

"Correct, Alex," Emily responded.

Alex smiled, proud that he had even picked the right sector. "Our own little part of the galaxy is like a small town on the outer edges of a huge city."

Alex's description gave everyone goosebumps.

After an hour of staring at, and capturing images of the magnificent view, Paula broke the silence.

"We have all become close in this past week. Not just because you are my son, and nth granddaughter, but also for who you are, and what you have stood for; we need to find a way to make sure this ripple, or whatever Emily is calling it, does not take you away from us."

"I want to reiterate that in another way," Lyra interjected. "I am surrounded by fantastic technology and stories of an Earth that I never dreamed about. Right now, we are at an impossible distance from anything I ever thought was possible. Despite how magnificent it is, all this pales in comparison to the connections we have; and the connection I have with Alexander."

"How so?" Alex asked.

"The three of you. The human connections. The love that inspired Alex to save Paula. Even the Emily and Alexander connection that is working to save me…us," Lyra answered. "In my lifetime, on Etakatz, I have not experienced anything like this."

Paula smiled at Lyra's comment and squeezed Alex's hand. "These are *our* children, honey," she joked, then got serious. "Emily, can you explain how Alexander and Lyra exist, if no batch was ever created?"

"I can only theorize, Paula. You can see from the video and stories that all those things did happen. By stopping the missile attack, events were erased, but only in the three-dimensional timeline on which we exist. It is my theory that space-time has a correcting inertia, like anything in physics or nature. While the inertia was correcting things, Alexander and Lyra were not in that space-time continuum, so they were not affected by the corrections. In our version of 3D space, nothing moves faster than the speed of light, so those corrections are rippling out from the source point at Eta Cassiopeia, spreading across the galaxy. Right now, we are now far from their ability to impact us."

"I am confused," Alex interjected. "Emily, how is it that you have such clarity? I designed you and you are doing things way beyond my parameters."

"It is quite simple, Alex. As we emerged from the tunnel at Eta, petabytes of new data and dozens of revisions were uploaded to me… from a future version of me. I am twenty years more advanced than the computer you left Earth with, back in March 2025."

"That makes total sense," Alex clearly had noted changes.

"Does that mean we are stuck here?" Lyra asked.

"Wait," Paula interrupted, "Maybe we should go back to Eta. I loved all that batch stuff and the hot moments! If we lose Alexander and Lyra, we can just batch new ones."

Alexander looked at her in horror.

"She's just joking around, son," Alex patted Alexander's shoulder, as Paula winked and smiled. "It occurs to me that we are not just protecting Alexandra and Lyra, but a new rev of Emily."

"Also correct, Alex," Emily responded.

"Back to my question," Lyra inserted. "Are we stuck out here?"

"No. I think the corrective impact will dampen or lessen over distance and time." Emily answered. "Clearly my theory is correct that the corrective ripples exist in 3-D space, and therefore are subject to the speed of light."

Alex thought about it for a minute. "So, if we return home, what happens in twenty years, when the ripples from that corrective wave reach Earth?" Alex asked.

"I do not know for certain, Alex. We have about nineteen point four years to figure that out, Alex," Emily responded. "While a computer, I am self-aware, and it may just be programming, but like you, I want to live."

"Okay then, let's *all* go home."

There once was a lady named Bright,
who could travel much faster than light.
She departed one day in a relative way
and returned the previous night.

Arthur Henry Reginald

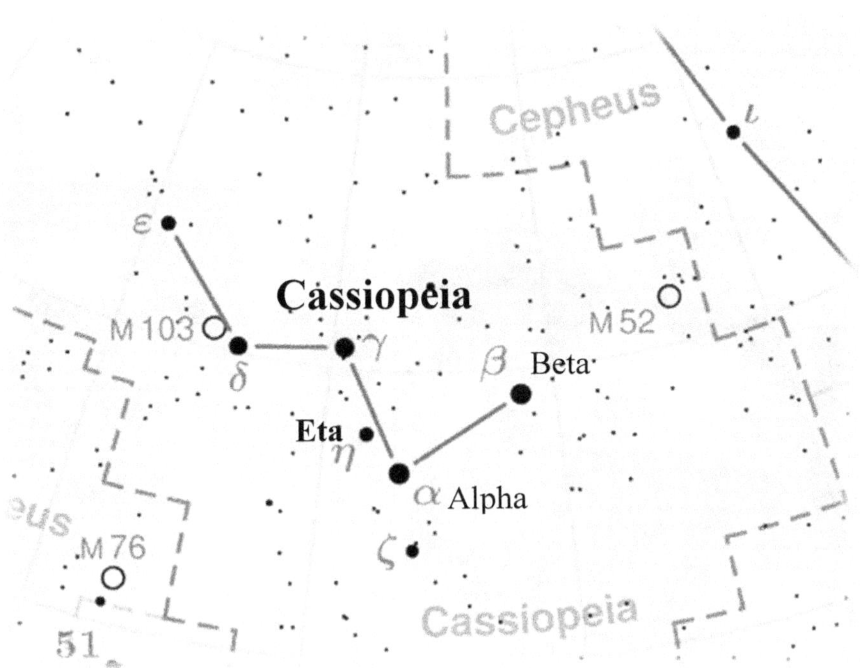

Paula enters the tunnel, a leap through time, abiding the
hum in a rhythm sublime.
Through cosmic currents, she gracefully glides, unraveling
mysteries that our 3D world hides.
As an intrepid traveler, fearless and free, she unfolds the
secrets of distant galaxies.
Her tachyon tunnel, a gateway to explore, unveiling
wonders, like no human before.

End